ABROW 25.00/15.00

STORM

PUFFIN CANADA

Published by the Penguin Group

Penguin Group (Canada), 90 Eglinton Avenue East, Suite 700, Toronto,
Ontario, Canada M4P 2Y3 (a division of Pearson Canada Inc.)
Penguin Group (USA) Inc., 375 Hudson Street, New York, New York 10014, U.S.A.
Penguin Books Ltd, 80 Strand, London WC2R 0RL, England
Penguin Ireland, 25 St Stephen's Green, Dublin 2, Ireland (a division of Penguin Books Ltd)
Penguin Group (Australia), 250 Camberwell Road, Camberwell, Victoria 3124, Australia
(a division of Pearson Australia Group Pty Ltd)
Penguin Books India Pvt Ltd, 11 Community Centre, Panchsheel Park,
New Delhi – 110 017, India
Penguin Group (NZ), 67 Apollo Drive, Rosedale, North Shore 0745, Auckland, New Zealand
(a division of Pearson New Zealand Ltd)
Penguin Books (South Africa) (Pty) Ltd, 24 Sturdee Avenue, Rosebank, Johannesburg 2196,
South Africa

Penguin Books Ltd, Registered Offices: 80 Strand, London WC2R 0RL, England

First published 2008

1 2 3 4 5 6 7 8 9 10   (RRD)

Copyright © Carrie Mac, 2008

*Publisher's note: This book is a work of fiction. Names, characters, places and incidents either are the
product of the author's imagination or are used fictitiously, and any resemblance to actual persons
living or dead, events, or locales is entirely coincidental.*

Manufactured in the U.S.A.

ISBN: 978-0-670-06602-5

Library and Archives Canada Cataloguing in Publication data available
upon request to the publisher.

Visit the Penguin Group (Canada) website at **www.penguin.ca**

Special and corporate bulk purchase rates available;
please see **www.penguin.ca/corporatesales** or call 1-800-810-3104, ext. 477 or 474

[Triskelia Book 3]

STORM
CARRIE MAC

PUFFIN
CANADA

*for Meredydd, sparkly full of glitter,
and a tenacious beauty to boot*

The heavens change every moment,
and reflect their glory or gloom on the plains beneath.

[ONE]

TRIBAN

1

***

So many had died, yet Zenith's death stood apart from them all. In the solemn hours after her passing, Eli had noticed the difference. The world had paused when it had never bothered to before. The air had lifted at first, then come down like a sudden fog, dense and transformative. He and the others had moved through this miasma all night. There was a unique finality to it, and yet, paradoxically, it held hope and promise.

Eli wanted to speak to this difference at Zenith's service, bring it to light. Suggest that her death carried its own blessing. He struggled with how he could put it into words. Zenith's dying felt *right* somehow ... as if it were meant to be. That's why he'd insisted on a memorial service. Her passing *would* be honoured, despite Seth and Sabine's protests that now was not the time, that the revolution was at hand.

And then the Guardy Commander had arrived with his gruesome bundle, as if proving their point.

Now Celeste collapsed to her knees at the sight of her husband's body, nearly unrecognizable from the torture he'd suffered at the hands of the Guard. She lifted his wrist, her face crumpling into tears. All four fingers, and his thumb, gone! Chopped off! She kissed the papery skin below the rotted stubs.

"What did they do to you, Pierre? What did they do?"

Sobbing, Sabine knelt beside her grandmother. "I'm so sorry, Nana."

Eli bent his head and asked his highers to welcome Pierre into their realm.

Seth could only stare at the corpse of the grandfather he hardly knew. Looking down on Pierre was like beholding the body of any stranger, but with one important difference. This dead man could absolve him. Seth knew it wasn't the time or the place, but he had to say something.

He gave the others what seemed like forever to fret and weep and wring their hands. And then he could wait no longer.

"You have to know this proves it now."

Eli, praying all this while, opened his eyes to glance at his brother. "Proves what?"

"Don't you see?" Seth turned to the others, but their eyes were either on the ground, averted from the horror, or locked on Celeste as she bid farewell to her husband. She keened there on her knees, snot running from her nose, white hair falling across her face as she wept.

Sabine looked up at him now as she held Celeste's thin, shuddering shoulders. "See what?"

"That I'm innocent!" Seth gestured down the street in the direction the Guard had gone. "The Commander said so himself! *Pierre* was the one who gave away Triskelia's location. Not me!"

Seth was speaking directly to Rosa now. What lay behind that look in her eyes?

Rosa turned back to Celeste and rested a comforting hand on her back. "Slow your breaths, Celeste. You'll faint otherwise."

"But don't you see?" Seth persisted, although he was hardly speaking above a whisper. "This means I—"

"Shut up!" Whisper or not, Trace had heard him. He took his arms from around his wife and stomped over to Seth. "Even now, it has to be about you!" he growled. "Where is your respect?"

"This man was a *stranger* to me...." Trace shoved him hard, but Seth didn't stumble. He stepped away, willing his fists to relax. He would not throw the first punch. He would not. "So I am *asking*—"

"Stop it!" Sabine cried out, just as Trace lifted his fists. "Enough!"

Trace let his hands drop, slowly. Nostrils flaring, he returned to Anya's side but kept his eyes, narrow with rage, locked on Seth.

And Seth kept pushing. "But all this time you people thought it was me!"

"I said *enough!*" Sabine yelled. "Go! Gather your army."

"No. Not yet." Seth folded his arms across his chest and levelled his sister with a cool, firm glare. "I will not go until you acknowledge my innocence. You people would have had me drawn and quartered if you could have proved I gave away the location. And here is your proof that I didn't, and you fault *me* for demanding a retraction? Absolve me in the matter of the Triskelian massacre, or I will not lend my soldiers to any battle of yours. I won't. No matter how you beg or plead, I promise you, I will not come."

Now Jack let out an angry laugh. "Innocent by blackmail. Nice."

Sabine glanced at Trace and Jack. Those two would set on Seth like a couple of rabid wolves if she denied his request. And there was no doubt that she needed Seth's army. There wasn't a chance of surviving any of this without those child soldiers. She hated the thought of so many boys—and even a couple hundred girls now, too—fighting against the Guard. But without them the fight would be short, bloody, and hopeless. She looked to Eli now, and he at her. He nodded, confirming their silent understanding.

"I'll make an announcement," Sabine said finally, turning to Seth. "I know ... we all know now ... that you weren't the one to lead the Guard to us. Now go."

Seth stood still for another moment, his jaw clenched. "I'll summon my troops."

"The highers be with you," Eli murmured.

"Save it, Reverend." Seth turned on his heel and set off at a run.

BY MID-MORNING, Zenith's body had been laid out in the coffin Trace had built. Her hands were folded on her chest, her hair plaited with pale blue ribbons, her lips lightly rouged. Sabine and Eli helped Trace and the others heft the coffin from the coliseum's sick room to just outside the main entrance, onto a makeshift platform with stairs off either side. As they carried it out, solemn and silent, they trooped past the main stage. There, in the yawning expanse, the trapeze and other circus gear hung in the stale air like the skeleton of a massive beast long since extinct, its bones reconstructed in a museum exhibit. Perhaps, now that they were balanced on the brink of war, the Night Circus itself would become extinct.

And yet the circus would go on. Even as she walked with Zenith's weight on her shoulders, Sabine knew they would light the three rings at least one more time. Zenith would want them to. They would rally the people for what was to come.

A massive crowd had already gathered outside, and now they parted respectfully to make easy passage for the Triskelians. People wearing hats removed them and set them over their hearts. Others prayed, some in whispers, others in anguished shouts. Those few who were bold enough reached out to brush their fingers along the coffin as it passed, hoping to find a blessing in the touch. Still, the pallbearers gripped the coffin tight, worried that the mood could shift at any moment. Sabine breathed a hearty sigh of relief when they finally set the coffin down on the sawhorses.

And now the first several hundred citizens took their turn, eyes downcast as they shuffled sombrely past.

Eli stood tall beside Sabine as they guarded the coffin. He couldn't help but stare in wonderment, though, at the soldiers arrayed along the entire perimeter of the coliseum: Seth's boys. They stood in carefully poised attention, hugging guns to their chests and bearing flat, watchful expressions as uniform-issue as their vests. Eli was struck by their austerity, their discipline. And by how at odds these qualities were with the chubby cheeks of receding childhood and the gangly limbs of early adolescence. He spotted only two girls among them—no wonder it was called the Boys' Army of Triban.

It was the first time he'd seen BAT in formation. Until now he hadn't believed it was altogether real. He hadn't thought anyone, child or no, would do Seth's bidding willingly, yet it didn't appear that Seth was using force. Thousands had heeded Seth's call and now marched to his orders.

It moved Eli to see their devotion, their readiness to fight. What had they seen in Seth to have followed him in such numbers?

"They're just children," he whispered to Sabine. "They're too young to fight."

Sabine eyed him sidelong. "Do you have a realistic alternative?"

As the mourners slowly streamed past, Eli settled into a routine of greeting each one, and then, when they'd had their brief time, ushering them along with a warm "Blessed be, friend."

Sabine glanced at him. Her nerves were taut as sinew, yet here was Eli, all placating smiles and patient blessings. Head down in prayer, shoulder to shoulder with a filthy man in coveralls who recited a labourers' hymn over the coffin. Finally the man reached in and gave Zenith's folded hands a quick squeeze. Sabine didn't want these grubby strangers touching their leader, but she supposed it didn't matter now. And Zenith had meant as much to them as she had to Sabine, or so she tried to tell herself, with little conviction. Zenith was their Auntie, their symbol of hope ... even if she had never set anything real into motion. No, Sabine chastised herself. In that, she was wrong. Zenith's very death would be a catalyst.

HOURS LATER, when night had fallen, the lineup still stretched down the street and spilled into the surrounding blocks. Thousands waited patiently in line, holding candles with wooden rings at the base to catch the dripping wax. More candles set in jars lined the street and perched on windowsills. It was as if the galaxy itself had descended to pay its respects to Zenith, surrounding her with a dappled glow that would lift her up to the heavens.

Sabine set a hand on the rim of the coffin, holding it down lest the stars wanted to lift Zenith up too soon. But lift her up where? A glance to the skies. Was there a place in the heavens where the dead congregated, a constellation of souls? Sabine didn't think so. She turned her eyes back to Eli, who was either silently praying or had nodded off standing up. His dog, Bullet, had long since curled up under the coffin and was fast asleep.

"You believe she's gone to her highers," she said to Eli, as if they'd been in mid-conversation on the matter.

He opened his eyes, not missing a beat. "I do."

"You believe she's in a better place. You believe she's with Maman, and Charis. And our grandfather. Everyone who died at Triskelia."

"Yes." With his hands clasped behind his back and a priestly nod to another set of mourners, Eli fixed her with a sideways look. Poised like that, his shoulders squared, his gaze steady, he looked far more authoritative than he really was. Did these people really believe in him as a spiritual leader?

Sabine's small scowl was not lost on her brother. "Care to debate the subject?" Eli said. "Or are you looking to pick a fight?"

"I—" Sabine wasn't sure. "I want to believe, but I just don't."

Not after everything. All the death and destruction. No higher power would sanction that. No higher power would have allowed the Keyland elite to oppress the Droughtlanders as they had for generations. It just wasn't logical. She told Eli as much, and he listened, nodding.

"I don't pretend to understand," he finally said. "But I *do* believe."

"And them?" Sabine swept her arm out, taking in the crowd. "You expect them to believe too?"

"Well, yes." Eli turned slightly to better behold the crowd. "These are, after all, the very same people who practically burned down the city. A city full of people who are high most of the time, or trying to get high, a lot of them criminals, even. But here they are, lined up like polite Keyland children waiting to sit on Santa's knee. Why do you think that is? A healthy fear and respect for their highers, when it comes right down to it."

"No." Sabine shook her head. "The respect is for *Zenith*. It has nothing to do with the highers."

"Maybe." Eli's thoughts were already returning to the memorial service he would offer tomorrow, after the viewing of the body. It would be his first opportunity to bring the highers to these people in any formal way. This was his calling. This was what he was meant to do. That Zenith had not called him crazy for it, that she'd practically christened him to do so, served only to solidify his faith. He could not be swayed. He would not deny the voice ever again. The highers were there to guide him, not confuse him. He had only to trust.

A girl made her way up the stairs, a line of smaller children marching behind her, each clutching part of a rope she'd tied around her waist to keep them all in order. Bullet awoke and wagged his tail as they reached out to pet him.

"I'm Effie," the girl said, without so much as a glance at Zenith's corpse. The children crowded around the coffin though, peering over its lip, standing on tiptoe to get a better look. "I'm looking for Seth."

"He's not here," Sabine said.

"But he's your brother," Effie said. "You know where he is. And he'll be coming back, right?"

"At some point. Why?"

While the girls spoke, Eli tried to keep the rambunctious group of children from climbing right into the coffin. One of the very little ones jumped up, complaining he couldn't see, and when no one lifted him up he let out a wail and started bashing the coffin with his fists.

"Excuse me—" Eli pointed.

"Bear! That's enough." Effie hefted the little boy onto her bony hip.

"Who are you?" Sabine gave her a once-over. The girl was about her age, wiry, her clothes filthy but in good repair. No sick scars that she could see. The children in her care had clean faces but were otherwise dirty. Each of them carried a little sack, and their hair was neatly tied back in two braids, boys and girls alike.

"I met Seth in the tunnels," Effie said. "Under the city."

"Tunnels?" Sabine and Eli exchanged a glance. Sabine turned back to stare at Effie. "What tunnels?"

Effie narrowed her eyes. "Why would I tell you anything?"

"Because I am leader of Triskelia now." Sabine pursed her lips. "You do know that much, right?"

Effie's lips thinned into a grimace. "I know a lot more than you're giving me credit for, standing there all mightier than snot. I can tell you all about the tunnel systems, and by the looks of it, you'd like it if I did. Wouldn't you?"

"You're right about that." Sabine couldn't help but smile. This girl was tough. "Truce, okay?"

"Truce." Effie's frown relaxed into a cautious smile.

Now the little girl at Effie's side piped up. "What's truce?"

"Never you mind, Rabbit."

"And how come she don't know about the tunnels if she's the leader now?"

A very good point. Seth had never mentioned any tunnels, yet according to this girl, he'd been in them himself. Sabine bristled. How could she lead the revolution without being informed of such things? Things about the very city they were trying to protect!

"Why don't you come with me and we can talk." Sabine ushered Effie down the steps before Eli could send them off with some kind of weird blessing. That prayerful look of his was altogether unnerving. "Tunnels or no tunnels, you're holding up the line."

Effie passed the little boy to the girl called Rabbit. "You take Bear, okay?" The girl hiked him up in her arms while the toddler whined and arched in protest. "Look," Effie said to Sabine as she steered her charges into the dark of the coliseum, "I have to talk to Seth."

"You can talk to me." Sabine took the hands of a pair of children who gazed up at her shyly.

Effie stared at her, and then, after a quick glance over her shoulder, she leaned in. "The Guard is under the city," she whispered. "That's what I came to tell him."

"In the tunnels you speak of?"

She nodded.

"How do you know this?"

"We live there. In the tunnels, me and the kids. There was a blast yesterday, but we got out. The Guard is moving toward the centre of Triban, marching through the tunnels. They're headed right this way."

Effie clammed up as Sabine led her and the children into one of the back rooms. With much complaining from Bear and Rabbit, Effie persuaded the children to go with Anya, and only after Anya had promised the warmth of the stove and something to eat. Sabine, meanwhile, summoned Jack and Trace to join them, and they all sat down and listened while Effie told them all that she had seen.

She'd been living in the tunnels for as long as she could remember, and had been taking care of some of the other kids who'd ended up there as well. She wasn't sure how many were down there, all told. Lots.

"Only, we don't see much of each other, you know?" Effie said. "We mostly just keep to our bit of tunnel. We did see a few running when we were. After the Guard came through. We was scared they'd come back for us, so we all skedaddled right after."

"Did the Guard shoot at you?" Trace asked. "Did they have weapons?"

"They had armour and guns and all, but they didn't use them. Not on us anyway." Effie shook her head. "It was as if they hadn't even seen us. They just marched by. One of the kids was tripped, on purpose or not, I don't know. But other than that, they didn't bother with us at all."

"They're advancing on the city as we speak, then." Trace's jaw was clenched so hard the muscles over his cheekbone tensed. "We'll have to ready ourselves for battle—sooner than we thought."

"We should send for Seth then," Jack said without enthusiasm.

"Not just yet," Trace said.

"We'll need him, Trace." Sabine stressed each word.

"Where is Seth?" Effie asked once more. The children were wandering back in from the kitchen. Bear climbed into her lap and planted a sticky kiss on her forehead. "He said he'd take care of us. I told him we didn't need help. Only, now we do. Will he take us in? We don't want to go back down below. Not right now, anyway."

"We'll send for him." Jack stood. "He's mustering his troops at his headquarters."

"When will he come?" Effie asked.

"I don't know," Sabine admitted. "But you can stay here until things get sorted out."

"Here?" Effie glanced around. "In the coliseum?"

"With us." Sabine smiled in what she hoped was a reassuring way. "It's the safest place right now, trust me."

"But what's happening? What's going on?" Worry creased the girl's brow. "Is it war yet?"

"Honestly ... I don't know."

"But it's not safe here, is it?" Effie's eyes fixed on the mid-distance, imagining the worst. "They'll be coming after you. They don't want nothing with us. I know that much." She stood and lifted Bear onto her shoulders. "Thanks for the offer and all, but we're getting out of here while we still can." Bear gave Sabine a final dour look before Effie turned out of the room, her wards trailing behind her like so many puppies.

Seth marched three of his regiments across the city to the coliseum, returning with muscle as promised. The going was slow. Triban was like a tangle of yarn, the influx of newcomers who'd come to greet the Triskelians snagging and knotting with the skein of restive city dwellers. The boys struggled to stay in formation, fought to keep their eyes straight and march in position. It took them five hours to clear a distance that should have taken a fraction of that. Seth was on horseback, as were the six boys in charge, a pair for each regiment. They saw no Guards, only the mass of civilians scurrying about, aware that something big was happening around them. Just as people had swelled into the city, now they clogged its streets in a steady exodus. Those who feared a violent uprising streamed outward, their possessions tied into bundles strapped to their backs as they clutched their children's hands, dragging them along in a haphazard line. Seth wondered where they would go. Even if the city was about to explode, it was still better than the Droughtland that lay beyond it.

The troops cleared the last corner before the coliseum just as Effie turned it in the other direction. She glanced up but did not see Seth, so awed was she by the sight of three thousand boy soldiers marching silently in formation.

"What's that?" Rabbit asked.

"An army. But not like the Guard. Don't worry, this one's on our side," Effie told her as the boys marched by, one-two, one-two. Bear puffed his chest out and swung his arms at his sides, but did not ask to be set down. The other children laughed as they marched in a tight little circle, staying close to Effie. Not Rabbit, though. She leaned against Effie, nervous of the stomping, of the orders hollered out in clipped barks. Then Effie thought to take a closer look. This was, of course, the Boys' Army of Triban. Seth's army. He'd be with them, wouldn't he? She stood on tippytoe and scanned the neat rows of boys in their colourful vests. By that time Seth had already reached the entrance to the coliseum.

2

I nstead of a hello, Sabine confronted Seth with news of what Effie
had told her.

"And you kept this from me?"

"It was before you came! Be reasonable, Sabine. I haven't had time to
even think about such things as what I haven't told you."

"But here we are, trying to organize. You can't leave anything out.
I should know every detail."

"Then you might want to note that I haven't taken a dump in two
days and I have a bellyache because of it."

"You know what I mean."

"Sabine, believe me when I tell you that the system is small. Most of
the tunnels have collapsed on themselves. The Guard can't get far." This
was true. He'd come upon countless logjams of crumbled debris while he
was down there. "I doubt even a quarter of the system is actually usable."

"Well, the Guard is making use of that much at least!"

"And only that much," Seth said. "They're bold enough to ride right
through the city to meet us—they can't get here via the tunnels."

"They can't?"

"There aren't any below this entire sector. It was built after the tunnels
had already been decommissioned. I would have told you if there were
tunnels leading here."

Sabine gave him a skeptical look. "We'll talk more about this later," she said as she turned down the corridor. "I'm going to check on Nana. She and Rosa are preparing Papa's body."

"Fine." Not even the mention of Rosa could knock Seth out of his carefully hidden dismay. So the Guard knew about the tunnels. Seth had used them himself to get to Regis, and he'd seen only a few ragged children down there. He'd *figured* it was too good to be true. Well, if the Guard were moving in underground, Seth would simply wait for them above, where daylight and space were cheap weapons and the ire of Triban's citizens cheaper still. And his BAT soldiers knew the streets and alleys of Triban inside and out.

But still. He summoned two of his boys to the coliseum kitchen, where they cowered, waiting for some kind of reprimand.

"I have a mission for you." Thrilled, they straightened up at once. "It's top secret, understand?"

The boys nodded and shared a quick, darting glance.

"I mean it," Seth snapped. "You mustn't tell anyone." He told them how to get into the tunnels from below the brothel. "I want you to go down there, take a good look around, then come back and tell me what you find."

"But what're we looking for?" the bolder one said.

"I'm not going to tell you. That way, you'll take notice of everything." The boys nodded.

"Now go. Make sure you have food and water for a couple of days. And do not speak to anyone else, understand?" Another nod. "Off you go."

With a salute, they were gone, leaving Seth alone in the room. He leaned forward tensely in his chair, drumming his fingers on the worn wooden surface of the kitchen table. What did the Guard know? What were they waiting for?

Suddenly the door creaked open and there was Rosa, with Sabine right behind.

"Rosa!" He hadn't seen her since those moments after Pierre's body had arrived, and before that, only fleetingly, just before Zenith's ... just before he'd done what Zenith had beseeched him to do.

Rosa paled. She murmured something to Sabine, turned on her heel, and backed out of the room.

"She doesn't want to see you." Sabine sat beside him.

"I just want to talk to her."

In the hall Eli was approaching. He could hear them talking. He hesitated, listening in the shadows.

"Well, she doesn't want to talk to you."

"It was all so long ago." But he could remember it so clearly, he and Rosa travelling across the Droughtland, spending the dangerously hot hours of the day in a sweaty knot of limbs and breath.

"Two days is a long time?"

Seth furrowed his brow. "What are you talking about, two days?"

"You know exactly what I'm talking about. When you were with Zenith last."

Seth rose to his feet and turned away from his sister in one swift movement. He busied himself with filling a mug with boiled water, thankful for the sulphuric smell of the purity drops they had to add. The smell kept his mind clear, or almost. Parts of those last moments came back: his pressing the pillow over Zenith's face, her mouth open in one last pull for breath. He'd killed her, yes, but she'd asked him to. Begged him, even. It had been merciful.

"Rosa says that you must've done something to Zenith."

Seth steeled his expression. "I did nothing."

"Ah, the common refrain."

"She was moments away from death. I only happened to be the one there."

"Hmm."

"What?" He banged his mug down, water sloshing over the lip. "Speak your mind."

From the doorway Eli watched Sabine pale. This was a corner his siblings should not turn just now. Eli knew what Sabine was talking about. He had his own thoughts on the matter. But now was not the time for them to disintegrate into a battle over ethics, when a real fight was so near. He stepped into the room. "What's there to eat?"

Sabine and Seth kept their gaze locked, neither willing to be the first to look away.

"Everything okay?"

"Fine," they snapped in unison.

Sabine looked away first. "You're still a guest here, Seth."

Seth stared at her. "My name has been cleared."

"That doesn't make you part of Triskelia—"

"You have no reason to exclude me now."

"No?" She raised an eyebrow. "And what about what we were discussing just now?"

"I suggest you drop it." Seth shook his head in disgust. "Move forward, or you'll lose this battle for sure."

Sabine could only look at him. Was that a threat? She had to give him credit, if it was. It had worked.

Eli brightened. "Maybe if we pray together—"

"Stay out of it, Reverend." Seth said it in the same way he used to call him *Eliza*. Same tone. Same scorn.

"Then let's just sit here without arguing, okay?"

"Why aren't you out there laying on your healing hands and speaking in tongues, brother?"

"Even spiritual freaks need a break every once and a while."

"Don't wait too long. The Guard is going to break this all apart, any minute."

"Maybe the Guard is letting the people pay their respects to Zenith, undisturbed," Eli suggested.

Sabine laughed. "You must think quite highly of the Guard if you believe they're 'letting' us do anything."

"No," Seth said without looking up. He stabbed a carrot and then punctuated his next few words with the fork. "They don't care about any of that. It's something much bigger. The circus. If I were the Guard, that's when I'd move in. There's no way I'd—"

Sabine interrupted him. "We're not cancelling it, Seth."

Seth shrugged. "Suit yourself."

"But I'm not," Sabine said. "That's the whole point. It's for everyone."

"It's for Zenith, really," Eli said. "It's the least we can do for her."

"And it's the most you can do for the Guard," Seth said. "You might as well give up now." Another shrug. "But what do I know? I'm just in charge of the entire military operation of this so-called revolution."

Sabine folded her arms and fixed Seth with her steely blue eyes. "You'll get to play war in short order, trust me."

"It's not play." Seth emptied his drink.

"You know what I mean." Sabine slathered a bun with jam to take to Celeste, and then another one for Rosa. "As for honouring Zenith, we do it now."

"Why not after?" Seth asked.

"What if there *is* no after?"

"Of course we need to honour her now," Eli said. "The people demand it, and it's only right. But there'll always be some kind of 'after,' Sabine." He wanted to approach his sister, touch her shoulder as he had for the mourners who'd come to see Zenith lying in state, but Sabine was practically vibrating with an energy that warned him to mind his distance. "We can't know what it will be exactly, but there *will* be an after. It is the one sure thing. As they say, this too shall pass."

"It all very well might *pass*." Sabine looked away. "But the question is, who will be here then?"

"I will," Seth said with a genuine grin. "I have every intention of it."

AS DAWN BROKE the next day people were already starting to convene for Zenith's memorial. Yet the service wouldn't begin until much later that afternoon, and would serve as a prelude to the circus performance. Eli had been awake all night, sitting with the last of the people to view Zenith's body and watching the crowd gather and settle in for the long wait. Today he would deliver the eulogy, and as he sat with his head bowed, silently rehearsing, someone handed him a small, warm bundle of baby. Eli looked down at the infant, and then up at his best friend.

"Nappo!" Eli gave him a one-armed hug as Bullet danced between them, delighted to see both Nappo and his little brother Teal, and giving Tasha and the baby a sniff each.

"May I introduce you to Emma." Nappo beamed. "My daughter."

"She's horribly ugly." Eli laughed. "Which makes sense, because she looks exactly like you."

"She's beautiful. And anyone who says otherwise is going to get a taste of my fists."

"She looks more like me," Tasha piped up. "Around the eyes especially."

Teal, meanwhile, tiptoed up to the coffin and peered in before glancing over his shoulder at his brother. "She *is* dead. For real."

"There were rumours on the road," Nappo explained. "All kinds of stories."

"Dead is dead, Teal. And we'll say our proper goodbyes at the service," Tasha said. "Come away from there now."

"Let's go," Nappo said then. "Doesn't feel right talking like this beside her."

As the small group descended the stairs, Eli turned to his friend. "Safe trip?"

"Not really," Nappo said with a shrug. "But we wanted to get here to see Zenith."

Tasha pursed her lips. "I told him he shoulda left Teal up the mountain with the other kids. It ain't safe down here."

"And I told you," Nappo took the baby from Eli and handed him to Teal. The little boy, now a six-year-old uncle, stood still, shoulders scrunched in concentration as he carefully positioned her in his arms. "That there's no way I'm letting my kid brother out of my sight. Not then, not ever. Same goes for Emma. I take care of them best."

Teal grinned up at Eli. "Besides, I'm old enough to fight too, right?"

"Not a chance." Nappo gave Teal a playful knock on the head.

"Have you done the naming ceremony yet?" Eli asked.

"We were hoping you'd do it," Nappo replied. "Would you?" A sly grin. "Reverend?"

"How do you know they call me that?"

"There's all kinds of news on the road."

"Even about me?" At first, only the Triskelians at the coliseum had called him 'Reverend,' and only because Seth had started it, and none too kindly. Soon though, and especially since Zenith's death, the moniker had taken hold. Farther afield than he'd thought, apparently. Eli felt a quick swell of pride.

"About a lot of things." Nappo poked him. "So, will you? Do the naming ceremony?"

"This from the guy who said I was going crazy?"

Nappo shrugged. "Things change when you've got a kid."

"You all of a sudden find your highers?"

Tasha bristled. "I never lost mine, whatever you're implying. I'm the one making him do right by the baby, get her named properly in the eyes of the highers."

Nappo winked at Eli. "Make the best with what you've got, eh?"

"Sure," Eli said. "Of course I'll do it."

"Not now, of course. What with everything. When it settles a bit." Nappo held out his hand, offering a handshake—verboten outside the Keys, an inside joke between the two. "Deal?"

"Deal." Something in Nappo's expression worried Eli. His friend had changed. He sounded happy, but the usual glimmer in his eye was gone. Eli looked from Nappo to Tasha, whose brow was furrowed, matching her pinched lips. She, too, was different from how he remembered.

"Come with me." He put an arm across Tasha's shoulders. "Let's find your little family a place to settle in, and some food."

Nappo and Tasha shared a cool glance. "All right," Tasha said finally.

"Food! Food! Food!" Teal chanted. He pushed the baby at Nappo, grabbed Eli's hand, and hauled him toward the doorway. "Let's go!"

HOURS LATER, Eli was back on the little platform, looking out over the largest crowd he'd ever seen. There was no end to the sea of people. Each side street held another fat tributary, and beyond that—Eli was sure—even more people. The whole of Triban, it seemed, had gathered for Zenith's memorial service and the circus performance that would follow. Eli scanned the crowd again as Seth's soldiers cleared a path for the Triskelians to make their way to the front.

Seth himself stood with his soldiers off to one side, while more BAT troops flanked the back and opposite side of the crowd. Eli looked over at him now, standing at attention as if he were at a military event, his soldiers doing the same. Seth wasn't here for Zenith. That much was obvious. He was here in his role as military leader. He was no Triskelian; he'd never be.

Finally, the crowd quiet now, Sabine glanced up at Eli and nodded. His heart pounded. The air was alive with anticipation. Eli took a steadying breath and began. "Droughtlanders, people of the city, supporters, all of you who loved and respected Zenith." As his voice rang out he lifted his hands, palms to the heavens, just as he'd rehearsed. "Welcome. We are gathered here today to honour her. Please join me in prayer ..."

It was Eli's very first eulogy, carefully prepared and now delivered in an ever-steadying voice to the masses of silent mourners. Thank the highers he'd memorized it; he'd faltered at first, so amazed and relieved was he by the crowd's rapt attention. He too must possess at least a little of whatever it was that made Seth's army do his bidding and that made a natural leader of Sabine.

By the time Eli finished, the sound of so many people weeping for their fallen leader had become a chorus in itself.

Eli closed the ceremony by inviting everyone to sing Zenith's favourite melody, "The Star Hanger's Song." Thousands of voices joined together, lifting their sobs into a real song. The sound was so beautiful that Eli got shivers.

... night after night, by and by, stringing stars up in the sky ...

The Triskelians hoisted Zenith's coffin back onto their shoulders, and still singing, made their way down the steps of the platform and into the coliseum. The deathminder would be coming for her body.

... for travellers as they roam, for the lost to find their way home ...

After the song ended, Eli's contentment remained. He'd done it: his first eulogy! He'd done right by Zenith.

But now, as the masses of people rearranged themselves into a lineup for the circus, the city's pallor returned, even greyer and colder than before.

"Outta my way!" A woman was trying to sneak up the line. "I was holding that spot!"

The man she shoved did not take kindly to her budging in. "Back off, woman."

"I was holding it. There was a handkerchief!"

He guffawed. "On the ground? That's how you was holding your spot?" He shook his head. "I don't think so."

The woman growled and launched herself at him, clawing at his face.

Eli saw Seth take notice of the scrap and break away from his post. As Seth made his way over, so did Teal and Nappo, with baby Emma asleep in her sling.

"At least they kept the peace while you were doing your thing," Nappo said.

"Thank the highers," Eli said as Seth pushed past them.

"Just going to stand there?" Seth said over his shoulder. "Typical!" Seth grabbed the woman by the collar and dragged her away as the man wound up for a swing at her.

"Anyway." Nappo ignored the skirmish. "You did great."

"They didn't say anything," Eli said. "Nothing at all."

"Who?"

"My highers."

"Well, that's good, right?" Nappo have him a hearty pat on the back. "Maybe you've been cured."

"There's nothing to be cured *of*, Nappo. I've gotten used to it."

"You don't have to get used to crazy."

"Maybe it's my calling."

Around them the lineup grew, eager for the circus to begin.

"I better go find Tasha," Nappo said as Emma scrunched up her face and let out a cry. "The baby's hungry."

"She was here for the service. Where'd she go?"

Nappo shrugged. "I don't know. And I wouldn't care either, only she's the one with the, uh, ta-tas." Nappo tugged the sling around to his front and snuggled his face into Emma's. "Isn't that right, baby girl? My hungry little chickadee?"

"I might be crazy, but I'm in good company. You've been reduced to a babbling fool, my friend."

"And so have you." Nappo's tone was kind, even if his words were harsh. "Only my muse is this beautiful baby and you're being dazzled by some faceless higher power."

Teal leaned against Nappo and glanced up at Eli, waiting for the two to keep arguing. But Eli turned, saying over his shoulder, "You better find your nursemaid then."

Eli didn't really want to talk to Nappo, not when he was like this, assuming some kind of instant wisdom along with his instant fatherhood. Who was Nappo to be critical? He had his life and Eli had his, and they'd never truly understand each other's reality. And if Eli could accept that, so should Nappo. Nappo was blessed in his own way, and so was Eli.

He no longer thought of his highers' speaking to him as a curse. It was a gift. He would not turn away from it, whatever his best friend said.

Eli had been looking forward to Nappo's return. He'd wanted to take him aside and share with him all his thoughts and fears. He wanted Nappo's help to sort them out, put them into some kind of sensible order, if there was one. But Nappo was busy with his new little family now, leaving Eli all alone with his thoughts. Those thoughts were not always good company. They drummed on his eyes and pushed at his temples, causing the worst kind of headache.

Eli knew he had to go and get ready for the circus performance, but he couldn't seem to make his feet walk back inside. He needed a few moments alone, out here, where the air wasn't fresh but at least the colours and the noise and the smells were a distraction from his thoughts.

"Reverend!" A boy covered in old sick scars waved him over to a burning barrel, a banner reading LONG LIVE TRISKELIA tacked up above the gaggle of Tribanites huddled around the warmth of the fire. Eli accepted the teetery stool they offered.

"Fine service," the scarred boy said.

"Thank you." Eli watched the man sitting across from the boy. He sucked in on a pipe, grinning at Eli as he did. The dust smoke was both sweet and acrid, and made Eli's eyes water. "Are you all coming to the circus?"

"Nope," said the man with the pipe as he let out the smoke through thin lips. "The BAT boys are going around asking anyone who's seen it to kindly sit it out so's others can have a look."

"And you've all been before?" Eli felt awkward making small talk with these people, but he wasn't ready to leave just yet either. His eyes followed the pipe as it was passed to the boy.

The group nodded.

"And you were all honest about it?"

The man shrugged. "We're good people, us Tribanites. You think we're all nothing but fighting and gambling and getting high?"

At this, the boy laughed. "We are, ain't we?"

The man gave him a rap on the head. "And we're more too, specially in times like this."

"Reverend?" The boy held out the pipe to Eli.

"Uh, no. Thanks."

"I ain't contagious. Haven't been since I was three years old."

"It's not that—"

"Too good to get dusted with the plain folk?" the man said with a sneer. "All well and good to preach to us, but too highfalutin to come down and actually get to know us, eh?"

The man had a point. Eli took the pipe. The bowl was warm, the stem moist from the boy's spit. He lifted it to his lips.

"It'll only help with your performance tonight if you're in the circus."

"I am," Eli said, more to buy time than to boast. "Will it wear off by then?"

"Even if it doesn't, it'll only give you a hand up, Reverend." The man smiled broadly at him, showing off brown, jagged teeth. Eli couldn't help himself. He wiped the pipe on his shirt, ignoring the disgruntled mumblings of his audience.

Would the dust make it easier? Not just the circus, but everything? Would it make the highers' messages clearer? Would it sort out his thoughts? Eli glanced around to make sure no one he knew was watching. He'd try it just this once, if only—he told himself quite convincingly—if only to know fully what he was preaching against.

He closed his lips around the pipe and sucked in. His lungs fought back and he coughed. He pulled the pipe away and wiped his lips with the back of his hand.

"Have another toke, Rev." The boy was nodding at him, grinning. "On us."

Eli was suddenly and keenly aware of all that was good in the world. This little group of people ... so beautiful! Triban, an oasis! He sucked in again, this time holding the smoke for a long moment until his lungs won and he doubled over, racked with coughs.

"Should make you the star of the show, Rev."

"Thank you," Eli coughed out, not sure what he was thanking them for. He stood, reaching his arms out to steady himself. He'd made a grave mistake; he couldn't even walk straight. How could be perform on the trapeze like this? But another dizzying moment passed and suddenly he felt not only steady on his feet but as if he could run across the city in one single heartbeat. "Thank you!" he practically bellowed as he made his way back to the coliseum. "Peace be with you!"

ELI RAN INTO TEAL, quite literally, just outside the back entrance. A shimmering light bathed the little boy in an aura of blue and purple. Eli blinked, and blinked again, but the vision remained. He looked away, and then back, and now along with the colours came dancing sparkles at the periphery of his vision. He loved this boy like a brother! Beautiful, brave little Teal.

"What is it, little brother?" He smiled at Teal and hugged him to him.

"Anya's looking for you to fit your costume." Teal looked up at him, his brow furrowed. "You okay, Eli?"

"Yeah. Yes! I am fine. You are fine. We're all fine!" He grabbed hold of Teal's arms and swung him around. Normally Teal loved this game, but something about Eli's manner made him uncomfortable.

"Lemme down!" He pulled away. "You dusted?"

"Did not." Eli folded his arms and gave Teal the sternest look he could muster. "It is possible that I was sitting at a fire and may have inhaled the smoke of the dusters around me. This is possible. This could be. Maybe."

"Anya's looking for you." Teal didn't know what else to say. Nappo had gotten clean with Eli's help, and Eli was always going on about how bad dust was. Teal was confused. "Let's go."

"Let's go indeed!" Eli slung an arm across Teal's scrawny shoulders and marched the two of them into the coliseum.

3

⚜

There wasn't much left to be done to the rigging: only a few bolts to tighten and the trapeze line to be checked for fraying. While the lineup outside hollered for the doors to open, most of the running around had to do with costumes and lighting and props. Teal told Eli that he had to be at the three rings in five minutes for a quick rehearsal, but not without his costume. Eli sprinted down the corridor toward the room where Anya was arranging the costumes, cobbled together out of what she could find and what they'd brought. He flung open the door to find Trace right up in Sabine's face, not exactly yelling at her, but almost.

"I want to be out there, on the front line!"

"There *is* no front line yet." Sabine did not flinch from his anger. "We need you here."

"Please, don't go." Behind the two, Anya clutched a swatch of fabric to her chest, her face white. *"Je ne veux pas que tu te fasse mal."*

"And what if Seth is right and they attack during the performance?" Trace's eyes were dark with fury. "You want all your best men in here?"

"I do, yes."

Trace let out a frustrated snarl when he noticed a bewildered Eli standing in the doorway.

"What's going on? Can I help?"

"Can you *help*?" Trace said, mocking him. "Can the Reverend help? Why yes, yes he can, by staying out of it! Go pray, you fool. See what good that does."

"Trace—" Sabine reached out to him, but Trace cocked his head, refusing her gesture.

"Calme, s'il vous plaît," Anya murmured. "Calm, my love."

Trace's shoulders relaxed, but only slightly.

"We need you here," Sabine said again. "After, you can fight."

"After—"

"Yes, after," Sabine said, her tone firm. "But for tonight, we need you to be ringmaster."

A moment pushed between the four when no one spoke. All looked from one to another, daring each other to be the first to break it.

"How do you say in English? The show must go on," Anya pleaded as she reached for a pile of shiny material. "Eli, your costume."

Eli embraced her in a hug. "Why, *merci beaucoup,* gorgeous!"

Sabine eyed her brother thoughtfully.

THE STANDS WERE PACKED long before the show was set to begin. During his patrol Seth happened to stride across the stage, and as he did, the crowd erupted in cheers. "Long live the boy soldiers!" Seth paused to give them a wave before he ducked backstage. That sent the masses into another uproar.

In the dim light of the wings Eli and Sabine were helping the clowns with their face paint. It would be an odd performance, given that all the Triskelian children who normally played the clowns were back at Cascadia. It was the clowns' job to distract the crowd, to tame it in anticipation of the performers' appearance. Tonight only six of the clowns had any experience, with another dozen having been accepted off the street and given a crash course in crowd control disguised as comedy and slapstick. Teal was the sole child among them, and he was quiet now, shy to be among the experienced and the streetwise alike.

"You think that helps, exciting the crowd like that?" Sabine asked Seth as she drew a fat red mouth around a new clown's stubble.

"They love me," Seth said with a shrug. "Can you blame them?"

"Never mind." Sabine eyed him with a frown. "Everything ready at your end?"

"As well as can be." Seth sat on the edge of the upended cable spool that was serving as a table. "Every able soldier I've got is in position, either right outside or at the various spots we talked about."

"And the tunnels?"

"I told you, the Guard aren't down there. At least, not anywhere that my boys could find."

Sabine finished the clown's makeup and waved him along. "And how do the stands look?"

Seth shrugged. "If you're wondering if I've found any Guardy spies among the circus goers, then no. But you should know that you're at four times capacity out there."

"How did that happen?"

"It was either that or cause a riot by turning people away. What would *you* have done?"

Teal peeked around the corner and gasped. "There's too many!" Even under his face paint he paled.

"What about safety?" Eli asked, his face stuck in a permanent grin. "Your friend the fire marshal won't like that, will he?"

"Does it really matter?" Seth laughed. "Considering everything?"

"Yes," Eli said. "Everything matters."

"I guess not," Sabine said, appraising Eli once again. She could see that he was different, changed since delivering the service. More confident, less grim.

Seth winked at Eli. "She's brighter than you. But then, that's not hard."

Eli, still marvelling at how everyone was bathed in a cloak of light, took great pride in holding up his end of the conversation. "It's a matter of principle. If a fire breaks out, or if any bombing starts, there's no way to get everyone out safely."

"Well, Reverend, how about you pray to your highers and have them keep everyone nice and calm tonight, the Guard included."

Eli set down his grease paint and embraced Seth. "I will, brother."

Seth shrugged away and gawked at him. "You're mad, Eli."

"Not at all."

"Keep an eye on him," Seth advised Sabine as he strode back out.

And now Sabine yanked Eli away from the others. "What's the matter with you?" she whispered harshly.

The light around Sabine was silvery blue. "Nothing's the matter." Eli forced his mind to order, even as the dust danced inside him, making him jittery. "I'm fine. Just excited about the performance."

A BAND had been patched together from the city's musicians, and it started up now in a corner of the coliseum. It was rough going at first, with an enthusiastic tuba player dominating the others and no one quite locating a recognizable beat, but after a few bars they found their pace. Now they were plunking out more of a polka than the atmospheric trance music the Night Circus normally performed with.

"That's awful." Sabine pulled aside the curtain to have a look. Letting it fall back, she shook her head. "This is going to be an absolute disaster, isn't it?"

"It'll be fine. A little higgledy-piggledy, but fine." Jack put his tattooed arms around her, the ink on his forearms rippling as he held her tight. Gavin joined in, encircling the two of them and resting his red head on Jack's shoulder. The couple had grown closer in the months since the attack, and with Gavin's little brother Toby in their care, they were the closest thing around to a true family. Sabine half envied Toby, having those two to love and protect him so fiercely. The little boy had been grumpy all day about not getting to go on stage, but he burrowed in now with a grin, clinging to Gavin's leg.

Sabine put a hand on Toby's head, regretting once again that she hadn't insisted on leaving him back at Cascadia, in relative safety, along with Althea and the other children. But Gavin and Jack wouldn't have it.

"Me too!" Teal squeezed in between the three, and then poked his head out. "Nappo, come on!"

Nappo, dressed in his clown's ripped pantaloons, striped stockings, and patchwork vest, ambled over and stood close, Emma cooing happily from her sling.

Eli gave him a shove. "Aw, get in there. You know you've turned into a great big softie since Emma." The dust must be wearing off, because Eli couldn't see the auras around everyone now. He still felt fantastic, but he wouldn't tell Nappo about it, not after seeing him through his mess of withdrawal.

Nappo feigned a shrug but then cut to the side and pushed Eli right into the group, sending them both staggering back a little.

Now Anya took a tentative step toward the huddle. She glanced back once at Trace, who stood sullenly with arms crossed, and then launched herself into the people pile. The group clung to one another, laughing and wishing each other a broken leg and a stellar performance.

"Okay, everyone." Sabine took a step back from the huddle. "This might be the last Night Circus for a very long time."

"If ever," Trace muttered. He was leaning over the group, despite himself still the protector he naturally was.

"We're going to go out and do our best and try not to think about what's happening outside these walls tonight," Sabine continued. "Tomorrow we're soldiers, but tonight we are the Night Circus."

Now she turned to Eli. "Reverend? If you would lead us in a prayer?"

Eli felt his cheeks flush. What to say? But then he closed his eyes and felt the calm brewing. "Highers, hear us now as you always do. Watch over us tonight, as you always do. Be with us—"

"Blessed be," Trace said, suddenly ending the prayer. Eli glanced up. Trace's expression wasn't cold, but still, he'd cut him off. The huddle broke apart.

"Thank you, Eli." Sabine gave him another hug.

Nappo sent Teal to collect Tasha for the baby's feeding, slipping out of the sling while Anya held the baby.

"All this hugging, feels like we're lambs to slaughter."

Eli clapped his friend on the back. "Ah well, you and me, we've been through worse."

SETH RETURNED BACKSTAGE to announce that they were as ready as they'd ever be at the front of the house. He glanced at his watch. "You all set back here?"

"You bet!" Eli gave Seth a matching pair of thumbs up.

"Sure," Sabine added brightly, even while her eyes said otherwise. "Let's do it."

Seth slapped a post. "All right."

Trace buttoned up his ratty tailcoat, ready to take on the daunting role of ringmaster. Anya pinned a silk flower into his lapel and kissed him on both cheeks. In return he swept her off her feet into one of his fierce bear hugs they'd all been missing since the massacre.

She cried out in surprise and gave him a playful swat. He set her down, and without another word strode out into the ring, into the spotlight, and into a deep, formal bow that silenced the stands almost instantly.

The triplets watched from the wings, Seth with his eyes darting from soldier to soldier, Eli staring off into the half distance, wondering at the beauty of it all, and Sabine gazing at the trapeze, muscles aching with memory and excitement. She couldn't wait to get up there once more.

Trace picked up his bullhorn, any earlier reluctance gone. "Good evening!" The dark makeup around his eyes made the whites of them pop in the spotlight as he came up from his bow. "Greetings city folk, Droughtlanders, Triskelians ..." He turned in a slow circle as his deep voice bellowed out. "Tonight you will feast at a buffet of delights! You will be amazed. You will be awed. You will put your hands together to welcome the one, the only ... the undefeatable"—a dramatic sweep of his arm—"Night Circus!"

The crowd was on their feet in a heartbeat, hollering and clapping and stomping their feet. Eli and the rest of his troupe held back in the wings, awaiting their cue. Sabine and Jack stood at the curtain, Gavin and Eli just behind them.

Gavin would normally mind the rigging, but with Lia and Zari gone from the troupe, dead in the massacre, he would perform tonight despite his shoulder injury. He and Eli both—Eli's arm still throbbed mercilessly on occasion—had had Rosa slather their shoulders in a numbing salve. And both were chewing on a willow-bark pill as they waved to the crowd on their preliminary circuit of the ring. Eli wound his arm up, testing it.

"Don't push it," Gavin hissed.

"As good as new." Eli swung his arm around one more time. "Can't feel so much as a pinch of pain. That willow bark works wonders."

"Willow bark my ass," Gavin growled. He gripped Eli's shoulders, forcing him to stand still. "You got more on board than that willow bark."

Jack and Sabine waved for them to keep up.

"You mess up tonight," Gavin said over the noise, "I'll kill you."

Eli nodded, knowing even through the dust not to argue with Gavin, who'd never had more than a frown and harsh words for Eli, no matter how hard he'd tried. He'd given up long ago; Gavin's animosity was just a fact of life.

They jogged to the far edge of the centre ring and stopped. In the middle, a pair of acrobats scaled the rope ladder in time to the band, which had shifted into a kind of bass-heavy, ambient melody. When the crowd spotted Sabine jogging around the ring the enthusiasm doubled.

"Sabine! Sabine!" they chanted, echoing the cries that had greeted her last performance, at Lisette's memorial, which now seemed so long ago. Sabine grabbed Eli's hand and raised it triumphantly, pushing the crowd into a near frenzy. Then she and Eli broke apart to take their positions at the bottom of the parachute silks, where the acrobats would descend.

Eli looked up at Lad and Aggie. He didn't know them well, but suddenly he loved them enormously. He gripped his silk—if either of the men slipped he'd catch them effortlessly in his own two arms, he was certain. Now Aggie and Lad were perched high up at each edge of the scaffolding, metres away from the silk. Then, without so much as a glance down, they leapt off in perfect synchronicity and were airborne, burly arms outstretched, reaching for the silk. The crowd gasped and grew quiet as they sailed through the air. Eli tugged back, the drape of fabric heavy in his hands, positioning it for Aggie's capture. Sabine pulled back on her own swath, and at the same second each acrobat took hold of his silk and hugged it, sliding down in graceful bends and twists and then slowing as the music followed suit, the beats mellowing until the duo came to rest.

And the music kept pulsing, the very life force of the coliseum. Eli had never felt so alive, so full of purpose.

SABINE, ELI, JACK, AND GAVIN were the third act in. By this time the crowd had settled into the show, and for that Sabine was grateful. With battle looming and the threat of death all around, thousands of Tribanites and Droughtlanders had congregated here, as much for the solidarity as for the Night Circus itself. These people were her allies. They wanted her, they knew she was next, and they chanted her name with a fervour that set her *blood boiling.* So much was expected from her now, yet she was not altogether convinced she could provide.

"*Sabine! Sabine! Sabine!*"

Her heart raced so fast she thought it might leap out of her chest and roll to a stop in the sawdust on the floor of the stage.

Sabine linked arms with Eli and Jack, and Jack with Gavin. They strode into position in the centre ring, stood in a row, and lifted their arms to greet the stands. As Trace brought the bullhorn to his lips, the chanting grew louder. "You may think you've already seen it all tonight. You may think you've seen the best we have to offer. But what we have next—"

"*SABINE! SABINE!*" The coliseum shook as the spectators pounded their feet in time to her name.

Trace lowered the bullhorn and glanced over his shoulder at her. "They want you."

To speak. To say something. Sabine pulled her arm out of Jack's. He nodded at her, and then the others did too, all of them giving her an encouraging smile.

She stepped away from her troupe and the crowd erupted in cheers. The girl manning the spotlight pulled it back, enlarging it until Sabine was bathed in its heat and could no longer see the crowd beyond the glare.

Trace held out the bullhorn to her. They'd salvaged it from the ruins of Triskelia, the same old horn that Night Circus barkers and ringmasters and Zenith herself had used for untold decades. The copper was smooth at the handle, warm from Trace's grip. The patina caught the light, the dents caught the shadows. Sabine closed her hand around it, and suddenly, as if she'd just cast a spell, the coliseum was cloaked in profound silence.

All the words she could think to say caught in her throat like fireflies trapped in a jar. Eli watched her open and close her mouth, trying to make them loosen. Sabine caught him watching and gave him a pleading look. She held out her hand, nodding for him to join her. When he did, clasping her hand in his, her words were freed.

"My brother, Eli. And I also summon my brother Seth, leader of the Boys' Army of Triban." There was a shuffling now as the audience craned and turned, watching for him. Seth strode out of the darkness and joined Eli and Sabine, standing slightly apart, stance squared as if he were being inspected by the Guard. Sabine took his hand and pulled him closer.

"If there was any doubt of my brother's loyalties, let me put those doubts to rest now.

"As most of you have heard, he was not the one who led the Guard to Triskelia." Sabine paused. "The one who gave away Triskelia did so under pain of torture and fear of death, and was executed nonetheless at the hands of the Guard. My grandfather, dearest friend of Zenith and faithful Triskelian. Pierre Fabienne."

This was not news. Word, of course, had already spread throughout the city like a vicious sick. What was a surprise, though, was Sabine's decision to clear Seth's name so publicly.

"Seth is exonerated of any suspicion. And we thank him for his army, for the muscle he brings to this battle." Sabine paused again. "Zenith, in her last moments, named Seth the body of the revolution." She raised Seth's hand in hers, sparking off a thunderous cheer. Beside them, Eli kept his expression even, despite the jealousy coursing through his veins.

But Sabine was lifting his hand too. "And in the same breath Zenith named Eli as the spirit of the revolution. Here's to the Reverend!" Another cheer, albeit more subdued, obligatory.

"And as your leader, Zenith named me the mind of the revolution. We are your triumvirate." The crowd faltered. Sabine realized they didn't know what the word meant. "Your trinity of leadership." With that the cheers renewed, but with an added frenzy.

"They've had enough," Seth leaned in to say. "Let's get on with it. There's no way of knowing how much time we've got."

Sabine nodded, but distractedly, as she raised the bullhorn again. "Tonight we perform for you. But that is not our sole purpose. Not by far. First and foremost, tonight is a call for unity! A call to arms! You are all soldiers of the revolution!"

This brought the throngs to their feet, but they didn't raise the din, so dearly were they hanging on to Sabine's words. "My people! Children of the revolution! We will win this war! We will triumph! And the world will be ours once again!"

The crowd could contain itself no longer. They stamped in place, yelled at the tops of their voices, threw the ribbons and confetti they'd brought for the finale.

Eli sucked in his breath as the whole building heaved, agitated and delirious with passion. He was surprised the stands didn't empty out into the street right away, nevermind the circus.

"That may not have been wise," Seth said amidst the din, speaking for both brothers.

"It was necessary." Sabine handed the horn back to Trace and brought her hand up to her throat. She fingered the medallion Pierre had made, one for each of them, their names carved on the sides of the Triskelian triangle. Instinctively, Eli did the same.

Scowling at them both, Seth strode back to the mouth of the main corridor where he'd been keeping watch.

"And now," Trace intoned, "without further delay, I bring you ... the royalty of the trapeze!" He stepped aside. The band struck up, and the spotlight swung dramatically in sweeping figure eights as Jack and Gavin ascended the rope ladder on one side and Eli and Sabine on the other. Now the music fell away, until only two clarinets taunted each other in the dark.

The troupe was rusty, no doubt about it. And worse, Eli didn't have the years of experience to read the others' silent cues. He watched as

Gavin took the swing out only to come back without Sabine, who'd been poised to fly across the distance and meet him in mid-air. Somehow they'd each known that Gavin needed another pass, more momentum, because at Gavin's next pass, and without breaking her stage smile, Sabine flung herself off the platform. Gavin caught her tight with one hand, but his other hand slipped slightly. No one else noticed, and by the time Gavin and Sabine were arcing back they'd picked up the routine again.

Sabine's heartbeat quickened. If it weren't for the band clashing back into action with a clap of the cymbals and a final tussle of the clarinets, she would have thought the audience could hear her pulse. She pulled her breath into her muscles and pushed through the air, her grip numbingly tight around Gavin's wrists. The sequins on her costume caught the light and dazzled her more than they should have. Nothing used to faze her up there. Her breath used to be steady, her movements sure and full of grace. She had to find her way back to that sense of magical flight.

From far below, the light caught the shimmery costumes, transforming Gavin and Sabine into two shooting stars wrestling against the night sky, the clarinets' melody a wake behind them. Eli watched the pair as he readied himself, gripping the edge of the platform with this toes, finding his balance. He wasn't experienced enough. He hadn't had enough practice. And as if to hammer the point home, his shoulder started to ache. The dust had definitely worn off.

Across the stage Jack held the bar in this hand, waiting for Eli's cue. Eli nodded. Now or never. The bar swung toward him. Eli reached out at the same time as notes from a third clarinet leapt above the other two. He could see his chalked fingers stretching out before him, the timing perfect, yet he was convinced he wouldn't catch it, that he'd fall to the net below. But then his grip tightened around the bar and he was soaring through the air, his heart leaping with excitement. The third clarinet followed Eli, the tune looping higher and then plunging down along with him.

Now Sabine swung past and let go, locking onto Eli's ankles and then not a second later releasing herself into a somersault and reaching out for

Jack's arms. Upside down on his bar, Jack grinned at Sabine as he clamped onto her and swung her up behind him, weightless now, sending her over the top and releasing her—just as Eli pushed toward her to collect her on his next upswing. The trio of clarinets knotted into their own intertwining notes, the drums beating between them, one pulsing soul for all. And again Eli ended up where he needed to be, his arms outstretched to receive his sister.

Her hands locked around his wrists, she grinned up at him, eyes bright and full of joy. Knowing only the pulse of their hearts and the rhythm of the trapeze, brother and sister flew through the air and back to the platform in exquisite tandem. Eli let go and Sabine landed as light as a nymph on the platform, clasping the rail with one hand and waving to the crowd with the other. The audience cheered, and then louder still as Eli returned and did the same, with only the slightest of stumbles. He stood beside his sister, drinking in the cheers. Across the stage, Gavin and Jack were waving too. There was no Guard, no battle to push through, no devastation, no massacre. Tonight, at this moment, there was only the circus.

4

※

The sun came up as the last of the circus goers filed into the street. Seth looked at his watch again. He didn't know why ... it wasn't as if he was keeping to any particular schedule. As if he had any idea of what would happen when. But he was anxious nonetheless, and as the hours had passed, it had only gotten worse.

His boys were the last to empty out of the coliseum. He did a head count and then got them into marching formation for the trip back across the city. He wanted to stay behind and talk to Rosa, or try to anyway, but he had told Amon he'd be back hours ago. Seth had received no reports of gunfire during the night, and only three reports of any disturbances at all. And those were all dusters, getting into predictable sorts of trouble.

He set off with his boys, his senses heightened to the slightest shift, anything that might give the Guard away. Their new commander—the man who'd dared come into the city, who'd dumped Pierre's body right at their feet—who was he, really? Seth knew his name; that hadn't been hard to find out. Vance. What was he up to? And was he another Regis—an arrogant, self-serving slave to his vices? Regis had been firmly tucked in Edmund's pocket, privy to almost all the Maddox family secrets. How much did his successor know?

If Vance was in his father's pocket now, it meant he could be bought, or persuaded. But Seth's gut told him that somehow Vance was a different kind of man. First, Vance had delivered Pierre's body himself. And second, he seemed to be taking his time, not rushing into anything—unlike Regis, who liked big, graceless plunders that showed off his might, his power. If Regis were still alive he would certainly have struck by now.

Since Vance had made his morbid delivery Seth had thought of a million things to say to him. He often replayed that moment when he'd laid eyes on his new adversary, heard the thunk of Pierre's body hitting the ground. He'd looked up, assessing the man sitting tall on his horse. His black hair slicked away from his face. Eyebrows that angled down sternly, a neatly trimmed beard. A stitched-up scar at his temple, still red.

This was no Regis, with his pasty complexion and glassy-eyed arrogance. Vance had looked Seth straight in the eye, fixing him with a hard, cold look that both challenged and humbled him. Intelligence gathered since had Vance pegged as a sly but honourable Commander. A man of cunning patience, but who spared no one once he'd been pushed too far. Not a man to be snuck up on.

With that thought came a flash from the night in Regis's tent, the moment Seth had crouched in the dark by his sleeping form and drawn the knife against his throat. The give of flesh, the hot ooze of blood. He couldn't expect such grim serendipity this time.

Edmund was enduring the annual legislature with a permanent fake smile. Everything seemed fraught. His whole life was teetering on the brink of ruin. Yet here he was in the Western Key, putting in his appearances and voting on the new bills and drinking the cocktails and making the small talk.

Like now, for instance—the last evening of the legislature. This ballroom, set for the gala dinner with tables draped in heavy cloths woven through with gold thread, each table crowned in the centre with a swan sculpted from ice. Edmund had forced himself to eat a small serving of braised lamb and roasted vegetables. While the others grazed the chocolate buffet, he sipped his wine and stared at the melting swan. It was a metaphor for his life, so clear and in his face that he'd laughed openly. No one at his table noticed, so engrossed were they in their own conversations, none of which had been opened to him. His wine had been emptied and refilled, and then again, and still the swan melted, losing definition, shrinking.

"All right there, Chancellor East?"

Edmund lifted slow eyes to the speaker. Only a server offering him more wine. Edmund lifted his glass in reply, narrowing his eyes at his table mates, deep in tedious discussions of law and the wordings of the new bills. Not another Chancellor among them. He'd been put at a table of senior clerks and policy analysts.

Since arriving without a Chief Regent, his second to die suddenly, Edmund could not help but notice the others regarding him through a cloud of suspicion. Nor could he blame them. Dead wife, new wife, dead children, new baby, and two dead Regents within the year?

Edmund sat back in his chair. Had it only been a year? What a busy one, then! His first wife, Lisette, had died in an explosion he'd ordered to root out the rebels. That she was herself a rebel had come as a shock, the first blow in the series of calamities that was to follow. He'd assassinated his last so-called Chief Regent—out of necessity, to be fair—after Nord's blackmailing. He'd lost his real Chief Regent to a mocked-up suicide attempt—thanks again to Nord. And as far as the other Chancellors knew, his two children had both died while newly enlisted with the Guard. Not one among them, however, was aware of the girl, of whose existence Edmund himself had only recently learned: a rebel like her mother.

A debacle. All of it. Edmund ducked his chin and lifted his wine glass again, a silent salute to the insanity of it all.

And now the annual legislature—usually a great opportunity to see old friends and build new ties between the Keys, to enjoy good food and smart company—had been an abysmal time. Either he was paranoid or his colleagues were casting him wary, calculating looks. And instead of invitations to join a cricket game or hand of cards, or even to share a simple brandy at the end of the day, he'd found himself with long hours of nothing to do.

He gave up on the gala and returned to his room, alone once more.

THE NEXT AFTERNOON Edmund was packing up his things when Vance rapped at the door.

"Errand completed, sir."

"Discreetly, I hope." Edmund ushered Vance in and poured him a finger of whisky. He offered him the glass.

Vance shook his head. "No, thank you, sir. I don't drink."

"Smart man. Liquor muddles the head." Edmund downed the shot. "Cheers."

Vance blinked, holding his expression blank. "Permission to speak freely, sir."

"Of course, please do. You're the only one who seems interested in speaking to me at all these days."

Vance did not let the moment pass. "And this surprises you?"

"I *beg* your pardon?"

"I'm only saying you've had an unfortunate time lately, and it's not a surprise if people start talking. Speculating."

Edmund had specifically chosen Vance for the chore of dumping Lisette's father's body. Vance, by all accounts, was a patient man, but not one who sat back and waited for the world to come his way. His patience was matched by an innate curiosity and a drive for success. He'd made the rank of Commander in only eight years of service, and the fact that he'd been given Regis's command over the volatile Triban region just proved he already had the trust and respect of the senior Keyland Guard. And Edmund had hoped that entrusting him with the task would establish a mutually beneficial relationship. He'd brought Vance into his confidence by telling a convincing lie about the boys being on a covert mission, embedded as spies but still loyal to the Key.

"Clearly you have questions of your own." Edmund suddenly needed to sit. "Am I correct?"

"You didn't mention you had a daughter."

"You're mistaken. I have two sons. Three now, with the baby. You know that."

Vance shook his head. "I do not make mistakes."

Edmund poured himself another drink, buying himself some time to think. He hadn't thought Vance would see the girl. This changed everything. This tilted the whole mess to Vance's favour. Edmund steeled himself. Vance might not realize the magnitude of what he knew. Edmund would hold on to the scale for dear life. It could not tip away from him.

"We all make mista—"

"*You* certainly do." Vance cut him off. "If I may say so."

"Watch your tone with me, Commander Vance. I don't take kindly to being toyed with. Say your piece."

"I will. Once you acknowledge the girl as your daughter."

"I know of whom you speak." With another fortifying slug of whisky, Edmund gave it his best shot. "She is *not* my daughter." Vance moved to interject, but Edmund silenced him with one finger, aimed just so. "Yes, yes, I understand your confusion, but she is not mine. I am sorry to say—" he could see the skepticism on Vance's face even as he cobbled the story together. "I am sorry to say that my wife had a bit of ... shall we say, *experience* before we met. She bore the child before I knew her and gave it away to save her reputation. We had a very brief courtship, you see. We married—she was already pregnant with the boys and it was the proper thing to do. I didn't find out about the girl until later. Much, much later."

Vance stood still for another moment and then reached a hand up to smooth his beard. "She's the spitting image of your sons." It came out as a statement, yet there was a question in the words too. One Edmund did not appreciate. "Eerily so. Interesting. Particularly since she's the Triskelian leader."

"Leader?"

"Since the old woman's death."

Edmund tried to add it up. He shook his head. "Explain," he said, with a gesture for Vance to keep talking, a kind of panicked churning of the air with his hand. "When did all this transpire?"

"I explained it at the debrief." Vance glanced at his watch. "Not even an hour ago. You weren't there?"

"I wasn't informed of any *debrief.*" Anger pressed at Edmund's temples. He massaged them roughly with his fingertips. "I was *here,* in my room. By myself. How was I to know if no one came to tell me?"

"I imagine that was left to the Chief Regents to do," Vance said.

There was a smirk in his tone. Edmund paused before speaking again. He would choose his words carefully, or not speak at all, and certainly not the venom that threatened to crest. Letting out his breath in a long, controlled sigh, he turned back to Vance. "Why didn't you think to call for me when you didn't see me in attendance?"

"The room was crowded. I didn't think to look for you specifically."

"Well." Edmund nodded. "I trust that the boys are capitalizing on the situation. And as for your debrief, what did you tell them? About the girl."

"I didn't mention the likeness to your sons," Vance said. "I didn't mention your sons at all, of course. I reported only that the old woman had died, and that a girl had taken her place as leader."

"I see." Edmund felt a swell of doom—a palpable sensation that he was about to be blackmailed. Again. This was bad news. Very bad news indeed.

And yet. Seth had done it! He'd promised to kill the old woman, and he had. Edmund let out a little laugh, half pride, half disbelief. Seth. His son. A boy of his word. A contender! He hadn't believed Seth had it in him to kill Triskelia's head clown.

Seth's offer to share power suddenly took on a real possibility. If this war played out, if the Droughtland uprising actually threatened the Key, if all was lost, perhaps not *all* would be lost. Edmund could see a sliver of hope. He could hold his power. Alongside his son. The son who'd proudly shown off his Guardy uniform the day he, Edmund, had dropped him off at training. But Seth had the scars now, Edmund remembered with a shudder. And he'd spent these many long months plotting against him. Could he really share power with Seth? Now, after so much dark water had passed between them? He could, he assured himself. And furthermore he *would*, if it meant survival.

"This is good news." Edmund grinned. "Tremendous news. Thank you, Commander Vance. For finding me and telling me."

"You must realize that it's only a matter of time before someone figures out the girl is your child—"

"My *wife's* child."

"Fine." Vance hesitated. "Your *wife's* child. It's only a matter of time before they connect you with her nonetheless, or look for ways to connect you with her. I suggest you prepare for the inevitable."

"The inevitable!" Edmund let loose one miserable laugh and began pacing the room. "If only we knew exactly what that would be." He spun back to look at Vance, one eyebrow cocked. "I don't suppose you're interested in becoming my Chief Regent, Commander?"

It had worked for Nord. Why not try the same ploy with Vance?

A pause. "Sir?"

"Ah, smart. Smart, Commander Vance." Edmund resumed his pacing with a nod. "Hide behind confusion rather than admit that any allegiance with me is doomed from the outset. This mission my boys are on for the Keyland—" Such pretense! Edmund shook his head at his own sorry state. Such elaborate lies! He could almost believe his own fiction. "The mission will have to be cut short. Give me a little more time, Commander Vance. I will sort this all out. You have my word."

"You're asking me to keep quiet for exactly how long?"

"Well," Edmund wondered how long he could ask for, but before he could answer, Vance was shaking his head.

"Disregard the question. *I'll* decide how long."

"But you'll be reasonable and give me adequate time?"

"Why should I?"

"Because I am quite senior to you and I demand it."

"That, sir, is not enough. I am a soldier. My integrity and honour are at stake."

"Why are you resisting me? This is a simple matter of honouring the chain of command. Why are you standing there, defying me?" Edmund knew he sounded petulant, but he was losing face to desperation. Buck up, stay strong!

With a sigh, Edmund summoned every air of authority he could. He squared his shoulders and brought his tone down to a commanding growl. "I trusted the first task to you because you had my respect. Now you would betray me? Betray such an important mission for the Keyland? Destroy civilization as we know it because you suspect me of some unspoken treason? If you hold to this, then tell me, exactly how have I lost your respect?"

"The girl—"

"And I have explained her, haven't I?" Edmund felt the cold talon of panic clutch at his throat. If he could not secure Vance's allegiance, the man could bring him down as easily as a crippled deer. "The situation, Commander ..." Edmund shifted to the brothers-in-arms approach. "The situation is volatile and complex. As a military man, you can appreciate such an environment. That is why I chose you to take the body into Triban. That is why I have trusted you with top-secret intelligence that would normally be well beyond your level of clearance. What I am doing now—if you could set aside the rigid thinking for just a moment—is simply offering you a reward for a job well done, for *when* it is done, which is not now. Soon. When the time comes, you can leave your uniform and the wretched theatre of war behind for the luxury and power of the position as my Chief Regent."

Vance's expression gave nothing away. Edmund held out his hand, but Vance did not take it. Edmund let his hand fall, and with it any last remains of the conciliatory smile he'd pasted on his face.

"I take your slight as a gesture of defiance."

Still, Vance did not falter from his soldier stance. "That is correct, sir."

"And tell me," Edmund cleared his throat, trying to free his breath that had suddenly become so thin, "why would you turn down such a promotion?"

"I have no respect for you, Chancellor East." Vance let his glance slide toward Edmund. His lips curled just slightly, but enough for Edmund to read Vance's disgust. "I believe this girl *is* your daughter. I saw her with my own eyes, and I am no fool. I am not the Guard's fool, and I am certainly not your fool. I am no fool to temptation, either, which is why your desperate attempts to placate me with position or wealth will fall on deaf ears. I am a Keylander, and I am a soldier, and I am a man of my word."

"As am I!" Edmund blurted. "As am I, and so I ask of you the gift of time—"

"And I will give it to you, but only because I can admit that I may not fully understand what you are up to."

"I am up to nothing other than protecting the Key we both love and honour." Edmund gripped Vance's arm. "How much time?"

"I'll let you know." Vance twisted out of Edmund's grip. "When it's up. And then I go to your peers. And don't think you can get rid of me. I've taken steps to ensure a full investigation should I come to an untimely death. Like so many people close to you as of late."

"I am deeply insulted by what you're insinuating."

Vance shrugged. "Better get started then, Chancellor." He headed for the door. Edmund wanted to run after him like a scorned lover, throw himself at his mercy, but he had to hold himself back, tell himself that some time was better than no time. The winds might yet shift in his favour.

Vance left the Western Key that evening, making his way back toward Triban with his legion. He'd played his hand well with Edmund. He would spend the next while letting him stew while he tried to get to the bottom of the Chancellor's treason. For if it was as vast as Vance suspected, he'd be only too happy to orchestrate the downfall of such a foul man.

For now, though, he must focus on his underground advance on the city. The work in the tunnels had been proceeding more slowly than expected. His men had been able to speed up over the last couple of days, what with the rebels planning their little circus.

Now, though, the Triskelians—and that damned boys' army—would be more vigilant. They'd be waiting for the Guard's next move. Vance would not disappoint.

5

Runners from Seth's army came to tell Sabine that Commander Vance was back in his compound on the edge of the city. Shortly after the news arrived, so did Seth.

"How was your night?" Sabine asked him.

"Pretty quiet, which makes sense if Commander Vance was out of town until now. I don't think we have to worry just yet, though. I've got boys posted at lookouts all over the place, and in the tunnels. We'll have advance warning when the time comes. Vance won't be able to take a step beyond his barracks without us knowing right away." Seth rubbed a yawn off his face. "Anyway. The worst of the vermin seems to have already cleared out of Triban. City seems pretty empty. There was a big exodus right after the circus finally wound down."

"Come to breakfast?" Sabine stifled her own yawn. "A cup of tea would do us both good."

Eli was already in the kitchen when Seth and Sabine arrived. He greeted his siblings with a nod as he shovelled in his oatmeal. He'd passed out after the circus, waking in a fog this morning, ravenous. On the other side of the table sat Jack and Gavin, and beside him Celeste was stirring honey into her tea. Anya and Trace stood at the sink, talking quietly.

"Any sign of the Guard last night?" Jack asked.

"None." Seth filled them in on the news.

"So now what?" Gavin crossed his arms and leaned back in his chair. "We can't just wait."

Nappo and Teal came in with "Good mornings" all around. Tasha trailed in behind them, the baby in her arms.

"The plan?" Gavin prompted, once everyone was seated at the table.

Trace angled a glare in Seth's direction. "You said they'd hit during the circus and they didn't. And you didn't even know Vance was out of the city."

"It's true that we missed his exit—"

"*You* missed his exit," Trace corrected. "None of us had the job of keeping an eye on him in the first place. You said you had everything under control."

"He must've left before we had the lookouts in place. I'm guessing he took off right after he dumped the body."

Everyone shifted their eyes to Celeste, who gave them a small, weary smile. "I'm not made of glass, children."

"Still, Nana—" It was Sabine's turn to glare at Seth. "His name was *Pierre,* and he was your grandfather. Show some respect, even if you have to pretend."

Seth wasn't stupid. He held his tongue. "My soldiers," he said instead, "are in position now. He won't get past us again."

"We should strike first," Trace said. "Catch him at his own game. Get the worst over with."

"Perhaps we should." Sabine glanced around the room at the tired faces, shoulders tight with worry. "The anticipation is far worse than the inevitable. Don't you think?"

The group shared wary looks. Anya put a hand on Trace's knee. "I'm not ready to lose anyone else. I won't ever be. *Certainement pas.*"

Trace covered her hand with his. "But we must fight, *chéri.*"

Eli didn't agree. There had to be a more peaceful way. They could retreat, rebuild Triskelia in another secret location. But as the others slowly began to nod, giving their silent consent, Eli knew he could not sway them. Not now.

Seth too was nodding. "I'll go back to my district, see what's happening there. Get an update on the Guard. Find out where Vance is at." He was clenching his fists now, looking around the table intently. "Once we know his position, we'll make plans to attack."

Suddenly Tasha piped up. "How will you know his 'position' if you don't know much of anything else useful?"

Seth looked at her, surprised. "My boys—"

"Right," Tasha said with a scoff. "We're taking the word of dusted little brats."

"They're soldiers."

"They're *kids*."

"You think they're too young to care about their future? The future of the continent?"

"No." Tasha laughed. "That's not it at all. I just can't believe you trust them."

"Well, I do."

"In my village, you weren't allowed to even have a say on *council* until you were into your twenties. *I* wouldn't even be able to have a vote yet, but here you are letting these brats run your army?"

"Feel free to go back to your village and do it the way you're used to." Seth didn't have time for this, and could tell by how the others were shifting uncomfortably that they didn't either.

"I would!" At that, Tasha stood. She handed Emma to Nappo and strode to the door. "Except that a certain *someone* refuses to leave you people and won't let *me* leave with the baby!" She stomped down the hallway, cursing as she went.

Eli looked at Nappo with a new sort of awe. His friend had indeed changed. The old Nappo would've sent Tasha and the baby on their way long ago, with a promise to visit that was never fulfilled.

Everyone at the table looked questioningly at Nappo, who answered Tasha's charge with a shrug. "I belong here, and so does my daughter. I won't be separated from her. Battle or no battle."

Jack and Gavin were quick to agree. Yvon, Gavin's younger brother, nodded his approval too. Gavin and Yvon had also refused to leave their littlest redheaded brother behind in Triskelia. Now Gavin pulled Toby onto his lap and kissed the top of his head.

Seth stood, feeling suddenly awkward. This group of people would never be fully welcoming to him. They all eyed him now, not with respect but with trepidation. They were trusting him, but only because they had no other choice. Seth would prove himself, he was sure of it. Even if, at this very moment, he felt about as alien from them as he ever had.

As he made his way back across the city, he tried to figure out why the unease had fallen over him in the kitchen. There was no simple answer, but a couple of truths were clear. There would always be a key difference between him and the Triskelians. Two, in fact. One: he'd never feel that familial tug for a bunch of strangers, and two, he'd never be content with peace ... not when power beckoned.

At BAT's sprawling headquarters the night shift was coming off duty as the day shift came on. Boys buttoned up their vests and shuffled bleary-eyed into position while others tucked themselves into whatever bed they could find, if only for a few hours before someone else shoved them out of the way to get a little shut-eye himself. A line of boys was waiting for the oatmeal to be ready, and still another line was waiting to take a leak in the long wall of pit toilets built up in the courtyard behind the kitchens.

George and Bal—one of Seth's pet pairs—stood in this line, shifting from one foot to another, both having to pee very badly. They would have pissed against the nearest wall they'd woken up to, but Seth was adamant that the boys use the pits—something about spreading disease and living like a pack of dogs, but no matter. They did what they were told, especially George and Bal, after Seth had made an example of them so long ago.

Unsure of their age—they guessed they were somewhere between eight and ten, with Bal being the older brother—they were littler than most of the others and so had to sleep on the floor, without even a blanket, after the one Seth had given them was stolen by an older boy. Still, they slept hard and dreamed deep. It was all they'd known anyway.

Bal, the dark one, was telling George about a dream he'd had. "There was a ladder that went way up into the clouds so I climbed up it and got on one of the clouds and then was hopping from one cloud to the next, kind of like hopscotch, only in the sky."

"You can't stand on clouds, stupid," George said.

"It was a *dream*," Bal said as they shuffled up in the line. "You can in dreams, stupid, and anyway I—"

Suddenly the ground rumbled behind them, rippling toward them like a heavy carpet being thrown down. The brothers looked at each other with terror and clasped hands. There was a muted bang, and then a larger explosion, and then the ground erupted under their feet like hell itself, throwing the brothers and the rest of the boys into the air and ripping them into pieces, arms and legs and gutted intestines showering down onto the quieted ground that was a crater now, the toilets blown to smithereens, shit and piss raining down too.

The boys who'd been smoking dust in the alley behind the compound—drugs were verboten with Seth, but of course their use still prevailed—were spared. Yet they would discover their friends and comrades blown to bits, and still others fleeing from the fires raging in what was left of the main hall and the kitchens and the sleeping quarters of five hundred boys. The bombs had all gone off at once. From below.

The dusters dropped their pipes. And instead of running to help those lurching toward them with bloody limbs and black, waxy burns and raw skin they fled down the alley, screaming at the top of their lungs.

SETH SAW THE MUSHROOM CLOUD burst over his headquarters, the dense smoke transforming into flying debris and raging flames as his ears rang from the blast. His horse reared up, kicking the air, nostrils flaring. Seth dug in his heels and brought him back down as he fought his own panic. The Guard! But how?

He tried to stop a group of boys fleeing in the other direction, but in their blank-eyed horror they didn't even recognize him as he shouted.

"Is the Guard there now?" he hollered at one pair of boys as they hobbled past, the one helping the other whose leg was in shreds below the knee. "Turn back! Go to the infirmary!" But Seth didn't know if the infirmary was even still standing, or if Dache was alive to administer whatever meagre knowledge he could. Seth's mind whirled in panic. He needed Rosa. He would send for her. She would come—not for him, he knew that—but for the boys.

Now an entire troop of BAT soldiers rounded the next corner, marching grimly toward him. Seth found Amon at the back—this was his regiment. Amon was so upset he forgot to salute Seth.

"It's the headquarters! They bombed it! There's nothing left!"

"Calm yourself!" Seth jerked his head, summoning Amon to his side so that he could speak to him privately.

"I don't want to go back there! We was out the west end, thank the highers, and we saw the mushroom cloud and then on the way back everyone was saying you were dead—"

"Well, clearly I am not dead. We have to go back and assess it for ourselves."

"I ain't going back there!"

"You are if you want to be my Sergeant! Now, buck up, Sergeant. Get your troop in order and start back to headquarters."

Amon nodded, his cheeks so pale Seth thought he might faint. But Amon nodded again, and bellowed at his soldiers. "Fall in!"

"Good man." Seth steered his horse back to his own escorts. "Onward!"

They rode at a canter, scattering survivors and civilians alike.

"They're all dead!"

"Your boys are gone!"

"Ignore them!" Seth yelled as the boy soldiers slowed for the rumours on the street.

The group took the final corner, Seth and Amon in the lead. Suddenly the wreckage lay before them. The horses reared up and the boys started panicking, some running head-on and others backing up, ready to flee once and for all.

"Stop!" Seth raised his arm. The boys hesitated, and finally all stood still, taking in the devastation.

The sight was awful. The main building had been utterly flattened. Flames formed a new wall behind. The air was thick with ash and dust. And everywhere lay the wounded and the blown to bits.

Screams lifted up all around, pleas for help, cries of pain and horror. It was Triskelia all over again and Seth reeled from it—he'd been buried alive there. His breath caught in his throat and he swung his head drunkenly from one side to the other, not sure where to go, what to do first. To his left, an arm clawed helplessly at the air, the rest of the boy hidden by a section of collapsed wall. Over there, a boy convulsed in a puddle of blood. And more writhed toward death like zombies, clutching chests and heads and guts, stumbling, teetering. Seth gulped for air and tasted only smoke and ruin and the rusty tang of blood.

He wanted to dig the buried out with his bare hands. He wanted to carry each of his boys to safety over his shoulder.

Soldiers who had been in adjoining buildings at the time of the blast now dug frantically through the rubble, yelling out when they found what might be a survivor, straining to hear each other through their temporary deafness from the blast. Seth turned his eyes to his boys once more. He took a deep breath and hollered: "You dare run away from this?"

The boys shuffled closer together, as if bracing themselves.

"Move! Go help your fellow soldiers! What are you? A pack of cowards?"

A few boys broke apart and wandered off to kneel in the muck and pull away rock and beams with a stunned lethargy. Seth spun around, shouted at the rest of his shocked soldiers. "You knew it would come to this! We've been preparing for exactly this!"

The boys listened, their faces ashen with fear. Seth hated that they looked so young suddenly. He hated the guilt that gnawed at him now when it hadn't ever before. It was useless, and poorly timed. There was nothing he could do about it now.

"And what about you lot? Are you cowards or are you soldiers?"

A pause, and then two boys called out tentatively, "Soldiers, Commander Seth."

"And the rest of you?"

This time, a more unified response. "Soldiers, Commander Seth!"

"That's right! You are soldiers. And this is your battle. And you will stay and fight and honour your city and your people and the future of Triskelia, right?"

Slowly, the boys' voices lifted into a more hearty cheer. "Boys' Army! Boys' Army! Fight! Fight! Fight!"

"That's right!" Seth nodded, forced himself to grin while the screams of the wounded echoed all around him. "Now, are we ready?"

"Yes, Commander Seth!"

Seth churned the air with his hands, working up his boys even as his gut threatened to explode with nervous vomit. "I said, are we *ready?*"

"Yes, Commander!" This time the response was loud and clear. "Ready to fight, fight, fight!"

"And fight we will, and soon...." Seth cut into the group with his horse, dividing the boys into two sections. "But first, we take care of our own. Amon will lead the search and rescue team." He gestured to his left. "You boys will dig for survivors. I'll take the rest." He indicated those on his right. "My team will salvage what remains. We need a clear idea of what we have left, boys. This is our war! We will own this battle!"

Amon thrust a fist into the air and roared. "Fight! Fight!" The boys joined in until they were all punching the air, chanting. *"Fight, fight, fight!"*

The two teams marched through the rubble. Seth heard himself order his boys off in various directions, on various missions, but he could not shake his sense of failure. How had the Guard gotten so close? No tunnels lay directly below, and soldiers had been watching the streets. An inside job? He surveyed the boys digging out the area above the gun lockers. Could one of his boys have been bribed? Were there plants in his army?

He blinked. Amon was at his side, saying something.

"What?"

"I said, there's another group of survivors waiting for orders."

Seth chewed his lip, looking hard at his right-hand man. *Could* it have been Amon? He pushed away the doubt. If he didn't stay solid, he'd lose even this last grip he had now, here in the wreckage of his army.

"Have you found Dache?"

"He wasn't there when the infirmary blew," Amon said. "He's already seeing to the wounded." Amon looked away, trying to hide his face. His eyes were puffy and his cheeks were pale. "Bad stuff, Commander Seth. Blown-up arms, eyeballs hanging out."

"We'll send for Rosa to come help him."

Amon wiped his face with his hands and looked up. "She'll come?"

"Of course." Seth nodded. "She'll want to do what she can. Arrange a perimeter out of the survivors. Except for Triskelians, no one comes in. No one goes out."

"How did they get to us, Commander Seth?"

"I don't know." Seth lowered his voice. "But I *will* find out. Now go get the perimeter in place. As quickly as you can."

"Consider it done." Amon saluted him as he turned away.

The sun was high in the sky now, but its midday glare was cut by the fog of dust and the smoke from the fires. Seth felt himself slowly teetering back to an even keel. He had to get control of his thoughts. He told himself that this was what he and BAT had been preparing for. Training for. Rehearsing for ages. He had to steel himself away from soft thinking. Regis would not blink an eye over a loss like this. He'd plow forward, as was necessary. Vance would too, Seth had no doubt.

The attitude among his boys had shifted sharply since the Triskelians had arrived in Triban, since the riot had erupted in the streets. Before then there had been a sense of playfulness to the training, a sense of make-believe. Seth could admit that. But after the riot, and then when Vance had dared march through the city, the boys had gained a singular purpose—they *wanted* to go to war. And now that it was here, in front of them in blood and bone and broken buildings, would they stand up and fight as they'd puffed up and claimed they would so often lately? They had weapons, and now they had rage. And they had nothing to lose.

This bombing was beginning to feel like nothing more than a calling card. An invitation to play. If the Guard had wanted to make a *real* impact, they could have.

"They're teasing us," Seth said out loud, marvelling. "They think this will scare us off."

Beside him, a pair of his boys stood at attention. "Commander Seth?"

"Yes?"

"The gun lockers got dug out and everything's there."

"Good. Good." Seth slid off his horse and put an arm around each of the boys. "Let's hand out the guns then, shall we?"

The bomb blast was felt across the city and heard even farther than that. Almost as quickly the rumours rippled like shockwaves, reaching the coliseum only minutes later.

"He's betrayed us again!" Trace was instantly apoplectic; the messenger had barely just paused, gasping for breath. "He let the Guard through!"

"No." Sabine laid a restraining hand on his arm. "That's not true."

"No?" Gavin turned on her now too, eyes bright with excitement. "Then how did they get through?"

"His *army* has been attacked. Think about it."

Jack stepped into the tense circle. "Right now, Seth needs us. So right now, we go help. We ask questions later."

"But what if they're on their way to us now?" Sabine spoke quickly. "What if we should stay here? Keep everyone safe?"

"Let's go!" Jack said, reaching for his gun.

"No." Sabine lifted a hand. "We stay here. Seth has all the help he needs with his boys. We don't know what the Guard is planning—maybe even to attack us as we leave to go to Seth. We must think before we act, Jack. You know better."

"I don't know better than fighting a good fight at this point," Jack growled. He lifted his eyes to Gavin and Trace, Yvon and Nappo, all four standing shoulder to shoulder, electrified with adrenalin. "And the battle isn't here, not now anyway. Am I right?"

The four sounded off in solidarity.

Not Eli, though, who sat quietly at the table, his chin on his fist, eyes droopy. He was ... distracted at the moment, enjoying the sparkly light show of the first hours after a fresh dusting, thanks to the fire-barrel boys. *Good to see you again, Reverend! Come, sit down a spell.*

"Jack's right." Trace's dark eyes blazed. "We should go."

"I want to go too!" Toby piped up from behind his brothers.

"And me!" Teal stood alongside his elders, feet apart, fists at the ready.

"Non, non." Anya swept a squirming Toby up into her arms and ushered Teal away with a firm shove. "You stay here with me. No fighting for little boys."

"I ain't little!" Teal protested.

"Me neither!" Toby puffed out his chest and copied Teal's stance.

"You are." Sabine cut the little boys' much older brothers with a sharp look. "Which is precisely why I didn't want them to come. This is no place for children."

Yvon spoke for them all. "We will not be separated from our kin, not at a time like this."

"But you're happy to leave them here, unarmed, while you go fight a battle that already has an army?"

Yvon and the others shared a look, and then it was Jack who spoke. "All right. If they need us, we'll go, but only after we've got the coliseum covered."

Eli was finding it hard to concentrate. Wherever he moved his eyes, his vision followed in a wake of shimmering light. Everyone, even Trace with his angry scar, was haloed with a crown of colour, dancing like aurora borealis across their shoulders, leaping from their brow, slipping over their ears. They were all so pure and magical. Their highers were blessing them right now, in front of his very own eyes, anointing them with this godly colour, illuminating their spirits.

"I can agree to that," Sabine said. "So long as we've got solid protection here. If so, I'll even join you."

Eli moistened his lips with his tongue. He was very thirsty all of a sudden. "No you won't."

"Good morning, Reverend." Jack cocked a disapproving eyebrow. "Glad you could join us."

"Sabine." Eli stood, spread his arms in protest. Each movement was followed by a comet trail of glitter. "You, of all people, must stay safe. At all costs."

"No." Sabine laid her hands on the table and leaned toward Eli, fixing him with a darkly determined stare. "I am a different leader from Zenith. If there was one thing she did that I'll do differently, it's getting my hands dirty—"

Jack let out a cheer. "That's my girl!"

"So if you go out there ..." Eli struggled to put together his logic. It all seemed muddled in an unhelpful heap. "Well, you simply shouldn't. You should stay where it's safe—"

"Are you okay?" Sabine frowned at her brother. "You're pale, and you're sweating."

Eli shook his head and sat himself down. "I'm fine."

"Let's go." Trace rose from the table, his hands spread on the old, oily wood as he leaned intently toward the others. "We solidify the soldiers around the perimeter: Triskelian, Tribanite, Boys' Army." He raised his fist and lowered his voice, deadly even. "Then we fight."

As one, Trace and the men strode out of the room. They were followed by Anya, herding a still-protesting Toby and Teal down the corridor to the playroom.

"Rosa, Rosa, Rosa," Eli mused to himself, apropos of nothing, as Sabine got up. "A lesson in forgiveness. Seth betrayed her, and she has forgiven him. We should be inspired by her."

"She hasn't forgiven him." Now Sabine stood at the door. She was about to follow the others, but Eli's mumbling had caught her attention. "What are you talking about?"

"Nothing," Eli muttered.

"What is wrong with you, Eli?"

"Nothing." He stood to demonstrate he was all right. But the room was tilting, and he had to grip the chair to stand upright.

"You'd do best to say a prayer for the victims of the bomb, Reverend."

"I will."

"And when you're done that, keep an eye on the children with Anya. I don't trust Tasha to keep them safe."

"Done."

And now Eli was alone. Highers *help* him, he was thirsty. He lifted an arm in front of his face. His fingers trailed that same shimmering light. He played with it for a while, flicking his fingers, making it dance around his wrists and across his field of vision. Then he slumped down into his chair and fell asleep, snoring loudly. Bullet whined at his feet, utterly confused by the state of his master.

Seth surveyed the damaged headquarters. The main building was demolished. He caught a glimpse of Dache in the courtyard, his arms full of towels. Dache had been gathering supplies in the market district at the time of the blast, and had set to work immediately with what little he had. But most of the five hundred boys who'd been in the building had perished. Dache's assistants had collected the dead and laid them out in a clearing behind the courtyard.

Seth headed off in that direction, ready at last to visit the dead. It would take some time to identify the boys—by the colour of their BAT vests, bits of clothing, old scars, the few trinkets they had in their pockets. They wouldn't be buried until Seth knew who they were. Meanwhile, if one boy of a pair had died, the surviving one would need a new partner immediately. The BAT boys had become so accustomed to their comrades that the singles who'd been left behind seemed reluctant to leave their dead friends. Some hovered silently near the collection of bodies. Others wandered like spectres, circling aimlessly. Still others, the ones who needed to *do* something, had organized a little brigade to clear away more of the rubble.

Although there didn't seem much point.

Seth gritted his jaw and ground his teeth hard, the creaking gnaw somehow comforting. He would mourn in private. He *would* not let his grief overtake him. Not here.

But he would pay his respects. Seth slowly made his way up and down the rows of bodies, some shrouded entirely, some with only their faces covered. He thought he saw a hand move under one of the palls. He squatted, lifted the dirty blanket, and fell away with a gasp as he startled a rat from its meal. *Keep moving.*

A pair of Amon's boys ran up to him. "Commander Seth?" one said with a salute.

Seth pulled his eyes from the death all around him. "Yes?"

The other one piped up. "Triskelia's lifeminder's here, Commander."

Rosa. She flashed across Seth's vision as if she were right there beside him, brushing her dark hair over her shoulder, parting her ruby lips to smile.

"She's with Dache, tending the injured in the courtyard," the first boy said, banishing the mirage.

Seth closed his eyes, willing her back to him. *Rosa.* Long-legged and slender, that delicious curve at her hip that begged for his touch, the dip at her collarbone perfect for kissing. *Rosa.* Kind and passionate, and in possession of several reasons to keep on hating him.

"Commander?" said the second boy. Seth was staring hard at where Rosa had appeared to him. He blinked, saw only the rows of bodies laid out at his feet.

Rosa would have to speak to him now, wouldn't she? She hadn't said a word to him since the night Zenith died. Correction: since the night he'd helped Zenith die.

Amon's boys looked at each other, waiting for Seth to say something. They'd heard rumours about this Rosa, about her effect on their leader. Evidently she could cast a spell from quite the distance.

"Thank you." Seth finally gave them a nod. "You may go." They backed away with matching salutes and equally matching looks of confusion.

Seth would wait. Hope that she would let him back in again. Back into the place they had shared in the worst regions of the Droughtland. They were meant to be together. He knew it—and deep down she had to know it too. She would be his again. When all of this was over, when he and his father shared the leadership of the new world, he would have her by his side. He could offer her the world then.

6

Eli woke up to a crick in his neck and a maw so dry he had to pry his tongue off the roof of his mouth.

Abstain.

His highers hadn't chimed in on his dust use until now. But why abstain? Dust brought him closer to his highers, and wasn't that his mission? Even Zenith had recognized his spiritual calling. Dust lifted him up to a better place. He imagined the afterlife was similar—devoid of violence, full of rapture, flooded in warm, brilliant light. The high without the drug. What was the difference, then, in attaining that same ecstasy now with a little help?

Purity is the path.

As his head cleared, shame filtered in. Wandering the hall toward the main arena, Eli realized he didn't know if the war had begun yet. How long had he been sleeping? He found a grimy window and looked out. The world was as he had left it however long ago, with the city bustling nervously despite the tension. Barrel fires and Seduce games. A pickpocket—barely three years old if he was a day—fishing in the satchel of a man slumped over, snoring off a night of drink. Eli rapped at the window. The kid glanced up. Eli shook his head, waved a chastising finger at him. The boy grinned, clutched his prize, and dashed down the lane, scrambling over two men locked in a fistfight as they wrestled in a slop of mud. All was as it ever was.

"Eli." Nappo came toward him, Emma in his arms.

"Nappo!" Eli grinned, but as Nappo neared, Eli noticed a gash on his forehead and a nasty scrape on his arm. "What happened to you?"

"Nothing, really. I was helping at the bomb site and a beam fell. I scrambled out of the way but caught the scrapes for it."

The bomb! Now it all came back to Eli.

Nappo looked at him. "You'd forgotten."

"No. No! I was feeling unwell and just woke up, and my head is a little fuzzy still. No, I hadn't forgotten." He gave Nappo a weak grin. "I'm just glad you're okay. And everyone else?"

"Seth's okay." Nappo explained what he knew. "Sabine and our boys are still over there. I came back to check on Emma."

Nappo steered Eli farther down the hall into the main arena, and with a gentle shove, sat him down on the edge of the stage.

"So ..." Eli looked around at the cavernous dark, sensing Nappo had something to say. "Now what?"

"Eli, come on." Nappo cradled Emma in his arms and shook his head. "How long did you think you'd get away with it?"

Eli avoided looking at Nappo's disappointed mug. "What?"

Don't lie to him.

"I don't have to tell you what a huge mistake you're making, do I?"

Eli tilted his head back and gazed at the trapeze rigging swaying slightly in the draft high above.

"Dusting." Nappo shook his head. "You, of all people."

"I don't know what you're talking about." Eli cleared his throat, nervous.

Nappo just stared, and hard. "You do so."

"This, coming from you?" Eli bristled. "I seem to recall you quite sternly telling me that I should at least try it before I trash it." A shrug. "So I did. Lesson learned."

"You won't do it again."

"No, if you're asking, except it sounded more like an order." Eli put his hands on his knees and pushed himself up. "I'm going outside."

"We're not done talking."

"Oh yes we are." Eli left his friend behind and walked quickly into the cover of the dim corridor.

As night fell Seth worked alongside his boys, digging in the rubble. The weapons inventory had been completed. Thankfully, the loss there had been minimal. Now it was a matter of clearing away the wreckage to find any remaining survivors and take a tally of the bodies. Now and then Seth would notice one of his soldiers gawking at him, surprised to see him in the muck, but Seth knew all too well the panic and fear of being trapped. He dug on.

Groups of boys clawed away at the rubble, filling buckets with debris and passing them back to be emptied onto piles. The fire chief and his men had managed to put out the worst of the fires, and were working now to keep them from spreading to the other barracks. Seth checked their progress with a glance over his shoulder. He didn't know much about the anatomy of fire, but to his eye the beast appeared to be contained.

The firefighters chopped at collapsed beams still glowing with dying embers. They dumped buckets of sand onto hot spots and cleared away any remaining fuel for the hungry flames that threatened the entire compound. Seth admired the fire chief's command of his men. It was clear that they respected him. He was a good man, a solid leader. Could he be convinced to join BAT? Not as a soldier of course, but as a sergeant answering directly to Seth.

"Chief!" he called to him across the rubble. "Could we have a word?" The chief gave Seth a wave and then strode toward him.

Suddenly Seth was blown back with a force that lifted him off his feet and punched the air from his lungs. He landed hard against the wall of a building, sliding down into a crumple on the ground. His ears rang and his throat burned. But he dragged himself up and staggered forward, trying to make sense of what had just happened.

Another blast. The fire chief lay sprawled in Seth's path. His legs were in four pieces around him like a frame, his skin taut with burns and his hair singed off. Seth lifted a hand to his own head. His hair was melted together, what was left of it. It registered with him now, the stench of scorched hair. His eyebrows were gone, but he wasn't burned badly, or not that he could see. The ringing in his ears flattened into one steady buzz he could barely hear through. Someone was calling for him. Amon.

"Seth!" Amon rushed toward him, checking over his shoulder, eyes wide with panic. "They're here! The Guardies are here!"

Seth strained to hear. The Guardies. He'd heard that much clearly. He pointed to his ears. "The blast. I can't hear anything."

"We're under siege!" Amon yelled. "The Guardies are here *now*! They've taken the whole western block. I've got all the weapons out to the boys I could find, but—"

The Guard had waited until the first blast had taken its toll, then struck again. Smart move. This Commander Vance was no idiot. That was unfortunate.

"Come on!" Amon pulled him by his arm, frantic.

"Round up as many soldiers as you can and empty the north arsenal before the Guard finds it." Seth heard himself give the order in a calm, firm manner. "Send a runner back to the coliseum and get the four battalions stationed there to march this way. They'll be ready to take over when your boys tire."

"They can't hold out that long!"

"Yes, they can! They're soldiers, and this is war, and you will lead them accordingly! Seth reached for the wall to steady himself as the ringing in his ears heightened, making him dizzy. "Now, go!"

Amon ran off, hollering something that was just a muffle to Seth. He turned, looking for uninjured boys. They were staggering toward him, wrung from the blast.

"Find your weapons, soldiers!" Seth couldn't even hear his own order; it merely reverberated in his head as so many syllables of white noise. *Don't let them see you falter. Don't give away your fear. Own it. Take charge of it. Use it as fuel.* He could hear Regis's words from his first days in his Droughtland regiment. So he *had* learned a thing or two from that devil. Seth gritted his teeth and scowled through the pain slicing through his head. "Delta formation! Now!"

The boys grabbed whatever they could for a weapon and scrambled into a tight line, several rows deep. Seth furrowed his brow, working to focus his eyesight. "Forward, ho!"

To his relief and astonishment, the boys marched forward.

They came upon the Guard not two blocks away, the uniformed men of the front line holding strong behind their clubs and machetes, knives and bows. No guns though. This is what Seth noticed first.

Seth fell back, waving for the boys to keep advancing. His pawns for their pawns. Save the fire power for the real fight.

It had to be done.

From the streets on either side came a war cry as a flood of locals rushed into the fray, some with boards or bits of metal as weapons, others with crude shields, but most with nothing at all, bare fists raised, ready for hand-to-hand.

Seth could see fear in the eyes of the Guardies. Fear! He grinned. They had no idea what they were getting into. Their clockwork *clomp clomp* slowed as they laid eyes on their opponents. All hail fear! Guardy officers atop their horses, well back from the front, sounded their horns. Two short blasts and a long one. Seth recognized the call to advance.

But as the riptide of Tribanites rolled forward amidst the repeated bleating of Guard battle horns, the Guardy pawns actually began to retreat.

Seth's hearing was much better now. Above the din he could even pick out the desperate cries of officers. *"Advance, you cowards! Advance!"*

The civilian posses rammed into the Guardy front even before Seth's boys did. The two sides clashed like shattering glass, soldiers and fists flying. Yells of rage rang out while men Seth had never laid eyes on before launched themselves into the tangle of battle as if they'd been shot from a trebuchet.

The boys at the front of his band of marching soldiers glanced in Seth's direction. Seth gave them the signal to keep going, a churn of his arm in the direction of the fight. The boys repeated it, and after the briefest of pauses, flung themselves into the melee with the war cries they'd only practised up until now.

Seth knew better than to jump into the fray; few would survive this first exchange. He glanced across the writhing mass of quickly bloodied bodies. One of his few girl soldiers was tossed out of the pit as if she were a rag doll. She stayed where she landed, blood pumping from the slice across her neck.

Where was Rosa? Seth scanned the crowd and found himself locking eyes with one Guardy in particular. An officer, Seth could tell from the stripes. He couldn't see which rank, though. The man tipped his head at him, gloved hand to the brow of his full-face helmet. A salute! An unmistakable salute! Seth gave a tentative salute in reply, and then the man atop the horse turned and rode away from the carnage.

Was that Vance? It couldn't be, not so close to the peril of the front line! But who else would make such a bold gesture? Seth tracked the man until he couldn't see him any more, and then he too backed away. First, he needed to make sure Rosa was all right. Then he'd work out the battle plan for his army.

TRACE STOOD before Seth at the entrance to the courtyard, eyeing his charred hair and singed brows. "Are you hurt?"

"No, no. How is Rosa?" Seth stood on tiptoe, trying to catch a glimpse of her. Over Trace's shoulder he could just see her in the distance, bandaging the stub of a boy's wrist.

"She's fine." Trace blocked Seth as he tried to push through the gate. "No one goes in there unless they're injured or helping. You're not injured and we don't need your help."

"I just came to see if she was okay."

"And she is. I've told you so."

A volley of cannon fire silenced their conversation. Seth turned and rushed back toward what was left of his headquarters. As he neared the building, Jack and Sabine drew up on horseback, a cart full of weapons behind them—rusty and cobbled together, but weapons nonetheless. Coming up directly behind the cart were a whole troop of men—Seth recognized only Nappo, Yvon, and Gavin among them.

"Mostly from Triban and the surrounding settlements," Jack said by way of hello.

"Ready and willing," Sabine said as she jumped down.

"Not you." Seth held out his hand to stop her.

"Don't argue with me, Seth."

"Stay back, help Rosa."

Before his sister could argue, another deafening blast sent them all diving for cover. When the tremors settled, Sabine, for once heeding her brother's will, wordlessly made her way to the courtyard infirmary.

7

⋘⊹⋙

While the battle raged, Eli prayed. Hidden with Anya, Tasha and Emma, the two boys, and Bullet in what had once been the warming cupboard off a laundry room, he prayed. Anya whispered stories to distract the boys and then sang songs to lull them to sleep. Tasha nursed the baby every couple of hours when she cried for it, which is how Eli kept track of the night passing.

Despite giving his word to Nappo that he wouldn't dust again, Eli had hooked up with the barrel boys just before all hell had broken loose, and now, so many hours later, his high was faltering. Actually, he was glad to be back to his right self at last. His highers hadn't spoken to him while he was stoned, and he sought their counsel now.

"Please?" he whispered, eyes fixed on the ceiling. Nothing. "Please!"

"What is it, Eli?" Anya rubbed her neck. She'd slept sitting up, there was so little room in the cupboard. They would need a better safe room if they stayed here. Eli said as much, stating the obvious and hoping to cover up the fact that he'd been talking to himself.

"Speak for your own dumb selves," Tasha said with a yawn. "I'm not staying here." She stuck Emma to her breast like a lid on a jar. "I'm leaving. As soon as it's safe. I'm going home."

"*Ah, oui,* but this is home for now." Anya reached to stroke Tasha's hair, but Tasha's look stopped her.

"No, it isn't. And it won't ever be."

Teal and Toby slept soundly, even as Emma fussed, flailing her arms, reaching for some invisible something. Eli knew how that felt. He took the baby in his arms and held her against his chest, with one hand cradling the warmth of her head. Tasha kept a wary eye on him, but soon her eyelids grew heavy and she slumped against the wall, asleep.

Across the city, dawn crowned the wreckage in a halo of mist. Had it been only scant hours ago that they'd been in the throes of battle, blocking blows and dodging bullets and taking cover where they could? Then, just as daylight crested, Seth had heard the Guardy sound the horn for retreat, and suddenly it was all over. Now bodies were strewn everywhere, as though someone had tossed a collection of toy figures into the road.

Seth would not keep track of the dead. There was no purpose in having a number. In truth, he was too horrified to know.

Instead he counted the Guardy bodies as he picked a path through the corpses. The core of the battle had been fought in one big intersection, spilling out from there onto the plaza on the west side and into the wreckage of his headquarters.

He spotted Amon from a distance, collapsed on a stoop on the far side of headquarters. Yet he was alive. No mortally wounded person sat like that, with his head in his hands and elbows on his knees.

"Amon!"

Amon lifted his head. "You're burnt!" He struggled to stand.

"Don't get up. I'm fine. My hair got the worst of it." Seth joined him on the step, quietly overjoyed to find that his ally had survived the night. The two sat in silence for a long moment until Amon spoke again.

"I'm sorry, Commander Seth."

"What for?" Seth clapped him on the back.

"I failed you."

"No!" Seth shook his head. "It's morning, a new day, and we're still here."

"But they're all dead!" Amon's shoulders shook with grief. He dropped his face into his hands again and succumbed to his sobs. "Gone! Dead!"

"No, Amon." Seth looked away from Amon's frank display and fought his own urge to cry. "They're not all dead. And the ones who are died for a good cause! This is war, and death is the price of war, and we will pay the price. But Amon, buddy, we will come out the other side and we will be free and your people will be free and we will have won!"

"No, no, no." Amon shook his head. "There's no point, Seth!"

"There *is*. Look." He gave Amon's shoulder a rough shake. "Open your eyes and look!"

Amon lifted his head.

"See?"

In the street, BAT boys were spreading out, checking for signs of life and collecting weapons off the dead. "Those boys are alive!" Seth whistled, waving for Ori and Finn to come over.

Amon quickly wiped his face and got himself under control. "I'm sorry I broke down like that, Seth."

Seth gave him a light punch on the arm. "Never mind."

"Commander Seth!" Ori and Finn greeted him with a salute.

"And one for Sergeant Amon here too."

"Sergeant Amon!" Another salute.

Seth stared up at his two little soldiers, his very first ones. The pair were covered in scrapes and cuts, and Finn had two black eyes and a swollen lip.

"We're okay!" Finn said stoutly, in answer to the concern in Seth's eyes.

"Good to go again, Commander Seth!" Ori made a gun of his fingers and blew imaginary smoke from the barrel.

"Where's your real gun?"

Ori paled, kept his eyes forward. "Lost it during the battle."

"Lost it?" Seth stood. "Or had it taken off you by a Guardy?"

"Not sure, Commander Seth." Ori dropped his eyes to the ground, his shoulders rounded with shame. "It was dark, and I was pounding this Guardy rat in the face with a brick, and Finn was kicking him and then this other one flew at us and grabbed Finn and they was rolling on the ground so I reached for my gun and it was gone. So I finished off the first guy with a couple more blows and then helped Finn. That's when he caught it in the face."

"Well." Seth brushed off his pants, a futile effort considering he was absolutely filthy, as were the boys, and Amon. "Good to see you two made it out okay."

Ori and Finn shared a look.

"I know others were not so lucky."

Ori and Finn nodded.

"But we are here to fight another day on their behalf." Seth wasn't sure what to say after that. Thankfully Jack and Gavin suddenly appeared before him, wanting to know what he had in mind for the dead BAT soldiers.

"Off you go." Seth dismissed Ori and Finn before turning back to the Triskelians. "Send for the deathminders. We'll start piling them on carts."

Seth managed to leave Jack and Gavin in charge of body collection and Amon in charge of mustering the troops.

Now he skirted the intersection, keeping his eyes off the bodies, and retreated into the quiet dark of the last building left standing on the block.

The stone wall felt blessedly cool as he leaned against it. He tipped his head back and closed his eyes. He'd lost.

He'd lost and Vance had won.

For the first time Seth worried that he'd taken on the impossible, that victory would not prevail. He turned, resting his hot forehead against the stone. He reached above him and spread his arms wide, letting them slide down the wall. He needed water. And food.

He needed help.

He couldn't do this alone. He didn't even know what *this* was.

"You're weak." He said it out loud, and then again, banging his head against the wall with each word. "You are weak!"

"Seth?" A voice behind him. Seth pushed himself away from the wall and focused on the redheaded boy standing in the door. Gavin's brother. He couldn't remember his name.

"What is it?"

"Sabine is looking for you. She and Trace are still at the field hospital. They want to know where you've got to put the Guardy prisoners once they're patched up."

"Tell her I'll be there in a minute."

Yvon made no move to leave.

"What?"

"She told me to make sure you came. At once."

"And I will!" Seth flexed his hands into fists, victim to a sudden, inexplicable rage. "Get out of here! I can make my own bloody way!"

Without another word, Yvon spun on his heel.

"Shit!" Seth knocked his head against the wall one more time, but it felt so good he did it again, and again.

SETH HAD TO ADMIT to Sabine that the only place he had to hold the prisoners had been bombed to smithereens.

"We'll take them to the coliseum then." Sabine couldn't help but stare at his ruined hair.

"They're *my* prisoners."

"They're not." Sabine had spent the night helping Rosa and was covered in blood. Seth found it hard to look at her, even though he told himself it wasn't her blood. "They belong to the revolution."

Seth's face did not give way from his steely glare.

"Don't tell me that you still fancy yourself on an entirely different page. We're doing this *together*, Seth. I can't believe that you, even you, would argue that this morning."

And he wouldn't. But it was still hard to let go, especially the prisoners. "I'll be in charge of the interrogations."

Sabine shrugged. "Fine." And then she scowled. "Hang on." She fetched a pair of bandage scissors and started hacking off Seth's scorched hair, right down to his scalp. When she was done, he ran his hands over the stubble. "Maybe now they'll consider answering your questions."

JACK AND YVON—having completed the grim task of arranging the deathminders and their carts—would now escort the injured Guardy prisoners across the city to a compound behind the coliseum that could be used as a prison. Eleven of the prisoners could walk; the other eight were too injured and so were piled onto carts as if they were already dead.

Seth assigned two pairs of soldiers to accompany them. Only once the cart was rolling did he allow himself to scan the rows of wounded, looking for Rosa working among them. Dache, kneeling beside a fallen Tribanite, glanced up and gave a little salute. Seth replied with the same.

"Your boys respect you," Sabine said, having observed the exchange.

"Where's Rosa?"

"She's sleeping. I ordered her to. She'd been up for two days straight."

"Where is she?" Seth said again. He knew that even just laying his tired, worried eyes on her would settle him, calm his jangled nerves. She had long since become a talisman to him, and he needed her now. Even just a glimpse.

"She doesn't want to see you."

"Still?" Seth shook his head. "How long will she keep this up?"

Sabine widened her eyes. "Is that all you can think about? At a time like this?"

"At a time like this ..." Seth guffawed. "What do you know about *a time like this?*"

"Not much. And I'd like to know more. Like how this happened in the first place. And how we can prevent another attack—"

"What makes you think we can prevent it?"

"Well, clearly we can't!" Sabine's cheeks flushed with frustration. She held her bloody hands out between them. "But maybe we could be better prepared next time so I don't have to have the blood of children on my hands!" She grabbed for Seth's, which were filthy and scraped, but with no blood on them. She dropped them, disgusted.

"I don't have to have their blood literally on my hands to have it there all the same." That sounded small. Desperate.

"How did this *happen?* Which way did they come?"

"I'm not positive yet, but my boys tell me that the original blast was set from a tunnel—"

"But you said—"

"Hear me out!" Seth yelled. "There *was* no tunnel there. They'd dug a new one. I couldn't have had boys on it, because it didn't exist."

"And you think there are more?"

"I don't know. But we'll put more soldiers down there."

"All this time, then—"

"They've been digging." Seth shook his head. "Like moles under the city, digging down there while we waited for them up here."

"I told you to check it out down there."

"And I did! Where I knew to, anyway."

"Effie tried to warn us."

"Who?"

"The girl you met down there."

"And we cleared them. We did!"

Suddenly they heard the sound of approaching horses, hooves thundering on the cobblestone. Four BAT boys came tearing up, their weapons slung across their backs, bouncing as they ran. "Guardies! A hundred of 'em! Headed this way!" It was Ori and Finn in the lead, sounding the alarm. Seth put a firm hand on each of the boys' shoulders.

"They're coming straight for us, Commander Seth," Finn panted, flitting his eyes toward Ori, who could only nod enthusiastically. "The big guy, with the stripes on his jacket like yours. And he says he's come in peace."

Vance.

Trace rushed to the gate, gun at the ready.

"Hold your fire!"

Vance and his entourage were flying white flags of truce.

Sitting high on their horses, boots polished, uniforms pressed. These men—there was nowhere near a hundred of them—were dressed in officers' garb with the same armour plates they'd worn when they'd delivered Pierre's body. Front and centre was Commander Vance himself, white flag propped in the holder of his finely crafted saddle. Everything about the group gleamed. The horses' coats, the armour, the rivets on the tack, and Vance's smile as he lifted off his full-face helmet.

"We should send for help," Sabine whispered. "Summon whoever is left protecting the coliseum! Rally the city!"

"No. They've come in peace." Seth grabbed her arm and clutched it tight. "Now is not the time."

She leaned in even closer. "Now is the perfect time! There's not that many of them. We could kill him now!"

"We follow the rules of engagement."

"What?" Sabine practically spat her rage at him. "Why? After everything they've done to us?"

"Good morning!" Vance pulled off his long leather gloves and tucked them under one arm. He ran a hand through his hair and grinned. "You'll forgive me if I stay atop my horse?"

"What if he kills us?"

"He won't." Seth gripped his sister's wrist. "Do not mess this up. Let me handle him."

With a scowl, Sabine wrenched her hand away and rubbed where Seth had left red marks.

"Quite the little spitfire you got there." Vance winked at Seth. "How did you fare? After our little bit of fun last night. Lost quite a few children, I hear."

"You're a monster—I'll kill you myself!" Sabine lunged for him, but Seth caught her around the waist and held her back.

"Whoa there, pony." Vance laughed. "Get a grip on her reins, Commander Seth. You and I are off to a fine start. Don't let her ruin a good thing."

"Good thing?" Sabine screamed, trying to pry herself out of Seth's grasp.

"Shut up!" Seth growled in her ear, and then let go.

"We haven't met, miss … ?"

Sabine strode toward Vance and stuck up her hand, as was custom in the Keys.

"Sabine Fabienne, leader of the Triskelians."

Vance took her hand and, just when Sabine thought he'd shake it, he bent and kissed it. *"Enchanté."*

She yanked her hand away and wiped it on her tunic. He'd caught her by surprise, and she hated him all the more for it.

"Commander Vance." Now Seth approached, his hand held out for a gentlemanly handshake. "Well done! It would appear you've won this particular battle."

This time, Vance hesitated.

"The scars, yes." Seth lowered his hand. "I understand the Keyland's ignorance."

Vance bristled, but quickly recovered. "I've come for my men. The ones you have as prisoners."

"No. No, we can't just hand them over." Seth smiled. "But don't worry, Commander, they are in good hands. The rules of engagement, after all, prohibit torture."

"What are you implying?"

"Nothing at all ... just rest assured that if or when your men are returned to you they will have all their fingers and toes."

"I had nothing to do with that man's torture."

Sabine stepped between the two, Vance atop his horse, her brother working so hard to appear calm. "What have you *really* come for? You knew we wouldn't give up our prisoners."

"You put up an honourable fight." Vance kept his eyes locked on Seth. "We may have taken the prize last night, but there will be other times to flex your army's might. You have an impressive collection of soldiers, Seth—"

"That's Commander Seth to you."

"*Commander* Seth. A fine assortment of children to play war under your marionette strings."

"*Commander* Vance ..." For the first time, Sabine took a good look at Vance. He was a handsome man, rugged and with broad, strong shoulders. But there was a flatness to his expression that gave her chills. It was a flatness she had often observed in Seth. "Tell us what you've come here for."

"You, young lady." Commander Vance cocked his head at her. "I've become quite curious about you. I wanted to see you for myself. To meet you, properly."

"Say *nothing*," Seth whispered to Sabine.

"You seem quite young," Commander Vance continued. He studied the girl. No matter what Edmund said, Vance could see him in the angle of her jaw, the shape of her lips. The small gap between her two front teeth. "Very young to have such responsibility resting on such delicate shoulders." He paused. "How old are you?"

"Old enough." Sabine put her hands on her hips "Why?"

"Older than your brother?"

"Sabine—" Seth willed her to be silent. If Vance didn't know she was his triplet, what else didn't he know?

"Why do you want to know?"

"Tell me how old you are."

Sabine stared at him. "Eight and three quarters."

The Guardy to Vance's left, still with his visor down, aimed his gun at her. "Answer him!"

Vance raised his hand and the man lowered his weapon. "Where were we?" Vance grinned at Sabine.

Suddenly the sound of marching made Sabine and Seth turn their heads to the street behind them.

"Call off your puppies," Vance barked at Seth. "Now!" he added when the bootsteps grew louder. "We are not quite finished here. You have my word no bullets will be fired today, so long as your boys stay well back. A good three hundred metres at least. Agreed?"

"Agreed." Seth sent a runner with instructions to hold the line. He didn't let his confusion show, but the truth was that he had no idea who was marching on them. The soldiers stationed at the coliseum were few, most having been seconded back this way during the night. More civilians from the city? Or was his grasp of his soldiers so tenuous that he didn't know who was where, or how many had even survived the night?

Seth glanced nonchalantly over his shoulder—and stifled a gasp. The street reaching across the city behind him was packed shoulder to shoulder with civilian allies, each with a red band tied around his arm in honour of their fallen comrades. Amon stood at the front of them all.

"Commander Seth!" He lifted a salute to his brow as he hollered. "Respectfully awaiting orders!"

Without betraying his glee, Seth turned back to Vance. "You were saying?"

Beside him, Sabine couldn't contain herself. "Look at them all! They've come to help. Ha!" She jabbed a finger in Vance's direction. "Shows you!"

Vance shared a smirk with his right-hand man. "I've come with an offer. Let's get on with it."

"Let's." Seth shot a glare in Sabine's direction.

"Or should I be speaking with her? She *is* the leader of Triskelia now, after all," Vance said. "Your sister? You do share a father, correct?" Vance knew Edmund was on his way across the Droughtland, back to the Eastern Key. What he was about to propose would be his way of reminding that pompous fool of their agreement. He'd send a messenger to Edmund, intercept him en route, to drive the point home and let him know his time was up.

Sabine caught Seth's eye, her own brow raised in a question. What was it Vance wanted to know? Or more importantly, what didn't he know? No matter, Seth would give him nothing. And neither would Sabine if she knew what was good for her, for them all. Seth and Sabine stared him down.

After a long, unbroken silence, Vance sighed. "Very well," he said. "I have come to offer a ceasefire. For one week."

Seth looked at him skeptically. "Why?"

"You can recover from this first attack. You can send the women and children—the ones who aren't fighting for you, anyway—away from the city before we take it for good."

"And we're supposed to believe you?" Sabine said with a scoff. "Tell me why I should believe you."

"My army is a real army." Vance straightened in his saddle. "Genuine soldiers, not toddlers with sticks and toy guns. Pillaging is no fun for them. They like an honourable challenge." He paused. "My views on the subject are just a few of the ways I differ from your friend and former colleague Commander Regis." He trained his gaze on Seth as he spoke. "May he rest in peace."

"May he rot in hell," Seth growled. "And as for your 'real army,' last night they looked like dusters you hired off the street for a packet of powder."

"Well, it wasn't a 'real' battle last night, now, was it?"

"My soldiers fought a real battle."

"Let's move on, shall we? Time is of the essence." Vance tapped his watch. "Deal or not?"

"I don't trust you." Sabine said. "And why would I?"

"Simple economics." Vance shrugged. "Fewer bullets, less chance of blood sicks. Fewer freaks and madmen to shake off while we take you down."

"We'll accept the deal," Seth said. "With one condition."

"But Seth—"

"I *said*, we'll take it." Another glare in Sabine's direction. "On one condition. You agree not to attack the hospitals. The field hospital here, beyond that gate, and the one at the coliseum."

"Conveniently located at your headquarters."

"My *headquarters* were right here." Seth walked a slow circle, indicating with outstretched arm the ruins surrounding them. "You know damned well what happened to my headquarters."

"Triskelia's headquarters, then." Vance shrugged. "You know what I mean."

"The hospitals. No-fire zones."

A long moment passed before Vance finally nodded. "I'll agree to that."

"I'm guessing you won't want to shake on it."

"Correct." Vance's horse shifted. "Besides, you're one of them now, aren't you? Isn't that sort of thing verboten?"

"Then we'll call it a verbal agreement, with your armoured cowards as your witness, and Sabine as mine."

"Fair enough." Vance nodded as he clicked for his horse's attention. "We will see you in one week."

"Where?"

"You'll know when the time comes," Vance said over his shoulder. His men lifted their weapons and aimed them at the crowd, warning them to stay back. "Until we meet again."

Seth gave him a look of steely indifference.

"Victory is neither earned nor genuine if it comes without contest," Vance added, as if it were something he'd intended to say and had forgotten until now.

He gave Seth a wink and then he was off, heading back the way he came, white flags fluttering.

8

Nappo unlatched the door of the warming cupboard, and before saying a word, took his daughter in his arms and kissed her. His hands and face were almost black with soot and muck. Anya scrambled forward, reaching for him.

"Trace?"

"He's fine. None of our people were badly hurt." Nappo rearranged the baby on one arm and hugged Teal to him with the other. "You okay, kiddo?"

"Yep. We heard the bombs."

"Thank the highers, everyone is safe and sound." Eli stepped out and stretched. He lifted Toby down after him, and then moved aside as Bullet shot out.

"Not everyone." Nappo gave Teal a little push. "Take Toby down to the kitchen and find something to eat."

"But I want to hear what happened."

"And I'll tell you all about it later, kiddo. Now go."

Teal dragged his feet as Toby hopped in front of him, singing a nonsense song about oatmeal and spiders. The boys weren't that far apart in age, but Teal had grown up in the Droughtland, and seemed all that much older for it.

"Tasha, the baby needs changing."

Tasha leaned against the wall, combing her hair with her fingers and yawning. "And I would've, only we were hiding in here all night and it wasn't safe to go wandering about looking for a nappy, was it?"

"It's safe now. So go." Nappo's tone surprised Eli. His words for Tasha always seemed harsh, but this morning they were particularly cutting.

Then it was just Nappo and Eli, alone, the warm yeasty musk of so many bodies in such a small space wafting out into the cooler air of the hall.

"What happened?" Eli asked. "Tell me everything."

Nappo leaned against the wall, lips moving as if he were about to speak. But then he pushed himself away and shook his head. "You weren't there. There's no describing."

"But our people are okay?"

"And thousands of people you've never met are dead." Nappo wiped his face, but only smeared the filth worse. "Shouldn't you care as much about them as about Jack or Sabine? Hmm, Reverend?"

"And I will pray—"

"I don't want to hear it." Nappo held up his hand. "I came back to check on the children, and to be sure Emma was being seen to."

"Tasha is taking good care of her."

"She's not." Nappo shook his head. "She doesn't seem to care about her. Not like I do!"

"She's doing her best—"

"Shut up, Eli!" Nappo's hands closed into fists. He punched the wooden door of the cupboard, slamming it shut with the force. He shook out his fist as he backed away. "I can't talk to you about this. I can't talk to you about anything! You've changed, Eli. I don't even know who you are any more. Go pray to your friggin' highers about that, okay? Just leave me alone!" He set off at a run, footsteps echoing down the dark hall.

Eli was stunned. When he could move again, he started after his friend. Of course he would go after him, talk to him, reason with him. Make Nappo see that he wasn't his enemy.

Let him go.

Eli stopped. But if he didn't go after Nappo, where would he go? Part of him wanted to crawl back into the warming cupboard and stay there until this was all over. Another, smaller part of him wanted to cross the city and pitch in. Maybe he could work with Rosa, see to the wounded.

What he really wanted to do was get high.

Eli made his way out into the morning, to the front of the coliseum where the barrel boys camped out. The fire had gone out in the barrel, but there, on one of the three pallets around it, lay the man with the dust.

"Mister?" Eli knelt and shook the man gently. "Wake up."

"Huh?" The man clawed at his blanket. "Wha—?" Slowly he focused on Eli. "Ah, you again. I got no more freebies for you. No more. You're a paying customer now. Like everybody else."

"Just one more time."

The man shook his head. "First time, I was being polite, Reverend. Second time, I was still being polite. You're brother to Sabine, brother to Seth, so I was showin' my respect and gave you a little step up, right? Third time you was pushing my patience, but now ..." He shook his head again and pulled the blanket over him. "No more."

"But I *can't* pay. I haven't got any money."

"I take trades. Barters, what have you. That medallion around your neck, maybe."

Eli touched his tunic where the medallion hung beneath. He'd never had it out in this man's company, had he? "No."

"Then off you go, Rev."

"Just one more time." Eli shook the man again, this time harder. "Please. *Please.* I beg you."

"Okay, okay." The man flung off his blanket and sat up. "And then you pay. Next time I won't budge. Even for a Triskelian."

"Next time I pay. Absolutely." Eli smiled at him. There would be no next time though, because Eli was going to stop. In honour of Nappo, out of respect for Zenith, in order to prove to himself and his highers that he could, he would stop. After this one last time.

Eli scurried off with the little pouch of dust. Once he was out of sight he rubbed it on his gums. He needed to be quick—he couldn't afford to get caught—and so he took it the way he'd seen other dusters do it, Nappo included.

The high came fast. Even before he licked the last of the dust off his fingers he'd been kicked in the gut by all things beautiful in the world. Eli was floored by the preciousness of what surrounded him, and yet he didn't care about anything at all. He swooned up into the high and grate-fully left behind Triban and the battle he knew so little about and the upcoming conflicts he knew even less about and his mother's death and so much ruin ... he held himself mid-air, floating, looking down on it all, his mother's charred face gazing up, the rubble falling around her ... and then he lifted his chin to the heavens and kept floating up, up, up.

As his mind and soul flew ever skyward, Eli flopped his body down on a bale of canvas, swishing his hands through the light and streaking the air with wakes of shimmering glow. He was thirsty, but other than that he was perfect. Perfection personified. Peaceful. Full of prayer. Pious. He savoured the words like boiled candy. *Perfect. Peaceful. Prayer. Pious.* He closed his eyes and Mireille was suddenly there. *Mireille!* He smiled, reached a hand out to touch her.

I miss you, she was saying while she floated in front of him. *When will you come back to me?*

"Soon, soon," Eli murmured. "I have to finish here, and then I can come to you."

I miss you, Eli. Mireille kissed the air. Eli stretched up to kiss her back, and as he did she morphed into Zari, but only for a split second.

"What was that?"

Mireille wasn't answering. She floated just out of reach, smiling, her dark hair framing her face, the pink of her cheeks, her plump lips parted ever so slightly, begging to be kissed. "Come closer, let me ..."

But someone was jabbing at his chest. Eli opened one eye. Teal stood over him, poking him with a stick.

"Stop it, brat."

"Who you talking to?" Another poke. And then two pokes at once. Eli pushed himself up on his elbows. Toby grinned at him, wielding his own stick.

"No one." Eli winked at Mireille. Mireille winked back from her watery perch. She lifted a hand to her bodice and tugged the ribbons loose. Eli pinched Teal's arm. "Go away."

"Ow! You were talking to someone." Teal hopped out of reach. "Only, there ain't no one here except you and me."

"An' me!" Toby poked him again. Eli swatted for him and missed. "Ain't no one but us."

"*Isn't* anyone." Eli struggled to sit up. He was stiff, his neck creaking as he looked around, trying to figure out where he was. Triban. In the coliseum somewhere, and he knew that only because Teal and Toby weren't allowed beyond its walls. He brought a hand to his throat. "I am so thirsty."

"Who were you making goggly eyes at?" Teal persisted. He did a little jig, hugging himself and making kissing sounds. *"Ooo, yeah, sweetheart, baby, baby."*

"I didn't say that."

"You did!" Teal kept smooching the air. "And you had a boner. I saw it poking up your pants."

Toby climbed up on the bale. "What's a boner?"

"I wasn't talking to anyone!" Eli barked. With that, Mireille disappeared in a twirl of light and colour. Vanished. He gave Teal a genuine shove. "Now look what you did! She's gone, just when I had her, she's gone."

"See?" Teal backed away. "You were talking to someone. Nappo's right." He turned on his heel. He looped a finger at his ear. "Loony!"

"Wait!" But the boys had disappeared around the corner. Eli slid his feet to the ground and stood. He wobbled back against the bale and thought better of standing again.

How humiliating. This was no way for a reverend to behave. He would change. He'd prove to the others he was worthy. Eli dropped his head into his hands. His forehead felt hot and his head throbbed, as if his brain was trying to tell him something and he was just not getting it.

"Why make it so hard?" he asked the highers. "Why?"

You make it as hard as you need to make it.

"And why the riddles?"

No reply.

It occurred to Eli then that he and Seth had as good as switched places. It was Seth and his army of child warriors who commanded respect among the Triskelians now. What had happened? Eli shook his head, but that just made the pounding worse.

He would gain back their favour. He hadn't realized how important it was to him. He would be the soul of the revolution, as Zenith had told him. He would find a way.

He didn't want to deny his highers, but he wanted his old self back.

Do not turn away.

"And I won't." He practically growled the words. "But this has got to stop."

Eli pulled the empty dust pouch from his pocket. He poked it open and peered in with a squint. He licked his pinky and shoved it in, scraping up the last specks of the dust into a little paste on his fingertip.

He would not dust again. This would be it. And with that he licked the last of the dust, swishing it in his mouth. He would be stronger next time—worthy of his position. He would become confidant, peer, counsellor to his people. And like all mentors he would speak from experience. He would know the desperation of rock bottom.

Eli lay back on the bale and closed his eyes again, the high a little flatter now, dimmer, but still glorious. He fell asleep watching plump white clouds on the insides of his eyes.

9

It had been a full day now with no gunfire from the Guard. Satisfied that the ceasefire was genuine, Seth had arranged for Rosa to return to the coliseum and work out of the infirmary there. She would be accompanied by hand-picked BAT boys and her new assistant, Stephane.

Seth quietly timed his day so that he'd run in to her en route.

"Look," Stephane said as Seth approached them. "It's him!"

"Keep going," Rosa snapped, keeping her eyes forward.

"But I haven't even met him," Stephane said as he waved. "Commander Seth! Over here!"

She sighed. Stephane was an eager kid, seeing the good in everything. He didn't know of her past with Seth. And what would she even tell him? *I loved him once.* Maybe still.

"Rosa." Despite the hammering in his heart Seth was careful to keep his tone even. "How are you?"

"Exhausted."

"But other than that? How are you, really?"

"Really *exhausted.*"

Seth could see she wasn't going to give him anything. This would not be the meeting he had hoped for. "Can I help in some way?"

"You could've left me at the field hospital."

"But under the ceasefire agreement—"

"Sabine said the agreement included both sites."

"And it does." Seth felt a rush of frustration. Here he was in a mundane conversation, Rosa's little peon drinking in every word, when all he wanted to do was lift her off her horse and take her in his arms. To someplace quiet. Where they could be alone. He glanced at the boy.

"Hi!"

Seth dismissed him with a slight roll of his eyes. "Rosa, could I speak with you in private?"

"You can say what you have to say in front of Stephane."

"I can't, actually."

"Then it will have to wait." She lifted her chin defiantly. "You wanted the less wounded settled in the coliseum. Personally, I wouldn't have moved them. But you're the boss. Who am I?"

"Who *are* you?" She was everything. He could stand the wrath of an entire land but couldn't bear her judging him. She hadn't let him explain. Not ever. "Rosa, I made that a condition of the ceasefire to keep you safe, don't you see? I want you to be safe. I want you to—"

"Stop." Rosa locked her cool, dark eyes on him for so long that Seth shifted uncomfortably in his saddle. "I have an official number of casualties."

"Don't tell me."

"You don't want to know?"

"I do, but—"

"But what, Seth? Tell me."

Seth allowed himself a small smile. When he and Rosa had been out in the Droughtland together, the way she would cut him off like that had driven him mad. Didn't the fact that she did it now just prove she still felt close to him? As if they were having a lover's quarrel? He just had to give it time. She would come back to him. She would let him in again.

"I should get going," he said at last.

"Whatever."

"But, but ..." Beside Rosa, Stephane couldn't contain himself any longer. "But he can't go yet. You have to introduce me, Rosa!"

Rosa sighed. "This is Stephane."

"Commander Seth!" Stephane was nearly bouncing in his saddle. "I am Stephane Zakary Aroca-Ouellette. An honour to meet you! I wish I was one of your soldiers, only I'm a terrible fighter and I have tired lungs and my mother *always* said I'd have to take it easy, so she gave me books to read, and she worked for a lifeminder—only as his cleaner, mind—but she'd borrow them and bring them home for me to read—"

"Good to meet you, Stephane." Seth did not have the time or patience for this kid. "I'm glad you're here to help."

"Anything I can do, Commander Seth. Anything at all! Your wish is my command."

"Heed Rosa, then. Whatever she asks of you."

"Of course, Commander Seth. And if I could just take this chance to thank you for everything you're doing for the people—"

"I really should get going." Seth brought his horse up close to Rosa's and leaned in. "I want to talk to you in private. As soon as possible."

Rosa stiffened. Her cheeks flushed pink. "Back off," she whispered.

Stephane gawked. How could Rosa talk to Commander Seth like that?

"I need to see you later," Seth persisted. A glance at Stephane. "Alone."

"No."

Suddenly Stephane knew. His own mentor and the Commander of the Boys' Army of Triban ... lovers!

"Just to *talk*."

"You do not want to hear what I have to say to you."

Now Seth grabbed her arm, leaned in, and said under his breath, "Tell me why you're acting like this!"

She wrenched free. "You know why!"

"I did not kill Zenith." He hadn't. He'd *helped* Zenith. He clutched Rosa's arm again. "I didn't!"

"Let me go," Rosa said through gritted teeth. "Now!"

Stephane watched, enthralled. A lover's spat! What about? But now Rosa pulled away and, with one final glare for Commander Seth, set off at a gallop, not even bothering to check that Stephane was following.

"What are *you* looking at?" Seth's eyes blazed.

"Nothing, Commander Seth!" Stephane tugged on his reins and peeled away from the daunting figure.

HOURS LATER, Rosa took the bandages from Stephane and pointed out the streaks of red around the soldier's shrapnel wounds. "What is this?"

"Infection."

"Right. So what could we put on it before we wrap it up again?"

"Berberry compress? Comfrey?"

"Let's go with the berberry." Rosa supervised him as he prepared the compress. "You think he's a god, don't you?"

"The soldier?" Stephane had meant it as a joke. Of course he knew she was talking about Seth. But his nervousness had gotten the better of him. Rosa looked at him, patiently waiting for a real answer. "Not a god, no." He applied the compress. The boy stirred, moaned, but then was still again. "But a hero, definitely. He's done so much for the people. He'll win us our freedom. I know it."

"Not alone, he won't. He's one of many responsible for what's happening right now. You have no idea, Stephane."

"I do so."

"You think you do, but you don't." Rosa washed her hands and moved on to the next bed. Stephane made to follow, but she waved him away. "Take the other side. I'll do this row."

Moving among her patients, she was as good as alone. She could go through the motions, ask questions, check dressings, dole out medicines and apply poultices, all the while following her own train of thought. She wasn't ready to be alone with Seth. She didn't trust herself. She hated that she couldn't shut off her feelings for him, even after what he'd done—or hadn't done?—to Zenith.

She glanced across the rows of patients to where Stephane squatted, talking softly to a boy with an oozing wound on his torso. She'd be sure to have him around, or Sabine, or someone. For if she were alone with Seth she would have no resolve. She closed her eyes and saw it all: he would reach for her and she would protest, he would pull her to him and she would resist, and then she wouldn't, and then she'd give up and let him kiss her, and then he would—

She clenched her hands into fists and told herself not to be stupid. Not for a second time around. Not when she knew better now.

10

⤜❧⤛

That night a strategy meeting was held at the coliseum. The only non-Triskelian in attendance was Effie, the girl from the tunnels. She and her gaggle of children had suddenly shown up again, having run out of food and with nowhere else to turn.

Eli was still passed out on the bale when they'd arrived; the cacophony of childish protests had woken him up. He lay there, not ready to face anything just yet, until Toby leapt on him.

"Anya's washing their faces and they don't like it."

Eli had gone to investigate and found Anya and Effie each wrestling a child into submission with washcloths and soap.

"*Allo,* Eli," Anya said when she saw him come in. "Come help."

"The meeting's in just a few minutes." But Eli caught the damp cloth she chucked at him, and without further protest grabbed the nearest snot-nosed toddler and attacked his face.

"They don't need you there."

Eli paused in his scrubbing. "What do you mean?"

The child Anya was washing pushed at her and squirmed, whining.

"They said you were to help me tonight, with the kids."

He glanced at Effie. "Is *she* going?"

"Yes," Effie answered. "*She* is. Because I know about the tunnels. Better than Seth. Better than anyone."

"I'm going to that meeting," Eli insisted. "They don't know if they need me there or not. Zenith would want me to be there, don't you think?

"Peut-être." Anya shrugged. "But more likely they will send you back here wit' me."

"I am just as much a leader as Seth or Sabine."

"No you're not," Effie said.

Eli let his charge go. "What's that supposed to mean?"

"All I'm saying is the city sees your brother and sister as the leaders. Not you."

"How they see it and how it is are two very different things."

"Very well may be."

But the truth was he *hadn't* been much of a leader. Not for a long while. Well, not ever really, and certainly not since taking up the dust. That would change from now on. He'd promised his highers. He'd promised himself.

"I'm going to that meeting."

Anya let loose one child and reached for another. How many were there? Eli tried counting heads, but none were still long enough to get an accurate number.

"Nineteen," Effie said, guessing what he was after.

NOW ELI MADE HIS WAY to the kitchen in time to get a seat at the table.

"We don't need you here." Seth looked worn out as he glanced up.

Eli didn't ask him about the battle. He didn't want to give away how little he knew.

Sabine frowned. "We wanted you to look after the kids."

Eli mustered a cool, indifferent look. "I've decided I'm better off here."

"And I'll say it again, we don't need you." Seth leaned over the table. That close, Eli could see how bloodshot his eyes were, how dulled with fatigue.

Eli clenched his jaw. "I'm staying."

The meeting was brought to order with no further comment. For highers' sake, even Tasha had been allowed to join in. Or she too had forced herself on them. Judging by the dirty look Sabine gave her as Tasha took her seat, Eli figured the latter was more likely.

Eli listened hard. He wanted to learn as much as he could, and silently vowed to everyone in the room that his beliefs wouldn't get in the way of doing his part.

"Do we have a tally?" Sabine was asking Seth.

"Several hundred injured," Seth said without looking up. He was carving something into the worn tabletop with his pocket knife.

"Can you be more specific?"

Seth shook his head.

"And dead?"

"No tally yet." Seth looked up. He was hiding something, Sabine could tell. She would ask him again, in private. Now she cast a glance around at the others. Nappo, Jack, Gavin, Yvon, and Trace had all been with her in battle. No number would surprise them. Rosa wasn't here. She would know.

The meeting moved quickly from topic to topic. A shipment of grain was coming in from one of the eastern townships.

"A donation," Trace explained. "We'll allocate it for the kids, mostly. There's another shipment coming in three days—a much bigger one. We'll set that one aside for the troops."

"They'll need armed escorts." Seth gouged out a sliver of wood. "I can put boys on both, if you let me know the details."

Trace grimaced, but Seth wasn't even looking at him. "Will do."

FOR NEARLY THREE HOURS the group planned for battle once the ceasefire ended. Where to get more ammunition, more machetes, more people to fight. Strategies for meeting with Vance—wherever that would take place. Eli listened carefully to it all. He hadn't once been called on, so he was surprised to hear Sabine finally say his name.

"Eli?" she repeated. "Are you listening?"

Now Seth looked over at him. "Maybe the good Reverend was deep in prayer."

"I wasn't."

"Eli, we're putting you in charge of evacuating the children."

Eli sat straighter in his seat. "Why me?"

"I can trust you with them."

"Why not Effie?"

"You'll have her, and Anya. And Tasha too."

Tasha yelped in protest. "But I've got the baby to look after."

Nappo let out a small laugh.

"I do!" Tasha hugged Emma to her as if to prove her responsibility. All this did was wake the baby up and make her cry. "See? I can't take care of a bunch of other kids."

"Yes you can," Effie said. "It's not all that hard."

"You're not a mother." Tasha put Emma to her breast. "You wouldn't know the first thing about it."

"I've taken care of kids since I could *walk*," Effie began, then caught Sabine's warning look. "I'll show you how."

"You will not. I'm not taking babysitting lessons from some kid."

"Yes you will," Sabine cut in. "We're all doing our part, and this is your part."

To this day Sabine hadn't found a good reason to like Tasha. She wasn't even a very good mother, and if it weren't for Nappo the baby would've been abandoned by now. That was Sabine's opinion, anyway. She saw Nappo doing all the work, changing her, rocking her. When Emma was left with Tasha, she lay in her blanket-lined drawer, ignored. Half the time Nappo had to remind her to feed the baby. Sabine had heard of women feeling low after having a baby, but this was a bit much.

"And who says I have to listen to you?" Tasha sneered at her. Sabine glanced at Nappo, who kept his eyes averted, his arms crossed in careful neutrality. "Why should I?"

"I am the leader, that's why."

"What about him?" Tasha jutted her chin in Seth's direction. "He's the leader too." She fixed her eyes on Seth. "What've you got to say on the matter?"

Seth set down his knife and appraised her with an icy look. "I say you're making a big deal out of nothing and you should be thankful I'm not shipping you out to cook porridge for my troops."

With a mortified gasp, Tasha tried Nappo for support, but he wouldn't even look at her.

"And him?" She jutted her chin at Eli this time. "He's supposed to be the finish to your magic triangle, right?"

Sabine and Seth held their eyes on him, waiting for more protest.

Eli sighed. "I'll do it. I'm happy to help in any way you see fit."

"Thanks, Eli." For the first time in a long time, Sabine grinned.

AFTER THE MEETING Tasha stormed all the way to the little room they'd been given. She waited for Nappo to catch up with the baby and then slammed the door behind him, setting Emma off on a fit of startled tears.

"You've upset her!" Nappo burst out.

"What about that cow upsetting me?"

"We all have to contribute, Tasha. This isn't going to happen overnight, and it isn't going to be easy."

"None of this has been easy!" Tasha grabbed her few belongings and started packing. "When I found you I thought we could be together, and that everything would be better. But it's not! And that baby doesn't even like me, I'm sure of it!"

"Tasha ..." Nappo leaned against the closed door, settling in for another one of Tasha's tantrums. He was never sure what to say. Everything he tried made her more upset, or just sad. Sad was worse. She'd crumple into a heap and weep for hours, crying even while nursing the baby or changing her diaper. "What can I say?"

"That you'll come with me!" She'd packed her bags before and threatened to leave. Almost daily. But she hadn't yet. And if she did—or more specifically, if she took Emma with her—Nappo would hunt her down until he had Emma in his arms again.

"No. We need to be here. Right now, anyway."

"I want to go home! I want to be with my family! I can't stand it here!"

Nappo rocked Emma and let Tasha stomp around, venting. "No one likes me here. Even from the start, no one did. That Sabine hates me and she has no good reason. None at all!"

Nappo didn't say that he didn't like her much either. He didn't say that he'd only hooked up with her at all because he'd been stoned. And that if it weren't for Emma, he'd have sent Tasha off with bells and whistles long ago. He didn't tell her that he kind of sometimes dreamed that she took off. By herself. Without the baby.

All this silence took the steam out of Tasha's tantrum. There she went, slumping to the floor, head in her hands.

Nappo counted. The tears would start in earnest in five, four, three, two ...

Tasha threw her head back and wailed. "I want to go *home*." Her shoulders shook and her nose ran and she didn't care. She didn't! There was Nappo staring at her like a dumb fool, and the baby gawping at her, always wanting, wanting, wanting! Taking, taking, taking! Her milk, her energy, her strength. She was being sucked dry! Used up! And she was just a *girl*!

Everything had changed with the baby's birth. She and Nappo never had any fun and the baby was nothing but work. And here she was, a million miles from home, and the only thing she wanted was her own mother. She just wanted to be tucked into bed and woken when it was all over.

11

꒰ঌ

E li had misunderstood about evacuating the children. He'd thought
Sabine had meant Effie's bunch. One entire day passed before
Sabine approached him in the hall, asking him how it was going.

"How many are you up to now?"

"What?"

"I haven't noticed many more. Where are you keeping them?"

She meant children—all the children. Eli gulped when it dawned on
him. Had he zoned out at the meeting without even realizing it?

Sabine spelled it out for him now, and then again for Effie and Tasha
and Anya when they were all together in the playroom.

" ... all the children you can round up by the end of the week. Not just
these ones, but as many as you can find. You're going to escort them up
to Cascadia for safekeeping. Take the orphans and street urchins first, but
if any Tribanites want to send their children with you, they can. Just keep
track of the child's name and who he or she belongs to."

Cascadia? The job was getting interesting now.

AS EFFIE DREW a detailed map of the city, she and Eli worked out how
to round up as many children as they could. Anya would stay behind,
keeping watch over the kids. Tasha would do ... whatever Tasha would
do. As Effie and Eli donned backpacks and prepared to set out, not an
hour after Sabine had set them straight, Tasha was nowhere to be found.

"Are you going to be okay by yourself?" Eli asked Anya as she dashed by, chasing a naked toddler.

"*D'accord,*" Anya said with a laugh. "Off you go. Bring back a hundred. *Mais non,* bring back a thousand!"

Effie stuck her fingers in her mouth and sounded a sharp whistle. "Freeze!"

All the children immediately fell still, even the naked toddler. Rabbit shushed a couple very little ones who didn't know any better, and Bear stuck a self-righteous fist on his hips, daring anyone to slight his Effie.

"If I get back and find out any of you were bad for Anya, I'll take the switch to you," Effie bellowed. "Got it?"

"Yes, Effie," came the collective reply, as if they were schoolchildren answering their teacher.

"HOW DO YOU DO THAT?" Eli asked as they set off into the street.

"I'm all they've got. They keep each other in line."

They passed the barrel boys and Eli pretended not to know them.

"Reverend!" The man ran after him. "What can I do for you today, Rev?"

"Sorry, I can't stop. I'm busy."

"You'll come looking for me later. I swear it!" the man called after him.

Effie eyed him. For a scrawny kid, she could sure lay on the disapproval with just one look. "Who's that?"

"No one."

"No one ... sure." Effie snugged the straps of her pack and quickened her pace. "Let's go. I'll take you to the squat I was telling you about."

Eli followed her, but his mind was back at the burning barrel. He should've got some, in case of withdrawal. But he'd taken it only a few times. Would he go through the same awful spell that Nappo had? The man wouldn't give him any more for free, so Eli was out of luck anyway. He glanced up, said a silent prayer to his higners, and then set his mind to the task at hand. Collecting the children of Triban.

Edmund arrived home in the Eastern Key to much less fanfare than he'd expected. No marching band, no banners or streamers enlivening the dull, tidy streets. Only a handful of people stepped onto their front verandas to watch him ride by. Arms crossed, they stared at him with the same look that a disappointed parent might give a child who's failed at an important task. Words like *impeachment, indictment,* and *inquiry* started flitting around Edmund's head like flies to a stench.

Vance was right—people had started to talk. Yet it was still all hearsay: chatter among servants, talk over tea. There was still hope. He'd received Vance's message about the ceasefire: so his "time had run out," had it? Ha! Edmund had since devised a singular plan. He would give Vance a little of his own medicine. Divert his attention ... elsewhere. Then Vance would think twice about just who he was dealing with.

He had his carriageminder take him straight home. His servants were lined up neatly, their smocks freshly pressed, shoes polished. Allegra stood in front, beaming. She smoothed her dress at her waist and held out her hands. He greeted her with a chaste kiss, appropriate in light of their audience. She took his hands and pulled him to her, for the kiss she preferred.

Remembering herself, she pulled back at last. "The baby has grown. Come see him?"

"Why didn't you bring him down to meet me?" At least his own son should be dressed up and bathed and brought out to see him home.

"He's sleeping." Allegra's glance travelled upward. "In the nursery."

Edmund let out an irritated huff. "Sleeping." He hurried past the servants—bowing or curtsying all, in well-practised form—and toward his office for a stiff drink.

Allegra grabbed his wrist. "Edmund, don't be angry. Come. Come upstairs and see Charlie."

Gritting his teeth, Edmund allowed himself to be led upstairs.

The creaks in the stairs screamed at him. The tick tock of the grand-father clock on the landing punched holes in him.

"What kind of message is that to the household, that you couldn't be bothered to have my own son brought downstairs to meet me? Do you really think an infant's *nap*time is more important than stately de*co*rum?"

They climbed the rest of the stairs in silence, until Allegra said simply, "You were late." She strode into the nursery, lifted the baby roughly from his crib, and thrust him at Edmund as he jolted awake with a fluttering cry. "Your son," Allegra said before turning to leave the room. "I'll send the nanny up. You can give him to her when you've had your visit."

Edmund held the infant at arm's length and marvelled at his little face, all scrunched up and damp with tears. Charlie took after him in more ways than Eli or Seth had put together.

"Shhh." He brought the baby to his chest. "Quiet, now."

The baby sucked in his breath and shuddered back his cries.

"There we go." Edmund sat in the rocker and laid the boy in his lap, supporting his head with his knees. After a quick, furtive look around, he leaned over and cooed at Charlie. "Final countdown, kiddo." He glanced at his watch. "Any time now."

Charlie churned the air with his hands and made bubbles with his drool.

A rap on the door. "Enter."

The nanny stood at the door, hands folded in front of her, head bowed.

"Go," Edmund said. "Send my wife up."

The nanny curtsied and then scurried off. The seconds ticked loudly on the mantel clock, the minute hand made its progress. Half an hour passed. Charlie was asleep in his lap. Edmund would not go find Allegra. She should come to him. Finally, she appeared.

"You wanted to see me?"

"Come in." Edmund knew he had no place in inviting her into her own child's nursery. No matter.

Allegra lifted Charlie, still asleep, off Edmund's lap and set him in the crib.

"What happened at the legislature?" She paused. "Even the house staff is talking. About a girl."

"What girl?" Edmund could feel his heart kick-start with fear. How could word of her have travelled all this way so fast? Even if she *was* leader, how could they know to connect her to him? This was worse, far worse than he could have imagined.

"You know what I'm talking about." Allegra lowered her voice. "They say the new leader of the Triskelians is your *daughter*."

Edmund shook his head. "Allegra—"

"Think!" Allegra was beside him now, on her knees, her skirts bunched around her. "Think hard about what you will tell me. We have a son to keep safe."

"She is not my daughter."

"They said there is no doubt."

"*They*." Edmund spat out the word. "Who are *they*?"

"Servants and staff, at the moment." Allegra's rich brown eyes bored into his. "Give it time and the entire Key will have heard."

"That won't happen." And even if it did, they still had time. A Chancellors' Court would have to be convened. It was the law. He reminded Allegra of this. "And that would take months."

"But it will happen?"

"Inevitably," Edmund finally admitted. "But we'll be long gone."

Allegra went pale. "Where will we go?"

He had no idea. No Key would have them, and even if he stepped down he'd be tried for treason. Allegra and the baby would never survive in the Droughtland, and nor would he.

"I'm not leaving." Determination had replaced the fear in Allegra's eyes. "This is my home. I won't be driven from it." And now her lip began to tremble.

Edmund reached out his arms and, after hesitating for a long moment, Allegra allowed herself to collapse against him. "It won't come to that," he murmured.

He glanced at his watch as he stroked her lustrous hair.

Any time now.

Seth stood outside the closed door, a bottle of wine tucked under his arm. He dug in his pocket and found a handkerchief to wipe his brow. He'd started sweating the moment he'd taken the bottle of wine from the crate of straw.

The crate held eight bottles—a gift from the father of one of his slain soldiers. Seth hadn't understood the gesture: why give a present to the person who'd led his son to his death?

"Thank you, but you take it and barter it on the street." Seth had pushed the crate back at the man, but he'd shoved it back.

"You took care of Eben when I couldn't, and I mean for you to have this as a way of showing my gratitude."

"Mister, I deserve no thanks." Seth could not for the life of him recall a boy called Eben, which only made him that much more uncomfortable about accepting a gift in his honour.

"My Eben died for a grand cause," the man continued. He backed away from the crate. "You're a good man, Commander Seth. You'll see us through this. I know it. My son knew it. The city knows it too. You and your sister ... you're the only hope we have."

Seth had sent the other seven bottles off to be traded for more weapons. A delivery was expected today from the south—likely nothing more than a few villages' attempts at pitching in. They'd had a drive, collecting what they could. He only hoped that a few good guns were among the rusty scythes and dull machetes and crooked pitchforks. Anyway. He'd kept this one bottle of wine to bring to Rosa. A peace offering.

He laid his ear against the door. She was alone in there, sleeping. Stephane had told him this. He was a good kid, eager to tell Seth whatever he thought he wanted to know. Rosa had been sleeping for several hours now. Long enough to be rested. He could wake her now. Talk to her. Put his arms around her and pull her to him, and—

He shook his head. Only if she would let him. He knocked.

Nothing.

He knocked again, and heard rustling, covers being thrown off, and then light footsteps padding across the wooden floor. The door opened and there were her dark eyes, appraising him, half-lidded.

"Yes?" She yawned, and then in another moment she was fully awake. Her gaze cleared and she tried to shut the door. Seth's foot was in the way.

"I only answered the door because I thought they might need me. If I'd known it was you I would've locked it from the inside." She pushed on the door, squishing Seth's foot.

"Rosa, please." Seth wedged his shoulder into the gap now. "Just listen to me."

She opened the door ever so slightly, only enough to stop hurting him. He could always count on that much from her. But she was hurting him now, in the worst way.

"Say what you came to say, and then go. I need to sleep. Stephane is all alone right now. I need to get back to him as soon as I'm rested."

"Let me in."

She shook her head.

"Rosa," Seth began. But what to say? How to communicate what he wanted her to understand? "I need you. This has gone on long enough. You know we're meant to be together."

"A Droughtland girl, a Keyland boy. A lifeminder and a warlord." She let go of the door and folded her arms across her chest. Seth took a step into the room. Beside the bed a small lantern cast a glow of warm light, illuminating her shape beneath her linen shift. "Meant to be together?" Rosa shook her head. "I don't think so."

"I'm sorry. You know how sorry I am. For everything."

"Go."

"Let's sit." Seth held out the bottle of wine. "Let's talk."

"I don't want it. And I don't want you." She turned, and now her face was lit—and he could see it in her eyes, in the tremble of her lips. She did want him. It would be as it was before. She would be his again. "Go. Please go, Seth. Please, please, please go."

Seth nodded. He set the bottle of wine on the table beside the lamp. The light reflected the deep red behind the glass, the colour of blood, the colour of heat. He took two steps toward the door before giving in. He spun back and grabbed Rosa around the waist, telling himself that if she protested, if she so much as laid a hand on his chest with the slightest push, he would stop. But she didn't. She crumpled into his arms and let him kiss her, and then she was kissing him back, moaning in his ear, and he whispering in hers.

"Let me in, Rosa." He ran his fingers through her hair, releasing the scent of the cinnamon oil she used. "Let me back in."

With a sob, she pulled away. "No!" She pushed him out of the room and slammed the door in his face. Seth could hear her crying, but he didn't knock, didn't try the door. He'd gone far enough, if not too far. Winning her back was harder than fighting this war, and at this moment he knew which battle he would not stand losing. She would be his once more. Death and strategy and hunger for power criss-crossed his mind like spider's silk, and he would tear it all down, turn away from it all for her. For a girl.

Seth set his hands on the closed door. He would set it all aside for a *girl*. He shook his head, marvelling at the state of himself. How had he come to this place? He was a soldier, wasn't he? Not a slave to his heart.

He strode down the hall, trying to convince himself that he was no slave to Rosa, only to his cock, which could be sated in short order by any number of girls.

Seth sent for a whore, but when she arrived, he sent her away again. There was no mistake. He wanted Rosa, and Rosa alone.

12

⛬

What Edmund's money and empty promises had bought him was a revolt. Small, strategic, and exquisitely timed. And who would even suspect it had been bought? It wasn't so hard to believe that the ceasefire wouldn't hold. After all, while Vance might have control over the Guard and Seth over the majority of the city, neither held the rest in check. Many in the city had fled. Of those who remained, a certain segment could be bought or sold, for a price.

Edmund had purchased what was left of Triban's private security firm, an offshoot of the city's police force before it had fallen prey to corruption and bribery. He'd sent a Guardy, disguised, into the city with a sealed letter and half the promised money. The letter spelled out what Edmund wanted done. First task: kill the messenger. Second task: break the ceasefire.

The messenger was a lowly Guardy Edmund had solicited back at the legislature, should the need arise for an errand boy. Unlike Vance, the man had gobbled up Edmund's promises of position and prestige. He'd been directed to a warehouse just below the brothel area. He'd delivered the letter, its seal intact, right into the hands of the captain himself, if he could be called that. Wearing a gun on his belt and a vest of heavy leather over his fat belly, the captain had read the letter while the other men at the table dealt out a fresh hand of cards.

That the captain could read at all surprised the Guardy. He was further surprised when the captain placed the letter on the table, checked the money in the pack, and drew his gun. The Guardy stepped back, fumbling for his own gun. He was dead before his hand reached the holster.

The men seated around the table didn't even set down their cards. The captain snapped his fingers, which brought his own errand man running. "Send for the duster. And get rid of that."

He assessed his hand of cards, then looked up and smiled. "Men, tonight we get wasted!"

A cheer erupted. Had the second half of the money not been well worth working for, the whole incident would have ended there.

Eli was preparing to escort the children out of the city when a tremendous blast sounded from far away.

Eli ran to the window. People stood stock-still in the streets, shocked. Others cried out and ran. And now screaming, confusion. The people camped around the coliseum were frantically gathering their things and fleeing every which way.

Another blast, no closer, but with an even greater reverberation: and now the great, thick coliseum walls that had stood for time immemorial shook in their very foundations.

Eli's mind spun. How could this be? They were in the middle of the ceasefire!

The children started wailing. They broke from their groups, clinging to each other even as Anya and Tasha hurried to tie the strip of cloth around each child's wrist with their name and age printed on it. They had left this until last, and now Eli wished they hadn't.

"There's no time for that!" Eli took the bundle of tags from Tasha. "We have to go."

"I'm almost done!" Shaking, Tasha squatted down to tie another one around a little boy's wrist. Now another blast resounded, this one much closer. Emma woke in her sling, her face crumpling into a grimace. Tasha's eyes were wide with fright. "What's happening?"

They had rounded up close to one hundred children. Now most of them were bawling and Eli couldn't think for the noise.

"We have to be quiet!" He gathered the older children, some of them nearly as old as he. "You have to try to keep the little ones calm!"

"I should've left!" Tasha cried. "We're all going to die!"

Anya, her jaw clenched, yanked Tasha into the corner. She gripped the girl's shoulders and lectured her in a quiet, intense mix of French and English, the gist of which was crystal clear. Buck up and shut up.

A fourth blast shook the building once more, sending plaster cracking off the ceiling. The children screamed, covering their heads as a window exploded, raining down glass.

Effie rushed into the room, trailed as always by Bear and Rabbit. Bear was crying and Rabbit was dragging him behind her, telling him to hush.

"The battle's only two streets over!" Effie yelled over the din of the children's wails.

"What about the ceasefire?" Eli said. "What happened?"

"Insurgents stormed the Guard camp at dawn, that's what," Effie hissed as they scrambled to get the children into some kind of line. Eli frantically counted heads as Effie's news tumbled out: an unknown troop had charged into Commander Vance's compound knowing *full well* they were in violation of the ceasefire. "It's *over*," Effie ended in a near-whisper.

Now the door was flung open and Gavin swept in with a screaming Toby in his arms. Behind them came Yvon, and then Jack.

"We have to get out there," Gavin said, but he did not set down his brother.

"Let Eli take Toby," Jack said urgently. "We can't keep him safe any more."

Gavin tightened his grip on the little boy and looked helplessly at Yvon. The two exchanged a long look. Finally Gavin bent down and set Toby on his feet. "We'll see you soon, little fox."

"We'll get the children to Cascadia." Eli strode forward and scooped a wailing Toby into his arms. "When this is all over, you'll find him there waiting at the gate for you."

The next staccato of gunfire sounded—far too close.

Go now, Eli. Go now!

"We have to leave."

"No!" Toby kicked, reaching for his brothers. Yvon and Gavin each hugged him, or tried to. Toby was so distraught to be left that he flailed and screamed and refused to hug them back. Jack planted a kiss on his head and then the three of them were off at a run.

"Into your lines!" Eli barked at the children. They fell into the groups they'd practised, looking every bit their own little army of ruffians. He'd take care of these children. He'd see them to safety. It was the least he could do.

WHEN THEY REACHED the mouth of the coliseum Nappo and Teal were waiting for them. Nappo held Emma in his arms as Teal fastened the sling behind him.

"We're coming with you." The brothers fell into line alongside Eli. Teal gave Toby his hand to hold, and this finally calmed him.

"I thought you were supposed to go with the others," Eli said. "I thought you were going to fight."

"This *is* fighting, in its own way. Right, Reverend?"

"But Seth said no one could be spared."

"Well, I'm sparing myself." Nappo clapped Eli on the back. "And I'll be damned by the highers if I'll be separated from Teal and my little girl."

Barely a block out of the coliseum and Toby was done with walking already, even with the company of his cherished buddy Teal. Eli swung him onto his back and kept walking, the little boy's arms clutching his shoulders. They'd barely made it past another block before a mortar blew off the corner of the building before them.

"Duck!" Effie screamed from the front of the line. The children dropped to the ground as they'd practised, their screams and the nearby bullet fire mixing into a terrible cacophony. Effie ran down the line, hunched over, arms protecting her head. "We can't go this way! It's not safe."

"Should we turn around?" Eli looked over his shoulder as he said it. A swarm of BAT soldiers was kicking a Guardy in the middle of the street. Another pop of gunfire and the boys scattered. The Guardy started dragging himself out of the clearing, but one of the boys turned, ran back, and clobbered the back of his head. The Guardy slumped, suddenly still.

And now another blast, a little farther away this time. Everyone ducked again.

Highers hear me now, prayed Eli. *Protect these children and guide them to safety.* It was part of a prayer from his childhood, one Lisette would sometimes have them recite if a child they knew was sick, or, he recalled now, after every visit of the Night Circus.

"Follow me!" Effie yelled over the rat-a-tat-tat of what could only be Guard guns. Try as he might, Seth had not managed to acquire guns with that much power.

ELI FOLLOWED the last child into the abandoned storefront. As his eyes adjusted to the dark, he whirled around in confusion. Why had Effie brought them here? One hundred and six children, all crammed into this small space. There was hardly enough air to go around. He pushed through and found Effie in a tiny back room stacked with dusty furniture and useless bits of this and that.

"Help me with this, will you?" Effie was shoving at a tall wooden wardrobe that stood against the wall. Eli moved aside a couple of broken chairs, leaned his weight against the wardrobe, and together they muscled it out into the narrow hall.

And then, on the wall where the wardrobe had been, he saw it: three planks fastened together and hinged at the top. Effie ran her fingers along its base until she caught a grip and heaved it up. Eli helped her, holding the makeshift door aloft while she found something to prop it open.

Cool, dank air pushed into the room. Eli got onto his knees and peered into the dim space, where a rickety wooden ladder shot straight down into the dark far below.

Effie was taking them into the tunnels under the city. He remembered leaving the Eastern Key down another strange tunnel so long ago. That one, though, had been wide and dry and warm. This one stank of rot and mould.

"I'll go first." Effie eased herself over the lip with Bear clinging to her back. The ladder creaked.

"It can't be safe down there," Eli said. Beside him, Bullet peered dubiously over the edge.

"Safer than up here." With one hand holding the ladder rung, Effie shifted Bear's weight on her back. He peered up at Eli with dubious eyes.

Eli shook his head. "But who's to say the Guard isn't down here too?"

"They dug their *own* tunnels to the barracks."

"But you saw them down here yourself," Eli pushed.

"I told you: they marched right by us, hardly even looked." Effie shrugged. "I don't think they want to waste their time with a bunch of kids."

"The army *fighting* them is practically all kids!"

"You know what I mean." Effie pursed her lips. "Just plain, regular kids. Not BAT soldiers. Come on, Rabbit. You come down after me. We'll help the others on the ladder."

To Eli's surprise, the children were delighted to climb the ladder down to Effie. She'd lit a torch and coaxed each one as they descended, until every last one had joined her. Even Tasha made her way down without complaint, followed by Teal, and lastly Nappo, with baby Emma snug in her sling on his back. That left only Eli and Bullet. He knotted a long rope behind Bullet's front legs and around his back before lowering the terrified dog into the dark. The children all called for him to be brave, but still Bullet yowled until Nappo let him loose at the bottom. Now Eli bade the daylight goodbye and grabbed hold of the top rung.

"You're sure about this?" he asked Effie once he'd joined the others, Bullet nervously licking his hand.

"I'm sure."

"Effie knows best about everything," Rabbit said. "She knows better than you, *that's* for sure. Let's go, Eff!" She took hold of Effie's shirtwaist and the trio started the crowd of children moving through the slop.

"We'll get out of the city way faster this way," Effie said, her voice picking up with pride and determination. "Come on, brats!" she hollered. Then she was off, marching in the mud, pleased as pie. And so the children followed suit, not at all bothered by the muck or the stench, happily slopping in the puddles. Effie starting singing, her voice echoing off the curved walls.

"The ants go marching one by one, hurrah, hurrah ..." The children joined in, making a much cheerier sort of cacophony than the misery up above.

Eli fell in at the back alongside Nappo and Teal as a muffled blast shook the street overhead, sending a rain of dust and dirt onto their heads. The singing wavered and then stopped altogether, but only for a moment. Then Effie, shakily at first but growing louder and stronger with every note, started them up again. Even Tasha chimed in off-key, along with Anya, who belted out the silly song as if their very lives depended on it.

13

S eth glared with disgust at the man who sat before him. "Any more dumb ideas you want to tell me about?" "You're the one with dumb ideas. You an' your stupid army." The captain was high on dust, and rather too fat for the thick leather vest he wore. His hands and ankles were bound and he sat slumped over in a chair, too kited even to hold his head up. "Might as well give up now."

"I appreciate your opinion, of course." Seth circled him. "But you broke a ceasefire that wasn't yours to break. So what I'd like to know is what exactly you and your little *security firm* were thinking. Hmm?"

"Oh, we was thinking." The man looked up, a small smile on his bruised, swollen lips. "You bet we was thinking."

"Tell me."

Another, wider smile. "Ask your daddy."

Seth paused. "What are you talking about?"

The man shrugged. "Wouldn't you like to know?"

Seth nodded at the boy twisting a black hood in his hands, waiting for orders. "Now, Finn."

Finn yanked the mask over the man's head and cinched it at his neck with rope.

"What's with this?" The man jerked his shoulder, trying to shake it loose. "Take it off!"

"Not until you've told me something worth knowing," Seth said. Another nod. "Roll up his sleeves." Finn, nervous, fiddled with the task until Seth snapped at him, "Tear it, cut it, I don't care, just bare his arms!"

"Why?" the man cried. "What're you going to do?"

Seth leaned in and growled, "Wouldn't *you* like to know?"

Finn sliced up the man's sleeves with his knife. Across the room, Ori was holding a poker to a fire burning in the long-unused hearth. "Why act now?" Seth continued. "You've sat on your fat arse for years doing nothing. So why now? Have you no respect for the law of inertia?"

"The wha—?" the man started, but then shook his head under the mask. "Someone should tell you that you ain't the friggin' king of Triban. Much as you might like to think so. Money is what talks, get it?"

Now Seth nodded at Ori, who solemnly lifted the poker, crossed the room with it, and laid it on the man's arm. The captain screamed as his flesh sizzled and smoked.

"Okay! Okay!" He wrestled against his restraints. "I'll tell you!"

"Enough for now," Seth told the boy. Ori was thankful for that. His stomach had churned when the smell of burning flesh hit his nose. He returned to the fire and set the poker against the coals to reheat.

"Ready to talk?" With a shove, Seth toppled the man and the chair. His head hit the floor with a crack.

"Okay!"

Ori and Finn tittered at the sight of the man still strapped to the chair, his legs in the air like a cockroach on its back, unable to right itself.

"You two are excused." Seth waited until they left before he spoke again. "What does my father have to do with this?"

"He paid us to do it."

"Do what, exactly?"

"Break the ceasefire. Start a revolt. Ruin your little agreement with the Guard."

"Why?"

"Dunno."

"Was the Guard in on this? Did Vance know?"

"Who?"

"Did the Guard know?"

"I don't know what they know," the man said from his position on the floor. "They was firing at us and bombing and taking prisoners, so I ran."

"You left your men behind," Seth said.

"Yeah. So what?" A defiant jut of chin from beneath the hood. "What about you, big man? Hiding out here while your little boys are being slaughtered like the little lambs they are?"

Seth called for Ori and Finn to come back in. "Watch him."

"And what about you, eh?" the captain continued. "Sitting pretty like the Keyland lord you fancy you are." The man twisted, trying to right himself. "You can take the asshole out of the Key, Commander, but not the Key out of the asshole." The hood bobbed as the man laughed at his own joke.

"Eloquently put," Seth said. "But irrelevant. A smart leader stays alive, any idiot knows that. And as for my past with the Keyland, it's just that, thank you very much. And I might add that, in my short time away from the Key, I've done more for your wretched people than anyone you could think of."

"Zenith—" the man began.

"Spare me," Seth said.

A rap sounded on the heavy door, a succession of knocks in the correct, complicated order. "Let him in," Seth said. Ori opened the door to Amon.

"Commander Seth!" Amon barked out. His face was ashen, his eyes darting. "The district is gone! The whole BAT district. They bombed everything. Nothing but fires burning over there. It's all gone, Seth. It's all gone!"

Ori and Finn glanced at each other, eyes full of fright.

"Not here," Seth said. Escorting Amon into the dark corridor, he said to Ori and Finn as he passed, "You're safe with me. Understand?"

The boys followed their nods with a "Yes, Commander Seth" directed at their boots.

"Eyes up, boys."

Ori and Finn obliged.

"That's better." Seth nodded. "You two keep an eye on him."

"Yes, Commander Seth." Two smart salutes and then Ori spoke for the both of them. "Want us to sit him up again?"

Seth shook his head. "Leave him where he is, better for the rats to chew out his cheeks."

"Wait!" The man twisted his wrists against the rope. "I'll tell you more!"

"I don't care to hear it," Seth said as he pulled the door shut behind him.

He and Amon raced up to the roof. Even with the spyglass Amon handed him, Seth could make out only spires of billowing smoke and a crumbled neighbourhood he no longer recognized. He was keenly aware of his senses ... smoke stinging his nostrils, screams and clatter banging his ears, the acid of panic at the back of his throat, the cool rim of the spyglass against his hot skin. But he could not summon one single thought. His mind was simply not available to him. Seth had no words, no plan, no idea. Nothing.

Long moments passed until finally Seth lowered the spyglass. He turned and looked at Amon, whose face was dripping with sweat, his neck black with dirt and soot.

"Commander Seth, we're not going to win this. The way things used to be wasn't so bad, was it? Here, I mean—not over the mountains in the real Droughtland. But that's them. We're us. Maybe we should give up."

Seth shook his head. He lifted the spyglass again and turned to the east. The main street was packed with Tribanites fleeing in panic from the surprise bombing. He and Amon could join them. Take off right now, with nothing but the clothes on their backs and the boots on their feet. But no. He was in too deep, and despite his doubt, he was exactly where he wanted to be. Nor would he demonstrate such profound cowardice. Not to his soldiers, and even more importantly, not to Rosa. He could picture it, his ducking out like a frightened officer of the Guard, Rosa staying behind to tend to his mess, dark half-moons of fatigue under her eyes, hands covered in blood. He lowered the looking glass.

"It may cost us every soldier, but I *will* win." He would win or die trying. "*We,*" he corrected with a murmur. "We will win."

Amon's eyes flitted over the devastation. "It's hopeless," he said.

"That's not true. And even if you feel that way, you have to pretend otherwise." Seth clapped a hand on Amon's shoulder. "You have to make them believe that you believe."

"Is that what you do?"

"Sometimes," Seth admitted with a nod. "Sometimes."

"I can't do it, Seth." Amon showed his palms, covered in cuts and dirt. "I'd rather crawl into a hole and wait for it all to be over."

"It won't be long," Seth said. What he didn't say was that the Boys' Army of Triban might become so decimated it could very well cease to exist. Seth glanced over at his companion. What would lie ahead for him then? Back to a life of dust? Or would he make something of himself, now that he'd seen what he was capable of? Amon caught Seth's gaze and returned it with a small, pained smile.

Seth and Amon stayed up on the rooftop for a long while, not saying much at all. When they finally returned to the basement they found that Ori and Finn had cut the rest of the prisoner's clothes off. They were laughing as the man thrashed away from what he thought were rats but were really just two young boys poking at him with sticks.

Trace was the one to tell Sabine the terrible news.

Gavin and Yvon had perished in a bombing blitz deep in the north end of the city. They'd taken cover in the ruins of a building, the two brothers running there together as Trace and Jack fled in the other direction, hiding flat on their stomachs under a fallen awning in an alley. A storm of gunfire followed. And then the Guardy had moved on to the next block, continuing their sweep.

After a relentless, horrifying hour under fire, Jack and Trace had emerged from their cover and run straight for the building. They found Gavin and Yvon in a stairwell, shot in the head at close range.

"Where's Jack now?" Sabine asked in a stunned whisper. To lose another lover so violently. First Quinn, and now Gavin. Jack would be devastated.

"He's escorting the bodies back."

"We can't—" She couldn't bring herself to say it out loud. There was no time, no way they could honour the brothers. Not now. "Is he all right?"

"He's not wounded."

"Trace ..." Sabine tucked herself into his strong embrace.

Trace silently held her as Sabine's mind whirled in shock. Poor Jack! Poor Toby, truly orphaned now. How much more of this could she take? How many more friends would she lose? The world was smaller without them. Sabine wanted to gather the loved ones she had left in her pockets like so many precious marbles.

"I should have been with them!" she sobbed, soaking Trace's vest with tears. "I should be with Jack now." Pulling away, she looked up at Trace. He was crying too, silently. "Take me to him?"

Celeste had come into the room. "No."

"But Nana ..." Sabine let herself be led to the couch. Celeste sat beside her and pulled her head into her lap. "It's my fault. I should go."

"Be strong." Celeste stroked her granddaughter's hair. "Gavin and Yvon are together at least."

"But Toby!" Sabine wailed. "He's all alone now!"

"He's not," Celeste murmured. "He's got all of us, and Jack especially."

"It's not the same!" Sabine lifted her head up. Celeste dabbed at her wet cheeks with a hanky. "Everyone's dying, Nana. Everyone!"

"Not everyone, my dear." Celeste tucked her hanky into her sleeve and cupped Sabine's cheeks with her hands. "Not you."

"Maybe I want to die." Sabine sat up, pushed her hair out of her face.

"Do you?" Celeste reached out, straightened Sabine's tunic.

Sabine struggled to smile. She didn't. Not really. But it had felt good to say so. She shook her head.

"Good." Celeste took her hand. "Because we need you to live a long, long life. We need to you to get through this and be the witness for those who don't make it. Someday you will be older than I am now, with your own grandchildren gathered around you, and you will tell them of these terrible times, and how freedom came once again."

"What if it doesn't?" Sabine wiped away new tears. "What if so many die and we have nothing to show for it after?"

"These are wicked days, child."

"So you think it could be like that? All of this ... all this death and ruin, for nothing?"

"Not for nothing."

"But maybe not for freedom either?"

"We aim for freedom. But if we fall short, it won't be for nothing."

"I just ..." Sabine's head ached, from the crying, from the grief, from all that lay ahead. "I just wish it were easier."

"There is nothing easy about it, child." Celeste stroked Sabine's brow, as if easing the tension away with her arthritic fingers. "Nothing easy at all."

"Easy or not ..." Sabine's gut flipped with a sudden surge of rage. She sat up, hair all straggly, cheeks flushed. "I want revenge. If we can't mourn, I want to make someone else hurt as badly as I do." She pushed herself off the couch and stormed out of the room, even as Celeste was calling for her to come back.

Sabine ran down the hall, ignoring everyone who tried to stop her. They'd all heard the news. They all wanted her to say something to make it better. They wanted her to listen to them, hear their sorrow, but she wanted only to fight.

She didn't stop for her leather vest that covered her torso with thick, protective hide. She didn't stop to collect a weapon from the cache. She just ran, foolish and haughty, into the street, fists raised. She spun around, eyes hardly focusing on the Tribanites camped out around the coliseum as if the Guard would still honour it as a no-battle zone.

"It's Sabine!"

"We need food!"

"Why haven't the water carts come by?"

Crowding around her, stinking of sweat and filth, eyes flashing with desperation, arms clawing at her, pulling her in every direction. "Stop!" she cried, not even trying to keep the panic from her voice. "Get off me, please!"

"Tell us what's happening!"

"My father! Have you seen him?"

"Feed us, Auntie!"

"Sabine!" A voice she recognized. Jack. "You shouldn't be out here." A barrow behind him, a heap covered by a tarp, crusty with dirt. The crowd let up just enough for her to push her way to him. He drew her to his chest and she laid her cheek against the smooth leather of his vest.

"All this playing at honour. It just isn't enough!"

"And so you'd have yourself killed to make a point?"

Jack's angry tone startled her.

"Gavin and Yvon dying?" he continued. "That's not enough?" He pulled away from her and gave the large barrow a swift kick. "And the two others in there too? You want to add your own body to the pile?"

"I just want to—"

"Go ahead!" Jack whipped back the tarp, revealing the pile of bodies. On the bottom, two red heads hung over the end of the cart. Yvon and Gavin. Atop them, two more bodies, charred beyond recognition. "Climb on!"

"Jack!" The anguish and horror on Sabine's face was request enough. Amid the crowd's shocked silence and wary stares, Jack folded the tarp back over the bodies.

"Not you too." Jack grasped the barrow's handles and lifted, his muscles straining, his face blanched with the effort. "Please. Not you too."

Sabine followed him inside, knowing Jack well enough not to offer to help. The gates shut behind them and he set the cart down once more.

"I don't know why I had to bring them back here." He stared dolefully at the tarp. "I know we're just going to send them off with the deathminder."

"We can bury them in the courtyard."

"That's not allowed." It was true. The deathminder dumped all bodies into vast pits outside the city limits—a rudimentary precaution against contamination and the spread of disease.

"I don't think that matters so much any more." Sabine hung her head and reached for Jack's hand, and he let her take it.

14

ﾟﾟﾟﾟﾟ

Afiter two days of trudging and one night of restless sleep, Eli
and the children emerged from the tunnels well beyond the
city. Eli had had a pounding headache for over twelve hours
now, and could hardly see straight for the pain. To make matters
worse, his stomach was knotted with nausea. It wasn't a bug, although
that's what Anya had blamed it on when she caught him retching his
guts out. It was from the dust, or lack of it. He had the runs too now,
and was constantly on the lookout for where he could rush if
his bowels cramped up again suddenly. Along with a serious case of
crawling skin, he was a mess.

Oh, and the joyful sound of children frolicking in the daylight, glad
to be out of the tunnels? Not at all soothing. If only they would Just.
Shut. Up.

So Eli kept to the back of the line beside Nappo, with Emma asleep in
the sling. Eli didn't particularly want the company, but couldn't think of
a good excuse to ask that he be left alone. Instead he turned his attention
to the crowds of people fleeing the city all around them. They plodded
along, meagre belongings strapped to their backs, or piled in carts, or
clutched in hand. It was a steady, slow procession. No one had the energy
to hurry. They looked like Eli felt.

"How do you think it's going back in Triban?" Nappo asked.

"No idea."

"Can't you squeeze your eyes shut, summon your brother and sister, and get some kind of psychic message?"

"It's not like that." Eli glanced at him, his headache following behind in a slow, painful wake as he turned his head. "And you know it."

"Then pray on it. Ask the highers."

"And it's not like that either."

Nappo was silent for a while, but then he started up again as if they'd been in mid-conversation. "I don't know what to do about Tasha."

"What about her?"

"Come on, you must've noticed, even with your head up in the clouds. She's miserable, and she won't do anything for the baby. I swear, if I had the ta-tas to feed her, she'd have taken off already by now."

"She hasn't though, so ..."

"I want better for Emma."

"And maybe you should've thought about that before sticking your prick in the first girl who'd have you at that party."

"Low blow."

"It's true."

There was a pause. "Well, what's done is done. And I wouldn't trade Emma for the world."

"Then you're stuck with Tasha too."

"She was nicer back at the foothills—"

"You were too corked to notice otherwise."

"I liked her."

"And you don't now?" This got Eli's attention. "Not at all?"

"She's different."

You reap what you sow.

"Mm hmm," Eli nodded in agreement.

Nappo thought he was agreeing with him. "So you think so?"

"Think so what?"

"Raise her on my own. If I had to, I mean."

"What do you mean?"

"I mean," Nappo lowered his voice to a whisper, "if I took her, you know."

"Kidnapped her, you mean."

"Well no, because I'm her papa. It wouldn't be kidnapping."

Eli swept an arm in front of him, taking in the steady stream of down-trodden exiles trudging toward nothing much better. "I can't believe you'd even consider such a thing at a time like this."

Nappo hardened his expression. "Why not? At a 'time like this' she's the only thing that matters. You'd get what I meant if you had a kid of your own."

"I'm only sixteen!"

"Still?"

"Still what?"

"You're still sixteen?"

"I think ..." Eli counted back. Nappo was right. He'd turned seventeen almost a month ago. "So what? Sixteen or seventeen. Either way, no thanks!"

Eli and Nappo were both scowling as their group crested a small hill ... and was stopped short at the back of a line of thousands.

"Guard checkpoint!" Effie hollered back to them. "What do we do?"

Now Eli noticed the fence, hastily constructed and entirely out of place, lining both sides of the road, funnelling them forward. Already the crowd behind them was catching up. He made his way up to Effie and Tasha, where he could see the blockade about five hundred metres away. Guardies on horseback were positioned outside the fence at tidy intervals, guns drawn.

"Should we turn back?" Tasha asked.

"And go where?" Effie said. "You were the one in such a hurry to leave in the first place."

"But this is no better! Not if they're going to shoot us all in the head and leave us for dead!"

The children within earshot started to whimper.

"Calm down, Tasha," Eli said. "The highers will take care of us."

"Oh give it a rest, Eli!" Effie let out an exasperated sigh. "There ain't no highers, because if there were we wouldn't be in this boat."

Bear tugged on her shirt. "What boat?"

"There's no 'boat.' And no one's gonna hurt us." Effie glared at Tasha. "There's no reason to panic. We're just a bunch of kids. We ain't no threat to them."

"Oh no, we're only the future, is all." Tasha rolled her eyes. "Nothing much." Even amidst the panic, Eli could see how Nappo was having a hard time liking Tasha.

"And you, you're only the *brother* of the leader of the Boys' Army of Triban and of the leader of Triskelia. 'My highers,'" she said, her voice heavy with sarcasm, "what on earth might the Guard want with you? I can*not* imagine."

Eli gave her what he hoped was a withering look. She scowled right back at him.

"Let me up on your shoulders," Effie said. "Maybe I can see a bit more from up high."

Eli squatted. Tasha cupped her hands and gave Effie a boost up. Eli stood straining under her weight, despite how scrawny she was.

"They're letting some people through," Effie said.

"What else?" Eli straightened even more, the better for her to see.

"They've got a corral kind of thing off to one side. They're sticking the ones they don't let through in there. And there's a camp or something. I can see tents lined up in rows." She tapped Eli's shoulder. "You can let me down now."

Eli squatted. "We'll have to keep going." Fresh dread trickled into his gut. "And pray for the best. Pray we're let through."

"We should disguise you." Effie dug into her pack and pulled out a long, pointed toque, knitted with thick yarn in sloppy rows of orange and purple.

"That's so ugly it'll make him stick out all that much more." Tasha scanned their group, looking for something else to use.

"It's a start." Eli put the hat on, long ago having given up his worries about sharing germs. "Thank you, Effie."

"Knit it myself," she said shyly. "From an old sweater."

"I know!" Tasha strode down the line of children, stopping at a boy not much older than Teal. He had spectacles that were too big for him and had one lens cracked straight through. Tasha yanked them off and brought them back to Eli. "These are perfect."

"But he needs them."

"He'll be fine. Put them on."

They were too tight on Eli, and made everything he looked at swim in a watery blur. "They'll give me a headache."

"Don't be such a baby." Tasha pulled off her red muslin scarf and wrapped it artfully around his neck. "You look pretty queer."

"It'll do," Effie said. "You should go to the back too, try to blend in. Take Bullet with you."

"Use your whistle if you need me." Back in Triban, Celeste had traded a few loaves of bread for a box of wooden whistles. Each child had one, and had been instructed not to use it except for the direst of emergencies. "Remember ... long, short, short, long."

The crowd shuffled forward now, ever closer to the checkpoint. Eli kept his head down to hide his face, but also to look over the top of the glasses so that he could see where he was going. He wove his way back toward Nappo. The children, all holding onto the rope that kept them together, laughed at his silly get-up. His headache was worse with the glasses pinching his face, and his guts still roiled. He tried to smile at the children, but he was worried he'd have nowhere to go but the fence if his bowels exploded. If only he could stop the symptoms. Even just until they were past the checkpoint.

Eli rejoined Nappo at the back of the group, where two little girls who seemed to enjoy working each other up into a flap were bawling again. Nappo had convinced another dozen or so strangers to stand alongside the children to protect them from the pressing crowd.

"Nice outfit," Nappo said with a smirk.

Eli leaned in. "It's a disguise."

"Ah. Right."

"How'd you recruit the help?"

"They've all got kids of their own," Nappo said. "They understand."

Eli took a closer look at the group of children. Indeed, it had swollen in number, the new children squeezed in alongside their charges.

"Parent to parent," Nappo was saying.

"What?"

Nappo glanced down at baby Emma, whose lip was quivering in the prelude to tears.

"Oh." Eli understood. He backed away just enough so that Nappo wouldn't keep yammering on about the joys of fatherhood. Eli didn't see what was so special about it, really.

Beyond the miracle of life?

Eli glanced up to the skies and had to force himself not to answer out loud. Where was the miracle in shagging some stranger, not pulling out in time or wearing a skin, and getting her pregnant?

The stench of body odour and drying mud pushed at his nose. The crowd shuffled forward again. Eli's fear grew with each step. *One more time,* he bargained silently with his highers. *Just one more time and I promise, that's it.*

No reply.

He'd take that as tacit permission. He did a little turn and surveyed the people nearest him. He picked out a likely person to start with.

"I'll be right back," he told Nappo as he headed into the throng, keeping his eye on the man he had in mind.

The man watched him approach with the glazed, red-rimmed eyes that had given him away. "Yeah?"

"Got any?"

The man glanced around. "No."

"Please—" He was going to launch into a sob story about needing it for a dying friend, and how he couldn't pay.

"That's Commander Seth!" a woman shouted, pointing at him. "Look!"

The duster narrowed his eyes, and then reached out and snatched the hat and glasses off. "It is!"

"No." Eli fixed his eyes on the ground. "You're mistaken."

"It ain't him." An old man pushed between Eli and the duster. "It's his brother. See? He's got no scars, and 'is hair is brown."

"So his brother then," the duster emended. "The Reverend, right? How about that. What you got to say for yourself, Triskelian?"

"Quiet!" An anonymous voice spoke up from the crowd. "You want him plucked out of here and strung up?"

"I'm taking a group of children away from the danger."

"He is, too," someone else piped up. "I saw them earlier, roadside."

The sound of hooves stopped the conversation. The Guardy nearest them was at the wire fence, his horse stamping the dirt. "What's going on?"

Eli grabbed back the glasses and toque, mashing them on as waited with bated breath.

"Nothing," the duster said.

"Just some spirited bartering, is all." The old man flashed a toothless smile at the Guardy.

"Hmph." The Guardy half-heartedly scanned the crowd, his eyes passing right over Eli. He clucked at his horse, turned himself around, and headed back to his position.

"Thank you," Eli said when it was safe.

"And you're welcome," the old man said. "You just see to it that your brother and sister make something out of all this, or else we're all out here for naught."

"Of course," Eli said. "And pray to your highers too—we can use all of your support."

"Oh, I'll pray until my knees are ruined. But I don't know how much good it'll do." The old man shifted away, and soon they were moving again. Eli fell into step beside the duster.

"Who's it for?" The duster spoke under his breath.

"Someone in the group," Eli said. "One of us minding the refugee children is going through a terrible withdrawal. I'm just hoping to ease it a little while he gets off it for good."

"*Someone,* eh?"

Eli nodded. "You'd be doing this *someone* an enormous favour."

"And what would this someone pay in exchange for a little relief from the beast?"

"I've got nothing," Eli admitted. "Nothing at all."

With a sigh, the man pulled a tiny paper packet from a pouch around his neck.

"A gift then."

"Thank you."

The man harrumphed and waved Eli away. Eli turned and bent over, pretending to look at something on the ground. A tap on his shoulder.

Teal, alone. "What you got there?"

"Nothing." Eli slipped the packet in his pocket and stood. "You're supposed to stay with the group."

"I'm old enough. I can take care of myself." Teal stuck his hands on his hips just as Anya did when she scolded any of them. "That's dust you got."

"None of your business."

In a flash, Teal made a grab for Eli's pocket. Eli grabbed Teal's wrist and twisted it up behind his head.

"Do not *ever* do that again, understand?"

Teal nodded. He had to pee all of a sudden. That sometimes happened when he was nervous, or scared. He concentrated on not peeing instead of the angry glare Eli fixed him with. He'd never seen him this way. He'd seen Nappo that way though, when he was still dusting.

"Go back to the group." Eli relaxed his grip, but then tightened it again. "Don't tell anyone, okay?"

"Okay," Teal whispered.

"I mean it." Eli let go. "If you do, I'll never talk to you again. I won't be your friend. Or Nappo's either. You don't want that, do you?"

A small shake of his head. Teal backed away. "I'm sorry, Eli."

"That's okay. Just keep your mouth shut."

Shame flooded Eli's heart, and he had to hold himself back from running after Teal and apologizing. He *would* apologize. When he felt better. His gut churned and he knew he couldn't hold it any longer. He hurried, hunched over with cramps, to the fence. Other people were using it as a toilet too, embarrassed or not. Eli stepped between the piles of shit, found a spot, and dropped his pants. Everyone there averted their eyes, so while his guts emptied, Eli opened the packet and brought a knuckle of dust to his nose, plugged one side, and inhaled the sharp, tangy powder.

With a spark of light bursting behind each eye, glorious and warm, he made his way back through the crowd.

"Reverend Eli." He bowed as he sliced through the crowd. "Reverend Eli at your service. Help from the highers at a holy cost of free!" He spun around, marvelling at the brightness of everything. Through the warmth, he remembered his costume and that he was supposed to be disguised. Eli kept his mouth shut for the rest of the way, determined to enjoy the high in silence. He even forgot about treating Teal badly, and so was astonished when Teal walked toward him and, with a ferocious glare, kicked him in the shin.

"Hey, buddy ... why'd you do that?"

"You're high. I know it."

"Shhh ... we have an agreement, right?"

Teal spun away, giving him the finger as he went.

"It's okay," Eli muttered. "It's all okay."

Nappo pulled him aside as soon as he was within reach. "Eli—"

"It's not true," Eli slurred. "Whatever he said."

"No one said anything—just listen. We're only a few minutes away from the checkpoint. Shut up and keep your head down."

"All righty." Eli gave his friend two thumbs up. He pushed up the glasses and squinted. "You look all blobby."

"Well, you look like a freak." Nappo pulled the ridiculous toque even tighter down over Eli's head. "And stop announcing yourself. You're supposed to be in a disguise, you idiot, so shut up."

And shut up he did. With a great big grin on his face.

ELI WAS STILL IN GREAT SPIRITS as they approached the wooden shed that marked the checkpoint. He'd come to quite like the toque, and it was kind of cool seeing everything in a blur through the eyeglasses. His floaty thoughts felt as if they were tied to his wrist like so many balloons on a string. He kept looking over his shoulder, thinking he'd catch sight of the colourful bouquet, and was surprised every time when all he saw were sad-sack Tribanites trudging along behind him.

Nappo had gone up to the front of their group to do the talking with Effie. Whatever they said didn't work though, because just moments later the whole lot of them were corralled through the gate and into the compound.

This was not good. Worse still, the dust was beginning to wear off. Eli fished the packet out of his pocket and was horrified to find it empty.

"Teal, you little brat!" He spun around, searching for him. "Get over here!"

"Tais-toi!" Anya hushed him. "Be quiet, for highers' sake."

Teal stood on tiptoe, way up at the front, and waved, a cheeky grin plastered on his face.

"But he—" Eli clamped his mouth shut. He wasn't about to admit that Teal had dumped the last of his dust. "I was just wondering where he was. That's all."

"He is with Nappo. Now shut up. *Nous devons faire attention.* Who knows what is happening."

Without explanation, they were checked for weapons—even the children—and led off by a fellow refugee down one of the lanes formed by the canvas tents lining each side.

"You can have these four tents." The man pointed out two on one side and two on the other. "You," he pointed at Nappo, "make sure you got a leader in each one to keep a handle on all these kids."

Eli wanted to tell him that Nappo wasn't in charge; he was. He kept his mouth shut. As the children broke away to claim their new homes, the man explained to Nappo and Effie that there was food twice a day and not to even bother trying to escape. He said he'd be back later to put them on the roster.

"How do you like that?" Nappo elbowed him as the man left. "Thinks I'm the boss."

Tasha pushed aside Effie to stake her claim to Nappo. "And why was he talking to her like she had anything to do with you?"

"Probably because the children treat me with respect," Effie shot back.

"I'm plenty older than you," Tasha said.

"Doesn't mean you're any smarter."

"Oh!" Nappo had to hold Tasha back as Effie sauntered off, Bear and Rabbit trailing behind her. "That little bitch!"

Teal laughed at Tasha, but when he noticed Eli glaring at him, he took off at a run.

THEY SPENT the rest of that first day sorting the kids into groups, with enough older ones to help keep an eye on the younger ones. There weren't many boys older than ten—most of them had joined Seth's army—but there were many little ones, and a horde of girls, who in Eli's mind were a lot smarter for not signing up for certain death. Nappo, Anya, Eli, and Effie each took a tent to watch over. Tasha headed off to join a Seduce game.

They'd all decided that Eli should stay in his tent. He was fine that first night, but after two days he was right back where he'd been on the road, his gut churning, head pounding, skin crawling and drenched with sweat. He told Nappo and the girls that he had a stomach bug, and they left him alone.

During a particularly bad spell of dry heaving, Teal appeared.

"Go away, Teal."

"I traded to be in your tent."

"Why?"

Teal squatted. "'Cause you need help. Right?"

Eli laughed, then swallowed back the resulting swell of nausea. "You could say that."

"'Kay then." Teal sat beside him and held out his flask. "Drink."

Eli took a sip. "Where'd you get it?"

"They bring it in."

"So they *don't* want us to die."

"Don't think so."

"What's going on out there?"

"Playin' soccer."

"I mean in the rest of the place."

"Dunno." Teal shrugged. "Waiting, I guess."

"Don't worry." Eli grimaced as another turn of nausea gripped at his stomach. "We'll get out of here, Teal."

Teal nodded, but as he did he backed away. He stopped at the flap of the tent. "What do your highers say?"

"That it will get better. We just have to trust."

"Yeah?"

"Yeah."

Teal stepped out into the daylight, leaving Eli alone with his cramps and headache and doubt. He'd just lied to Teal. His highers hadn't spoken to him for days. He missed the guidance. He missed the company.

ONCE HIS HEAD CLEARED of the last tendril of dust, Eli felt nothing but shame. He was weak, he told himself. He'd been lured by the devil. He'd been tested by the highers and had failed them. Was that why they'd abandoned him when he needed their guidance the most?

On the third day, he rose with Teal's help, donned his disguise, and joined the others in Nappo's tent.

The kids in Nappo's charge were playing Seduce, the ones who knew the game teaching the little ones. The sun was just going down, and the tent was still bright and warm.

"Thank you," he said as Teal brought him a bowl of mush. It was like oatmeal, only Eli wouldn't trust that it actually was. No matter, it filled the gut. They were provided with a bowl of it in the morning, and another at dusk. Eli took a seat in the doorway and looked up.

"Praying?" Teal dug into his own bowl.

"Nope."

"What're you doing?"

"Watching the sun set."

"Oh." Teal licked his bowl clean.

"Thanks, Tealy."

"You don't want yours?" Teal pointed at Eli's bowl.

"I mean thank you for helping me."

"Sure."

Eli tousled his hair. "I mean it. You're a good friend."

Teal grinned.

"You can have mine." Eli handed him his bowl. "My stomach is still a little funny." It wasn't, but it was the only way he could think to thank the little boy.

[TWO]

THE DROUGHTLAND

15

T wo weeks later and Triban was a corpse. The city limits marked the edges of a gigantic graveyard of rubble, the crumbling buildings its tombstones, the streets mere winding paths between them. The fires still burned heavy and foul so that a roof of smoke pressed down on the remains, sandwiching a thin slice of sky between its bleak layers. Seth kept his eye on that narrow slice of freedom, the air that belonged to no one, unlike the weather, the city, and its people.

He and his army of boy soldiers had held out as long as they could—until nothing was left to fight for except power itself. For a long time Seth had thought that by the end he would have at least gained that power. Not now, though. He stood on the same rooftop from where he'd looked over the city just two weeks before, trying to convince Amon they could prevail. They hadn't. They'd failed. He'd failed. As hard as it was to admit, they hadn't stood a chance from the beginning. And the numbers were staggering.

All this time Rosa had been keeping track, sharing numbers with the deathminder for a tally of dead and wounded. Rosa, who still refused to talk to him. So how could he know how many they had lost? The truth was he didn't want to know. He knew he'd find out eventually, and now was looking like the time.

Sabine sat across from him in the kitchen at the coliseum. Vance had stayed true to his word and hadn't bombed the building. When the remaining civilians figured it out they'd flooded in and now took up every nook and cranny, practically sleeping in piles, not an inch of floor space left. Every seat in the bleachers had been claimed, and the aisles were line with blankets spread with goods to trade. The main stage had been staked out early on as the place to play Seduce; several games went on simultaneously around the clock. The noise was never-ending, even if it did quell to a dull roar in the darkest hours of the night.

Celeste had managed to keep the wing containing the kitchen, infirmary, and a few small rooms off limits to the Tribanites. Two sets of BAT boys guarded the infirmary. Ori and Finn were there now, along with a pair of boys Seth had recruited from the sea of people camped in the coliseum. Only a fraction of the original BAT soldiers had survived the two weeks of fighting. Now he was filling his ranks with whoever was willing to step up.

Seth didn't feel as though he had much control over his new recruits, but they acted as if he did. He knew that, despite his losses, admiration for him had grown strong. He knew that the people of the city looked up to him, expected him to bring them out of this triumphant. Yet in his own eyes he'd let them down. His reputation was far larger than his own self now.

Sabine stared at him. Trace and Jack sat beside her, all on one side, making him feel as if he were facing some kind of tribunal. Behind them, Celeste stirred a big pot of stew. It was just potatoes and carrots and herbs, but it smelled like a meal fit for a king. The Triskelians were eating only slightly better than the people in the coliseum. Trace hunted down donations of grain from the outlying areas, so there was always some kind of gruel, but other than that the people shared what little they had, or bartered for better.

"When do we eat?" Seth asked.

"Not long."

"How can you be hungry?" Sabine shook her head. "I can hardly find my appetite at all lately."

"You better find it quick," Celeste said. "The stew won't wait. And you need to eat, my dear."

"I need answers first." Sabine focused on her brother. "I need to know what's next."

"We keep fighting," Trace said.

"With what?" Jack spread his hands on the table. "We need more. More of everything ... people, weapons, ammunition. Spirit. Will. Hope."

Sabine leaned forward. "Has she told you?"

"What?" Seth played dumb, although he knew what was coming.

"Has Rosa told you how many of your soldiers have died? What the total is, as of today?"

He shook his head. "She won't talk to me."

"That's weak," Trace said.

"Guess." This from Sabine, arms crossed, challenging him. "Guess how many."

"To be honest, I don't see the point." Seth returned the look, squaring his jaw. "Does it matter? Really?"

Sabine gasped. "Of course it matters!"

"Why, so that I can feel worse?" Seth scraped his stool back and stood. "So that we can lie awake at night thinking about all those bodies rotting in the pits?"

"Yes, quite frankly." Sabine stood too. She leaned over the table, thought better of it, and came around so that she was standing toe to toe with her brother. "Four thousand, six hundred and forty-two."

Seth winced. Each number was a rock that hit him in the temple.

No one said a word. The stew bubbled quietly on the stove. "And civilians?" Sabine seemed to be actually taking some pleasure in this. Relief, at least. "One hundred thousand," she paused, "nine hundred and sixty-eight."

Seth lowered his head. He'd known, or sensed, or understood the numbers without being told. He'd been in their midst for the last two weeks, seeing them fall. Of anyone, he'd seen the most die.

"And what am I supposed to say to that?" He raised his eyes to his sister. "You're going to attack anything I say, right?"

"Probably."

"Damn right." Trace slapped the table. "Let's hear it."

"Fine." Seth shook his head. "I give up. How about that?"

Sabine shoved him hard. "Oh, no you don't."

"Then what?"

"We take the battle to the Keys."

"Just to finish the rest of us off?"

"To finish *them* off. To topple the Group of Keys!"

"Sure."

"The momentum is there, Seth. You still have many boys. And I bet we could rally everyone here in the coliseum, plus every other soul we could find. We can't stop now. And you don't want to. I know you well enough to be sure of that."

But she didn't know him. She didn't know that he'd made a power-sharing deal with their father—and that, stupidly, he'd held on to that outcome like a talisman for the longest time. And she didn't know just how crazy he'd been to believe that Edmund would ever permit it. So here he was at the helm of a sinking ship. But Sabine was right about his not wanting to quit. He'd rather sink to his death than give up. But where to go from here?

The city was lost. The Guard itself had left, leaving behind only a small contingent to make sure the city stayed defeated. This thought made Seth laugh. Who'd want the city now? It would be like setting up house in the decomposing corpse of a dinosaur while all around you skin rotted off its bones and maggots crawled over you as you slept.

"Seth, come eat." Sabine took his hand. "You'll feel better after." Celeste served out bowls of the stew now, the steam rising as Trace and Jack dug in.

"I'm fine."

"Well, I'm going to eat." Sabine took her seat. "And then afterward, we'll figure out what to do next."

Seth sat in front of his bowl, but didn't lift his spoon. The chunks of potatoes and rounds of carrot swum in a murky broth. Vance was probably stuffing himself right now with roast meat and fresh bread and a carafe of wine. And here was Seth with nothing but gruel to eat. He didn't want to feel sorry for himself, but he did. Had it gone differently, had the ceasefire not been broken ... what the *hell* had Edmund intended by that? If his soldiers had had that extra time to prepare, to gather more arms ... Seth shook his head. There was nothing for it. They'd lost.

And the fact that Vance had spared the coliseum made him feel even worse. It felt like charity.

Celeste had asked him a question. "Pardon me?"

She held out a pan of bannock. "Would you like a piece?" she said again. He took a warm lump of fried bread.

"For dipping in your stew." Celeste finally sat. She ripped up her bread and plopped it into her bowl. Seth could see that she'd taken only broth; she'd given them all the vegetables. "That's the last of the flour. I picked out all the weevils myself."

The door to the kitchen pushed open, and Rosa stepped in. She usually ate in the infirmary, but now Seth noticed the extra bowl, the bannock set aside. His heart jumped when, with a frown of acknowledgment, she sat down beside him. He watched her eat. Took in the long line of her arm as she lifted her spoon, the flex of her throat as she swallowed.

Sabine picked at her bannock, observing Seth and Rosa as if they were animals in the wild. She could see that a fire still burned between them. It was plain as day: Rosa would not look at Seth, and Seth could not look away.

"We'll split up," Sabine said now. "I'll take the Eastern Key."

"What?" That got Seth's attention. "No. The Eastern Key is mine."

"Absolutely not. You can have *any* of the others, for all I care. But not that one."

"I'll break ties with you altogether if you do not concede the Eastern Key."

Now Rosa looked up. She turned to Seth, lips curved down with disappointment.

"It only makes sense," he carried on. "I know the Key inside and out—"

"They're all the same."

"But I want to confront Edmund on my own."

"Edmund is mine." Sabine's eyes darkened. "That's final."

"But Sabine—"

"But nothing! I deserve the chance to *see* him at least, Seth. I want to talk to him—"

"And what would you say? Hello, Father, how'd you do? And if you wouldn't mind apologizing for being such a prick?"

"I'm going to kill him." Sabine's voice was calm and steady. Only her eyes betrayed her as they darted back and forth, uncertain.

"Sabine!" Rosa reached across the table for her friend. "You wouldn't!"

"I have every intention to. I want the chance to see what I'll do. I take the Eastern Key."

"I really don't think that's the best idea, Sabine." Jack leaned forward to catch her eye. "Seth does know it better. And he's travelled the Droughtland before."

"I have too!"

Now Trace piped up. "Not on your own, you haven't."

"I won't *be* on my own!"

"Well, you won't have any of my boys if you go." Seth folded his arms, defiant. "If you agree to any other Key, I'll send them with you. If not ... " He shrugged. "You're on your own with whoever you can scrounge up."

"That won't be a problem."

"You better hope it's not."

"Stop!" Rosa grabbed his arm. She had hold of them both now. "Seth ... give your sister the Eastern Key. You know she deserves a chance to confront her father. But Sabine, you mustn't kill him. Promise me you won't."

Seth looked down at Rosa's fingers pressing into his skin. He could feel each tip as if it were sending shocks of electricity to his heart, his gut, his groin.

He took a deep breath, easing the sudden lump at his throat. "Fine."

"Good." Rosa let go. Seth silently kicked himself. He should have argued, and then she would have held on longer. He was stupid. And even more so for giving Sabine the Eastern Key with so little fight.

He reeled back whatever pride he could. "You're on your own, though. I mean it."

"I have no doubt the people will come with me."

"Not if I ask them first."

Celeste rapped her spoon on the table. "You won't, Seth."

"And even if they did," Sabine spat, "I don't want your child soldiers fighting for me."

"They've been fighting—and dying—for you this whole time!"

"No more." Sabine shook her head. "Do you *want* them to die? Are they nothing more than pawns to you?"

"It's not a matter of want. It's a matter of measure." Even as he spoke he could feel Rosa's disappointment focus on him like a scope. "If one hundred people have to die to save one million, is *that* acceptable?"

The question landed on the table, where no one laid claim to it. It sat there like an elephant, heavy and cumbersome.

"Enough," Rosa said. "We will go mad like this."

"We've already gone mad." Sabine half laughed, half sobbed. "We're all mad."

AFTER SO MANY DAYS of mush for breakfast and mush for supper, the Keyland Guard suddenly left the refugee camp. With no warning, no hint, the whole lot of them loaded up a few carts and took off in two neat rows atop their horses out the front gate. After several stunned moments the crowd rushed the gate and the fence on either side, toppling both with one collective heave, and spilled onto the road that ran alongside the camp.

"What's happening?" Teal yelled as their camp neighbours stampeded past. "Where's everyone going?"

Eli stood beside him, watching the exodus. "I don't know."

"Why are we waiting?" Tasha threw back her head. "Let's go!" She and a few stray children leapt into the throng. Nappo, with Emma sleeping peacefully in the sling, grabbed two of the kids, and Eli the third. But Tasha was already beyond reach. She did not look back.

"We'll meet you at the gate!" Effie yelled after her, stretching up on her tiptoes to catch the last glimpse of Tasha's head bobbing along in the mass. "Wait for us there!"

"Maybe you should go after her," Eli said when Nappo made no move.

"I don't want to risk getting separated from you guys," Nappo said, and Eli heard the unspoken echo: *I don't care if I ever see her again.*

"What do you suppose is going on?" Effie asked as hundreds more pushed their way to the gates.

Eli shrugged. Nappo nodded, as if giving it all a great big think. "No more use for us, is my guess."

Effie allotted Anya a chronic wanderer for each hand and organized the rest of the children into their own two neat rows. Instead of joining the traffic toward the gate, they knocked down a section of fencing nearby and filed along the length of the camp until they reached the front where the gate used to be. The fence had been torn to bits. Tasha was nowhere in sight.

"Now what?" Effie said. She and Rabbit stared at Eli while Bear sat atop her shoulders, his filthy hands holding hers.

"Look for Tasha, I guess." Eli turned in a circle. So many people.

"We should get going," Nappo said, half-heartedly looking about.

"We have to wait for Tasha." Eli looked sternly at Nappo. "We *are* waiting, Nappo. I don't care what you have to say about it."

"I didn't say anything." Nappo arched his brows. "Did I?"

AND WAIT THEY DID. The sun arced across the sky, the children complained of empty bellies, and then the day cooled off as the sun neared the horizon. Finally even Eli had to admit that Tasha had truly gone. The crowd had thinned, most having walked off in whatever their original direction had been, yet a substantial number had hung back. Eli asked them why. "This is as good a place as any for now," was the common answer, "what with the shanties set up and firewood from the fence, and Triban no longer even fit for rats."

"And the coulee for catching rabbits and the road for bartering," said one old woman with four children in her care, all with her long nose and far-apart eyes.

"But what if the Guard comes back?"

A shrug. "They fed and watered us decent enough, didn't they?"

Eli had to agree, but still, as the sun slunk lower in the sky, he and Effie and Nappo marshalled the children onto the road. At least they might crest the far hill before giving up for the night.

"What do you think happened to Tasha?" Eli asked Nappo as they trudged along. Despite the dark, Eli could see Nappo shrug. "What about feeding Emma?"

"I'll figure it out," Nappo said, although without a shred of bravado. "Been keeping my eye out for a wet nurse."

"A what?"

"You know," Nappo said under his breath, as if they were talking about something filthy, "a girl who's already got a kid and can feed the both of them, on her ... her ta-tas."

Eli paused. "I see," he finally said, although he didn't. Here was a little girl without a mother, and Eli knew what that was like. She'd know the feeling of loss, even if she wouldn't be able to place it as she grew up. If she grew up. Without telling Nappo, Eli had asked the old woman to tell Tasha, if she ever met her, which way they'd gone.

"No contenders yet," Nappo muttered.

Eli could hear the worry in his voice. He turned his gaze to the swath of stars in the night sky above. What were the highers planning after all this suffering? Why couldn't they deliver them from all this strife? Surely whatever lesson they, or even just Eli, were to learn was fully grasped by now. *I'm humble, I try to be obedient to your word, I pray ... and still you've abandoned me?*

The stars blinked silently above.

Eli let out a sigh.

Nappo eyed him. "What have they got to say about it all?" he said, gesturing up.

Eli shrugged. He didn't want to admit that they weren't speaking to him any more.

"Have you got an inside track on a wet nurse at least?"

"Why don't you just go ahead and pray for yourself once?"

"Don't know how," Nappo admitted.

"Just *pray*," Eli said. "Don't tell me you've never prayed for anything in your whole life, not even when your parents were dying, or when Teal was sick?"

"Why would I pray to something I don't believe in? What's the point?"

"But you want *me* to pray for you."

"You believe."

"Why don't you?"

Nappo laughed. "Let me tell you something, Reverend." He gestured at the line of tired, grumpy children trudging along in front of them. "We're alone, in the dark, responsible for all these kids, and we have no food, no water, and no hope. What kind of higher plays a joke like that?"

"There's a bigger picture," Eli said. "You just have to trust that it'll all work out in the end. For the greater good."

"I don't see it." Nappo shook his head. "I see us dropping like flies, one by one until the last kid is stranded in a crowd of bodies, his nappy hanging wet to his knees and nothing but his thumb to chew on."

Eli looked back up at the stars. Were the highers up there, residing in some actual, celestial place? Or more of an all-over nowhere, everywhere-all-at-once existence? Wherever and whatever, he wanted them back. "I'm sorry," he whispered, sending the apology up into the night on his breath. "Please. Come back."

16

⚜

Vance's convoy was making good time across the Droughtland. He sat back, allowing himself to enjoy the triumph of Triban's defeat. His men had been tidy, quiet little moles, digging under the city, carving out a path right to them. And then, when that crazy little band of insurgents had broken the ceasefire, well, his Guard had simply taken it in stride and come out with guns blazing. And if, as he suspected, it *was* Edmund who'd been behind it—and what a feeble ploy *that* had been—all the better when he arrived in the Eastern Key to orchestrate the man's fall from grace. As if Vance would ever want to be a Chief Regent! It was a position for weak, sissy benders too afraid to do the real work of military men.

Vance smiled to himself, picturing the Star Chamber's response when he told them all he knew. They'd convene a Chancellors' Court right away to try Edmund. He'd made sure that Seth and the girl, Sabine, survived the battle. Actually he'd wanted them captured, but no matter. He could keep track of them easily enough. As for the other boy, Eli, he'd lost track of him. But he wasn't important. In fact, only the girl was, really.

Word had reached him that the Guard had abandoned the refugee camp and fanned out to protect the Keys. Good move. What pansy Keyland leader had thought up the camp idea anyway? Much better to attack outright. The Droughtlanders, en masse, had been shocked or scared or infuriated into action, and now, from the relatively containable city of lowlifes and addicts, their battleground was leaching out over the entire continent.

But nothing would stop Vance from revealing the biggest scandal in Keyland history. He would secure his place in the history books as the one who'd brought the proud Chancellor Edmund Maddox down like a twenty-point buck in the forest. If only he could have Edmund's head to hang above his mantel.

Edmund sat in his office, hands folded on his desk, thoughts large and scattered.

Triban had fallen and there was no word as to the exact whereabouts of his children. Reports had reached him that Seth and his army had fled the city, and that Eli was somewhere amidst the quarter million refugees wandering about who knows where. As for the girl, Edmund had no clue. And Vance was on his way.

He could kill Vance. Or pay someone to do it, perhaps. Or he could flee? He shook his head. He would not, repeat *not*, be frightened away by some military goon, Commander or no, secrets or none.

He'd never been a coward, and would not fall prey to such weakness now. He could still fight. As long as he was still alive and breathing he'd find a way to bring himself and Allegra and Charlie through this and out the other side. And he would still be Chancellor East. At all costs. Whatever it took.

A knock at the door. Edmund took a deep breath. "Enter."

Francie brought in a tray of food, none of which looked appetizing. In fact, one sniff of the egg salad sandwich turned his stomach. "Take it away," he said as she set it in front of him.

"Yes, sir." Francie retraced her steps to the door and then murmured "Yes, sir" once more when Edmund asked for tea to be brought instead.

"No milk today. No sugar," Edmund added. "Just plain tea. Make it chamomile, actually."

"Yes, sir." Francie let herself out of the room with a curtsy.

BACK IN THE KITCHEN, Cook furrowed her brow at the sight of the untouched lunch.

"He's not feeling well," Francie said as she set the tray down and helped herself to the sandwich. "I can't say for sure, but he looks a little off. He asked for chamomile tea. I don't think I've ever brung him chamomile tea."

"It's his tummy then," Cook said. "Looking for something to soothe it. All that fighting out west, I imagine. Stresses a man in his position." Cook turned back to the pastry she was working. She scattered a fist of flour on the countertop and commenced rolling out the dough with her sturdy old pin. "All that state business on his mind. Probably giving him an ulcer. All the gossip since he got back."

Francie said nothing. She knew more than Cook, much more. Perhaps only she and Gulzar—outwardly maid and stableminder, in reality rebels to the core—knew just how close the unrest was. The Keys were doing a good job of downplaying the Droughtland uprising, but she and Gulzar knew it was likely only a matter of weeks, maybe days, before the conflict would reach their Key.

It had been over a year now since she'd pretended to be Gulzar's secret love. That one spontaneous, desperate declaration had saved him from Edmund's accusation of an affair with Lisette. But it had had another, unintended, effect: she and Gulzar had become lovers after all. She couldn't have known what comfort it would bring to be with another rebel, someone who knew the truth, someone who, like her, wanted life to be different. She'd been permitted to move into Gulzar's quarters above the stables; they were to be married. Francie wore a simple white-gold ring with a diamond solitaire that had been his mother's. Cook was nothing but thrilled for her.

Now Francie watched as Cook pressed the pastry into the pie plates with her knobby fingers. Such normal things they did every day, making meals, cleaning, washing up, but all the while Francie had felt the tension pulling as taut as the air before an electric storm. There was no telling what life would be like after. After what, exactly?

Cook glanced up. "Grab that bowl of apples?" Francie lifted the bowl of sliced fruit and held it to her chest for a moment. "Ta, dearie," Cook said, taking it from her. "You all right?"

"I'm fine," Francie said, rousing herself to start on the stack of dishes waiting in the sink. "Just tired."

"You and Gulzar are being careful, right?" Cook said to her pie shell. "This is no time to be having babies. Count your days and double check, mind."

"Oh yes, we're careful." Francie sunk her hands into the water and fished for the washing brush. "Very careful."

Sabine and her troops emerged from the mountains at last and made their way toward the Foothills Market. They numbered in the thousands now. In every town they'd passed through they'd picked up more volunteers, sometimes virtually emptying villages of able-bodied Droughtlanders eager to take up arms against the Keys. And with every new group of volunteers Sabine would warn that the going would be harsh, that food would be scarce, and that she could not even promise water for her soldiers. Yet still they joined.

The entire continent was now one giant incendiary device.

The people had a rage she had never seen. Rage that boiled into nearly hysterical cheers when she stopped to speak to them, whether to a market of traders or a gaggle of refugees at the side of the road. She'd spoken at enough rallies in enough different markets and camps that the words rolled off her tongue easily now.

"Unite! Fight! Take back your country! Topple the Keys!"

The defiant cheers carried her from town to town, gave her energy when she faltered. Now, as they were about to cross the scorching plain, she could only hope to sustain their strength.

She and Jack strode ahead of the troops toward the market, escorted by Tasha's father, the breadminder and unofficial mayor of the community.

"How's our girl?" Thomas asked at once.

"I haven't seen her in some time," Sabine said, careful to keep her disdain for Tasha out of her voice. "But she and the baby were doing well the last time I did."

Thomas and his wife shared a look. "Baby?" he asked, turning back to Sabine.

"What baby?" his wife echoed.

"Oh dear." Sabine's small smile was circumspect. "I'm so sorry, I just assumed you knew. You haven't heard?"

"No." Thomas's own smile vanished and his eyes went dark. "Who's the father?"

"Nappo," Jack offered without hesitation.

Husband and wife shared another look, and then the wife grabbed Sabine's sleeve. "Tell me everything! When did she have the baby? Where? A boy or a girl?"

"A girl," Sabine said as, thankfully, they entered the market. "She's called Emma. Tasha and the baby left the city when the children were evacuated. They were held in a camp for some time, but then the Guard abandoned it. I don't know where they are now." Sabine could see the breadminder's cheeks redden with anger. No wonder where Tasha got her fiery temper from. "They were originally headed to a safe spot in the mountains," she offered. "I don't have any reason to think they haven't resumed the trek, but I can't say for sure."

"But you're the leader, ain't you?" Thomas boomed. "Auntie All-knowing, right?'

"And so you should know where your people are at!" his wife cried.

Beside her, Jack bristled. Sabine put a hand on his arm and spoke slowly to the distraught parents. "These are dire times, friends. We are all doing the best we can." And with these words Thomas and his wife finally found some comfort.

LATER, AS NIGHT FELL, a band struck up a mazurka in the central square, where lanterns had been hung to mark a dance floor. Thomas quickly got drunk, raising toast after toast to his new granddaughter. Now he raised his mug yet again. "I never met my Emma but I love her fierce already!" With that he threw his head back and chugged his ale.

Jack guessed the market was the kind of place that welcomed any reason to throw an impromptu celebration with drinks and dust all around. He sat with Sabine off to the side in the dark while the crowd revelled in the guests' company.

"You think they party more because they don't know what's going to happen next?" Sabine asked as a couple jigged drunkenly through the crowd, toppling over into the dirt and laughing. "Or because they do know what's in store and want to make the best of things now?"

"I don't know." Jack put an arm across her shoulders. Since Gavin's death, he'd grown quiet, withdrawn even, but he still noticed things. He still watched, took note, observed keenly. Without Gavin, and with Toby in Eli's care, his main concern now was Sabine, supporting her through all that lay ahead, whatever the outcome. He'd done his mourning as he'd battled the Guard, with each bullet fired pushing the sadness further into hiding.

Thomas stumbled over with two sloshing steins of ale in each hand. He thrust one at Jack and one at Sabine. Now with one in each hand, he raised both.

"To Emma!" He cracked a stein against Jack's and took a long swig. "And to Emma again!" He cracked the other against Sabine's and took a swig from it too.

"Cheers!" Sabine couldn't help but laugh at Thomas's antics.

"*Salut,*" Jack said half-heartedly as Thomas backed away, flinging himself into a boisterous do-si-do with a woman whose skirts were tucked into her knickers, all the better to kick up her heels. That is, until Thomas's wife took notice and hurried to cut in.

THE NEXT MORNING Jack and Sabine were perhaps the only ones to wake without a hangover. While the others slunk around with bloodshot eyes and flushed cheeks, the two made plans for striking out into the Droughtland. Normally they wouldn't travel during the day on this side of the mountains, but time was of the essence. So they would carry on through the heat, under the burning sun, covering themselves as best they could and stopping only to switch horses. They would take as many people as they could, leaving the rest to follow in the standard way of Droughtland travel: advancing only during the night and waiting out the brutal sun during the day.

Careful not to let on what they were doing, Jack and Sabine tried to select the stronger among the many, the ones without the red-rimmed eyes of the dust, the ones who had the sick scars and so were immune. They discreetly asked for those who'd travelled the Droughtland before to come forward; these would guide the others through the perils ahead.

"I've got directions to the next village," Sabine said. "We'll trade out the horses there."

"If they've got them to trade." Jack hitched up one of strongest horses. "That's a lot of blind hope. If they can't replace the horses, we'll be stopped until these ones are well enough rested."

"I hope we won't have to do it too often in the villages," Sabine said. "We'll aim for the transport-train route and use the horses from the depots along the way."

"You think they'll give them up to us for free?"

"I do." Sabine gave her horse a nuzzle with her hand. "And if they don't, we'll help them make the right choice."

Jack shook his head. "And to think you were once such a nice girl."

Sabine punched him. "I still am!"

"We'll call you Sabine the Terrible," Jack joked.

"And I'll call you Jack the Bad."

Two more hours of arranging horses and carts and people and the speeding convoy was off, Jack and Sabine riding in front, facing the empty plain that lay before them.

17

⚜

They might have reached Cascadia by now. But Nappo's insistence that he knew the route had cost them a three-day detour, only to end up that much farther from the mountain trail leading up to the weather station's castle. Nappo admitted defeat only when they approached the very same village that had helped them as they'd fled the Triskelia massacre so long ago. Eli's heart sank when he spotted the little grove of trees where Sabine had had them all tie prayer cloths to honour those who'd died. The bright strips of fabric fluttered in the branches as the children ran ahead to explore the strange sight.

"Sorry." Nappo addressed the ground as he said it. "Screwed that up. And I was so sure."

Eli sighed, but as he did felt his heart lift up a little. The last time he was here he'd battled against what he thought were crazy voices. Now, though, he had accepted his unique connection with his highers as a blessing. He would pray at the trees once again, only this time with a peace of mind.

Besides, he knew the way to Cascadia from here. And he knew the villagers would be kind and generous, two things the children could use now. They'd been eating whatever they could scrounge along the way, yet still they were starving. Anya had let Emma latch on to her own breast until the milk that had dried up after Anya's baby died returned and she could breastfeed once more. It made Nappo uncomfortable, but what else could they do? Anya herself often wept quietly while Emma nursed.

"It's all right," Eli said. "We're here for a reason."

"You *would* say that." Nappo rolled his eyes.

"Everything for a purpose, my friend." Eli strode after the children, who were climbing the trees and swatting at the strips of cloth.

As they trudged up the hill, Teal ran back down toward them.

"The village!" he hollered as he waved his arms frantically. "It burnt down!"

Eli and Nappo shared a quick look of dread before breaking into a run.

And now Eli stood transfixed, staring at what was left of the village below. Except for a couple of buildings spared, it had been razed, and some time ago. Not a wisp of smoke lifted away from the huts' charred remains.

"What do we do?" Effie moaned.

"You and Anya stay with the children." Eli's skin prickled with fear as he scanned the devastation. "Nappo and I will go down."

"I'm coming too!" Teal started toward them at a run.

Eli began to protest, but Nappo stopped him. "He's seen worse, Eli."

So the trio made their way down to the village that had harboured them when they'd needed it the most. They did not run. Something—Eli would say it was his soul and Nappo would say it was his gut and Teal wouldn't know what it was—told the boys that they were walking into a graveyard.

And it was. Bodies were strewn where they'd been gunned down or axed with machetes. Whole families lay together in piles, having died in each other's embrace. Eli and Nappo did not let Teal come with them into the little buildings the villagers had called home. Instead, he waited in the road with Bullet while Eli and Nappo checked each building still standing for signs of life. There were none. From the bloated, decaying corpses it was clear the village had fallen several days before.

"Which means," Eli laid a hand on Nappo's shoulder as they carried on to the next hut, "that if you hadn't gotten us turned around, we may well have been here when it happened."

Eli could tell by Nappo's sudden pallor that he understood just how important his lousy sense of direction had been.

At the end of the village stood the little worship hall, untouched by fire. A trio of arched windows lined up along either side, its steepled roof pointing directly to the heavens. Eli felt a pull toward it. To pray, he thought.

But no. As he pushed open the heavy wooden door, he knew: he was there to bear witness to yet further atrocity. The holy place had become a mausoleum of bodies.

"They thought their highers would keep them safe." Nappo's voice behind him was taut with anger.

"This isn't the highers' fault," Eli said quietly as he steered a curious Teal back to the road.

"I want to see," Teal said.

The two older boys shook their heads. "No, Teal. You don't."

Halfway back to the hilltop where Effie watched the children, Eli stopped. He hadn't said a single prayer for those people.

"I'm going back."

"Want me to go with you?" The pain in Nappo's eyes made the answer easy.

"No."

Eli returned to the worship hall with only Bullet for company. But once he pushed the door open and the stench wafted out, even Bullet knew better than to go in. With a whine, he sat himself in the dirt to wait. Eli entered the dim chapel, careful to breathe through his mouth. He swore he could still smell the rotting bodies, no matter how hard he pinched his nose closed. They were crammed into the pews, huddled on the floor, leaning against each other in death as they probably had in life. Mouths agape, flies buzzing, women and children forming the majority. Eli saw them, but not as corpses. He made his way down the centre aisle, and he was not afraid. He saw light around each one, shimmering auras that sent a wash of peace over him. Eli kneeled at the altar with the stained-glass wall behind it, broken in places but not destroyed.

The rays of light came up from the floor, all reaching up, up, to form a pair of hands, palms spread open to the highers.

Give thanks.

At last: his highers had returned to him.

"I do give thanks," Eli prayed. "For keeping the children safe. For taking the people of this village into your arms. Into your care."

Eli felt dizzy. He fell forward, resting his head on the stone floor. There was a ringing in his ears and nothing but light pressing at his eyes, even if he squeezed them shut. Then he could see clearly, but not the altar. Not the stained glass. Not the cool, stone floor. Something else entirely. He let the vision pass through him until it took hold in his memory and was as clear as if he'd lived it.

He blinked. He was in the worship hall again. The vision was gone. But the feeling of profound sureness stayed with him. He knew what to do now. He'd been called.

EFFIE HAD GATHERED the children from their play and sat them in fidgety rows, ready to get back on the road upon Eli's return. Several of the older ones were crying, and ran to Eli for comfort as he joined them. Eli beheld the anxious faces of the children he'd come to know. They looked up to him, and would come to him for little things, like lacing up shoes, and also for the big "Why" questions so many children ask. Now, though, Eli was too numb to speak.

As he and Nappo took up the rear again, Eli was silent. Nappo would only mock him if he told him of the vision he'd had. Tell him he hadn't been the same since the massacre.

Well, fair enough. None of them had. And he, for one, was better for it.

The highers had given Eli a task that seemed impossible. He would have to tell Nappo sooner rather than later. And Mireille too. They would both play a part.

He glanced at his friend. The horror in the worship hall had humbled Nappo, or frightened him, into an uneasy quiet. He held Emma in his arms instead of packing her in the sling, as if he wanted her even closer, skin to skin. Emma's new favourite thing was to smile, and she shone a big one at Eli now, stretching out a tiny hand as if she could read his mind and was trying to cheer him. Eli shook himself from his thoughts and asked Nappo if he could hold her for a while.

"Not just yet, Eli." Nappo kissed the top of his daughter's head. "Okay?"

"Of course," Eli said. He understood. Emma was a fountain of life, and Nappo was drinking from her to refill the emptiness.

A little while later, Nappo handed her over. Emma was still too little to hold her head up very well, and she was lighter and smaller than Charis had been when he'd met her, but still Eli could not help but think of Trace and Anya's little girl. Thoughts of Charis hurt as if he were being stung by so many bees. He glanced at Anya now. A toddler strapped to her back, the two wanderers firmly in tow. She met Eli's gaze and returned a small, tired smile, but a smile nonetheless. Of anyone on this journey to lead the children to safety, Anya was holding up the best. Her life had taken shape again: she was once more a mother, but to many children now.

Anya's charges were whining, pulling away from her. Even Eli could see they were on the brink of one of their tantrums. Anya, not missing the shift, started in on the ever-effective marching song.

"As we march, march, march through the bush, bush, bush!" small voices sang, fumbling as they caught onto the silliness. "We will sneeze, sneeze, sneeze," was one verse, along with exaggerated sneezes. "We will skip, skip, skip ..."

Eli glanced up. Was it blasphemous to sing? When so much death was still so close?

Rejoice.

He couldn't. Not yet. His head spun with images from the worship hall. Bits of skull from where the mice had gnawed away hair and skin. The gaping mouths, frozen forever in screams of terror.

Eli squeezed his eyes shut, willing back the light and clarity of the vision. He would cling to that instead.

THEY SLEPT ROUGH that night, as they had many others since fleeing Triban. It wasn't as cold as the last time Eli and Nappo had passed this way, and Teal insisted this to anyone who would listen, but the older children wanted to know why they'd left the Guardy compound in the first place.

"They say that at least there were tents and food," Teal reported back to where Eli and Nappo had settled in to sit watch during the night.

"But we were prisoners," Eli said, although they weren't, at the end.

"And as for the food ..." Nappo spat on the ground. "Hardly."

"Better than nothing," Teal countered.

"Watch your mouth, brother," Nappo growled. "No one's in the mood."

A pause, and then Teal pushed a little more. "We got nothing? No jerky? No hardtack? No nothing?"

The look Nappo shot at Teal sent him scurrying to Anya. Now it looked as though she was telling the children a story. Absentmindedly she tousled Teal's hair as he cuddled close, letting a toddler claim his lap and tossing a grimace in Nappo's direction. Nappo, though, was busy whittling a stick, flicking the shavings away with his knife. He would try to catch fish in the stream while Eli sat watch. And then they'd switch, and maybe by morning the kids would have something to eat.

BY DAWN they'd caught eight trout between them, using big fat worms for bait, tied with bright yellow string and one of the earrings from the girls as a lure. The children ate the fish hot from the fire, picking at it with their fingers and making sure each of them ate even just a little. It was hardly enough to sate a hundred children's appetites, but it, along with a few salal berries each, would have to do. Effie had gone off early with a handful of older girls to collect the berries, and although they were tough and soapy tasting, the children were delighted.

Then they were off, even as the fog hung low across the trail, threading through the forest like spirits.

Mid-morning they ran into a group of travellers who shared what food they could and told them of a market up the trail that they should reach by nightfall.

"It wasn't there before," Eli said, hoping they were on the right trail to Cascadia.

"You're right." The man nodded. "They're survivors of that village south of here. You folks must've seen it."

They shared more news. Eli told them about fleeing Triban and the bizarre camp they'd been held in. The travellers told him that Triskelian fighters were on the move now, and were aiming to take out the Keys one by one.

"Word has it that the Droughtlanders are joining up to fight too," the man said, his face beaming. "This could really be it. Sabine is leading them across, to take the Eastern Key with her own hands!"

"And Seth?" Eli worked to keep his face expressionless.

"Marched out with his soldiers. Heading for the Western Key."

Nappo glanced at Eli, waiting for him to claim his connection. When he didn't, Nappo did it for him. "This is their brother. Eli."

"The Reverend Eli! We've heard about you." The man called for his friends. "Come meet the Reverend!"

"Nappo ..."

"What? You should be proud!"

"Of course!" The man put it all together. "Then these are the children you led out of Triban?"

"Yes," Eli said with a sigh. There was no point in denying it now that Nappo had shot his mouth off.

"You've got allies in us, friend." The strangers gathered around him. "Come on, give us a blessing before we go on our way, Reverend."

"I, uh ..."

"Go on," Nappo said with a grin.

Eli lifted his hand, and as he did, the men dropped to their knees. Nappo stifled a laugh.

"Go in peace. May your highers keep you safe."

After a moment, the man looked up. "That's it?"

Eli nodded. The men stood. "Well, thank you, Reverend. And say hello and bushels of thanks to your brother and sister when you see them next."

"I will."

"Hi from Burt and his gang."

"Will do."

"She's going to do it, I tell you. Her and Seth. I know it in my gut."
He poked his belly. "I know it in my head." A poke to his brow. "This is
the revolution. For real. For *keeps.*"

As the travellers took their leave Eli closed his eyes, trying to summon
Seth and Sabine. He clutched his medallion and tried again. Nothing.

"Let's go." Nappo pushed Eli ahead of him. "The sooner we make it
to the market, the sooner we can get some real food into these kids."

Eli nodded and let himself be swept into the group as they resumed their
way up the trail. Sabine would be only halfway across the Droughtland
at best. Eli knew how bad it could get on the plains. How would she
endure it? Who did she have with her? Had the other Triskelians survived
the fighting in Triban?

Give me strength, Eli prayed.

THE MARKET, when they finally reached it, was just a row of dirty tents.
The few survivors of the village massacre told Eli that the Guard had
indeed swept through just a few days earlier—and had made it clear
it was punishment for having helped the Triskelians.

Yet these weary, grief-stricken survivors still wanted to help, scrambling
to find extra food and beds for the children. Eli's heart could break from
it. He felt a terrible, heavy weight in his chest and sat down on a rock for
a good long time.

He might have sat like that forever, with moss growing up his legs and
birds building nests in his filthy hair, but someone shook his arm.

"Eli?"

As slow as earth, Eli turned to look. A young man he did not recognize.
Eli nodded, brows furrowed.

"We've been waiting for you." The boy took a step back to let Eli draw
himself onto his feet. "I'm Louis. We met at Cascadia. I was at the gate
with Yvon when you came."

Louis told him excitedly about the gathering forces heading out
in different directions across the continent. Then he paused and searched
Eli's face. "We lost Gavin and Yvon. In Triban."

Eli felt a hard pang of grief for the brothers. Toby's brothers. Toby must not be told. Not now. Not yet. Eli took a deep breath to steady himself. He would speak to Anya. She would be the one to tell Toby. Eli could feel it: Anya would have the right words for that little boy. She would know when he was ready.

Now Louis gestured for Eli to follow him.

"Have any of the Keys fallen yet?" Eli asked as they walked.

"Not that I've heard."

Louis led Eli to a small tent, where they sat on a worn carpet and talked some more. Mireille was doing fine, Rainy not so well. Louis must have sent someone for food, because a tray was handed in through the opening with a simple bowl of soup and bread and a teapot of something that smelled like chicory. Eli could feel the warm swallows of soup land in his belly. Louis, although younger than Eli by a year or two, spoke confidently, instilling a quick trust in Eli. He clung to the feeling.

"We can fit the little ones in the carts and have the older ones walk. I hadn't expected this many, but we can make it work. We'll ration the food supplies a little tighter, that's all. Find a couple more tents before we get going."

"When can we leave?" Eli said when his bowl was empty. He wanted to see Mireille. He wanted to be atop the mountain so magically removed from the world. He could picture Mireille, with that thoughtful tilt of her head that gave her a look of constant wonder, her bright green eyes dancing with curiosity and intelligence. Above all, he wanted to tell her of his vision. He needed her for it. He'd have to convince her somehow.

"Tonight, or first thing tomorrow."

Tomorrow. Let the children rest.

Eli told Louis they would set out at sunrise.

18

⚜

The trek up to Cascadia seemed to go much more quickly than the last time Eli had come this way. They camped two nights, with the children in high spirits. When they finally caught sight of the impressive stone building that was Cascadia itself they broke into a run toward its gates, whooping and hollering. Althea ran down to meet them, and after delighted greetings and hugs all around, Eli left the children in Anya and Effie's care while he and Nappo walked toward the castle to find Mireille.

On the way they spotted Rainy wandering in a circle halfway up the north ridge. Eli called out to him, but the old man looked up only briefly before starting his circular pacing again.

"Seems odd," Nappo said as they carried on. "Hardly cares that we're back."

"Mireille says he's going senile," Eli said. "That's why she didn't want to leave the mountain to come to Triban."

They found Mireille setting iodide plumes on the narrow bluff beyond the stable. The wind was furious and loud, whipping her dark hair across her face and flapping her jacket as she knelt, configuring one of the plumes. It wasn't until she glanced up to assess the clouds overhead that she saw Eli and Nappo. With a wave, she got up and ran down the hill to greet them.

"You're back!" She hugged Eli so hard he stumbled.

He held her tight for a moment before giving her a timid kiss on the cheek.

"And Nappo!" She hugged Nappo with the same enthusiasm, Eli noticed in dismay. "I'm so glad you guys are back. Rainy's been so out of it lately, I've been doing absolutely everything by myself."

Nappo and Eli shared a look. "We saw him," Eli said.

"In the lab, I hope?" Mireille scratched Bullet's head as he pranced at her feet. "He hasn't wandered off again, has he?"

"He's out front. On the ridge."

With an exasperated sigh, Mireille started quickly down the hill. Eli and Nappo followed her.

"What about the plume?" Eli asked.

Mireille stopped, brow furrowed.

"You'll miss the weather."

"But Rainy—"

"I'll go get Rainy," Nappo offered. "You finish up here. I'll meet you two at the lab."

"Thank you, Nappo." Mireille smiled weakly. "I really appreciate that."

Eli wished he'd thought to offer as he watched Nappo jog purposefully down the hill.

"I've found him seven times now," Mireille said as she and Eli headed back up to the abandoned plume. "After he's wandered off. Once I discovered him in his underlinens lying in the dirt with his hands behind his head, happy as anything even as he was freezing to death. He told me he was organizing the clouds."

"That's what he does, though, right?" Eli said, trying to reassure her.

"Not really, no," Mireille said as she bent down over the plume. "We don't 'organize' the clouds at all. And certainly not half-naked in foul weather. He's losing it, to be blunt. We might have to lock the lab. I found him in there last week, taking apart the plumes."

Mireille handed Eli the pin that locked the mechanism. Stepping away, they watched the plume rise up into the wind.

"Now let's go see how dear old Rainy is doing." Mireille sounded weary. "See what he's gotten up to this time."

NAPPO MET ELI and Mireille in the castle's front hall. "Rainy went down for a nap."

"Oh, good." Mireille beamed at him, and Emma too, snuggled in his arms. "And who's this?"

"My daughter, Emma." Mireille, to Eli's surprise—he'd thought her a bit too academic to be into babies—turned to mush as she lifted Emma from him and ogled over her. Nappo beamed as he recounted their difficult journey to Cascadia, which made the story seem almost pleasant.

"And where's Emma's mommy?" Mireille asked Emma herself, in a singsong voice.

"We don't know," Nappo admitted. "She took off."

"She left her baby?"

Nappo bristled. "In good hands."

"Oh, I'm sure … it just seems awfully rash, doesn't it?"

"She knows where we were going," Nappo reasoned. "She can find her way here, I'm sure. If she wants to. Who knows …" He petered off. Eli glanced at him. He didn't want her to come back, that much was plain. There was also no doubt about the way he was looking at Mireille, with the same goggly eyes she was giving the baby. Adoration.

Since when?

"So, Mireille. Nappo." Now was as good a time as any to shove them off the topic of babies and mommies. As they made their way to the lab, Eli began. He'd kept it to himself long enough, and was practically bursting to share his vision. "I'm going to tell you something very, very important. I need your help. I won't be able to do it without you."

Nappo and Mireille stopped and raised their eyebrows at him.

"You been keeping something from me, friend?"

"I thought we should focus on getting here before I told you."

"Well, we're here," Nappo said flatly. "Fire away, Reverend."

"What is it, Eli?" Mireille bounced the baby, waiting.

Now Eli hesitated. The vision had been clear and simple in his head, but he hadn't yet described it out loud, or tried to explain it.

Emma grinned at him. Oh well, he had one admirer at least.

In the village where the massacre happened, when I went back alone, I had a vision—" Eli watched his friends closely. They shared a glance.

"And with it, a calling."

"Really." Mireille tilted her head. "A vision?" She was already making assumptions, Eli could tell. He pressed on.

"I've been called to destroy the iodide depot."

"Hmm." Mireille tilted her head the other way.

"Huh?" Nappo's brow furrowed. "What do you mean?"

"We're to go to the main depot."

"Really!" Mireille handed Emma back to Nappo. "That's the stupidest idea I've ever heard. And coming from you, Eli!"

"What," Nappo said, "a slave to your highers now? Even if they send you on a suicide mission?"

"It will work." Eli said. "I know it will. It will free the weather."

"Just like that?"

"Yes."

"There are other depots, Eli."

"This is the one I'm called to. We could be there in a week."

"We?" Mireille's jaw dropped. "What do you mean *we*?"

"You and Nappo were in the vision. Plain as day."

"We've tried storming depots before, Eli. Three years ago. We failed. And two of our people died in the effort."

"This will work. I know it as sure as I know this floor is stone."

It is a sacred mission.

"It's a sacred mission." Eli echoed his highers, but the moment the words left his lips he knew he'd pushed it too far.

"Sacred?" Mireille's eyebrows arched and she began walking again, taking the lead as they turned the corner toward the lab. "Eli, come on. Listen to what you're saying." She turned her eyes to Nappo. "What do you think about all this?"

"I don't know." Nappo shrugged. "Eli's my best friend."

"But in general, do you believe there's anything *sacred* about it?"

Another shrug. "I trust him." His tone was firm. "I trust Eli."

Eli had to resist lifting Nappo off his feet in a big, nelly hug. Instead, he just smiled. "Thank you, Nappo."

"I'd follow you anywhere, Eli. I know you'd do the same for me."

Mireille scoffed. "Well, this is just stupid."

They'd reached the door to the lab. Mireille glanced in the window and then stepped back with a frustrated huff.

"So much for his nap."

The boys looked in the window. Rainy was sitting in the middle of the floor, his notes spread end-to-end around him in an obsessively precise spiral that filled the room.

"We'll talk about this later," she said as she pushed open the door. "But I can't even leave him for just half an hour, so I can tell you now there's no way I'm leaving him for weeks. Sacred mission or not."

Eli held his tongue. He'd let her think. She'd come around. His highers would make it so.

"My papers!" Rainy cried as the gust from the door scattered them.

"It's okay, Rainy." Mireille stepped carefully between the rows and offered her hand to the old man. "I thought you'd gone for a nap?"

He crossed his arms and let out a growl. "It's not okay!" he yelled, refusing to budge. "Put them back. Just as they were." Then he noticed the boys. "What are you looking at? Get to work!"

Mireille knelt beside her mentor and laid a hand on each shoulder. "Think, Rainy. There's no point in your papers being like this."

"Their order is vitally important." Rainy would not move. "And if you cannot know why, then you are nothing but an imbecile."

"Rainy ..."

"You are an idiot and a disappointment after years and years of training. You are a failure."

"Okay, Rainy." With a sigh, she stood. The boys followed her back out into the hall, where she pulled the door closed shut.

"I'll see you two at supper." Tearing up, she kept one hand on the door. "I'm sure there's lots to be done with the children."

"Will you come with us?"

Nappo gave him a sharp look before giving Mireille a softer one. "Never mind him. You do what you need to do."

Mireille did not look at Eli. "Thanks, Nappo." She gave Emma a quick kiss, and then opened the door and went in to Rainy, who was now on his knees, rearranging his papers just so.

The two boys stood in the hallway for a moment.

Eli grimaced. "That went well."

"I can't believe you didn't tell me this sooner." Nappo gave him a punch in the shoulder. It didn't feel altogether playful. "Freak."

"But you said you'd come."

"Only to let you save face in front of Mireille."

"You won't come?"

"I will. Even just for the hell of it, now that Emma and Teal are in good hands."

"Thank you."

"You can bet *Mireille* won't, though."

"She has to come," Eli said. "She's part of the vision."

"You can't make her do it, Eli." The boys headed for the great room, where they could hear the noisy bustle of the children settling in. "What are you going to do, kidnap her?"

"She'll come." She simply had to.

"Not likely, buddy." Nappo punched him again, this time less hard. "Pretty clear to me she thinks you're stark raving mad. And she already has one crazy person to deal with."

MIREILLE AVOIDED ELI for the next two days. Every time he caught sight of her she was with Nappo. Eli tried not to be jealous, but he hated seeing them together, even if Nappo was only being Eli's ambassador. Eli once saw them sitting side by side in front of the fire in the great hall, a blanket over their laps. One blanket! Over both laps!

When she finally spoke to him again the three were at breakfast, Mireille sitting between them. A little closer to Nappo than to Eli, he couldn't help but notice. *Highers help me,* he prayed, willing down the hot poker of envy.

"I talked to Rainy about what you said—"

"But Rainy's going crazy, Mireille."

"Maybe you are too," she snapped.

"Mireille ..." Nappo said, drawing out her name like a warning.

"Sorry, Eli. But it is possible."

"I am not crazy." Eli pushed the hash around his plate, suddenly very un-hungry. He slid his piece of bread to Bullet under the table.

"But look, crazy or not ..." She finally glanced up. "I'll come with you."

"You will?" Eli felt a flood of relief. "That's fantastic—"

"But I don't want to hear about your highers, or even your vision." Mireille lifted a hand and shook her head. "I'm going because I'm curious. And I'm tired. Rainy is testing me, and I need a break."

"It won't be easy."

She glared at him. "I know that. I knew the two men who died, Eli. And I'll be armed, and so will Nappo, so don't even try to fly your pacifist flag on this one."

No one had died in his vision. But he wouldn't bother using that as a way to placate her fears.

"The apprentices below me will look after Rainy," she went on. "You can thank Nappo, Eli. He's the one who convinced me to come."

"Thank you, both of you. I know this will work. I know it. The highers—"

"I said I'd go, Eli." Mireille dropped her hands into her lap, frustrated. "As far as I'm concerned, this is strictly a scientific quest for the greater good of the whole continent."

"You don't believe it's a sacred mission."

"Not in the least."

Eli caught Nappo's eye. "And you?"

Nappo shook his head. "I don't."

"But I have your word that you'll come with me?"

"I swear." Nappo hardened his look. "Now, can we eat?"

"Mireille?"

Mireille swallowed before answering. "I swear too."

"Thank you both." Eli wanted to leave the table now. He should feel grateful, he told himself. But all he could really feel was sadness and frustration and that awful, overwhelming jealousy. Oh, it had all been so embarrassing. A girl like Mireille would never be with someone like him. She thought he was insane, obviously. And he had no one to blame but himself. And maybe his highers, for making him come off as such a kook.

He took a fortifying breath and bade himself to stay and feel all the uncomfortable feelings. There would be no Eli and Mireille. His instant connection with her when he'd first come to Cascadia must have been only an early recognition of her role in this task. He had mistaken a premonition of purpose for love. His highers had cheated him as a means to an end.

THE NEXT MORNING Nappo handed Emma to Anya for safekeeping while they were gone.

"*Je vais prendre soin de elle.*" Anya arranged the blanket over her. "She is safest here, of course. She will be waiting for you when it is all over."

"We'll take good care of her and Teal." Althea hugged Nappo. "Don't you worry about them."

Teal had to be held back. "I hate you!" He struggled to get free. "I hate you!"

"Nappo, he can't come." Eli could see his friend falter. The brothers had never been apart before.

"Trace would often have to go away for a time, and he was always sad to leave Charis ...." Anya kept her eyes on the baby as she spoke. "And Charis ... *ma chère petite enfant* ... was always happy to see him when he came home."

Eli and Nappo shared a look. This was the first time Anya had mentioned Charis without becoming either hysterical or catatonic.

After a final goodbye to Emma and Teal—which won Nappo a kick in the shin and a volley of curses from his little brother—they went to collect their packs.

"You don't think Anya's going to do anything weird like start calling her Charis and claiming Emma is hers or anything like that, do you?"

"No," Eli said, although he wasn't all that sure she wouldn't. "Let's go find Mireille and get going before Teal's on the loose again."

THEY MET MIREILLE in the stalls and were soon off down the mountain on the three strongest horses. It would be a long ride to the depot, with who knew what kind of obstacles along the way.

19

⚜

S eth and his soldiers pushed toward the Western Key. The nearer
they got, the bigger their army grew, with Droughtlanders from
far and near falling into step alongside the remaining BAT
soldiers. Now, mere hours from the Key's walls, Seth looked behind him
at the forces he'd amassed. He could not even begin to imagine the
number. It was a veritable sea of determined faces, and from that
he took comfort.

Seth also took comfort in the fact that Rosa was among them. She hadn't
even told him she would join him. Nor had she said more than a handful
of words to him since, but there she was, riding at the back with her cart
of supplies, and that was all that mattered.

"How many do you think?" he called back to Amon.

"Thousands," Amon bellowed over the din of the march.

"And all of them willing to fight." Seth stopped his horse for
a moment just to behold the Droughtlanders passing him, armed with
whatever weapon they could find or cobble together, many with no
weapons at all. Amon wove his horse through the ceaseless crowd until
he was at Seth's side.

Few among the throng spoke, fewer dawdled. It was as if they had
together formed a river of bodies with an unstoppable current. It came
to Seth that his approach back in Triban had been all wrong. Why could
he not have motivated this kind of revolt there? Why were they amassing
now, after the city had fallen?

"Or maybe it's *because* it fell," Seth said out loud. Maybe he had only failed to anticipate the effect of losing Triban. If the city had become his, perhaps these people wouldn't have felt compelled to join him now to topple the mighty Western Key. Not a single part of Seth thought he'd fail here. There would be many dead in the end, but Seth would win. There was no doubt.

"What?" Amon said, not following.

"I was just thinking how it's all come to this." Seth gestured at the passing fighters. "Triban was the call to arms."

"Okay ..." Amon still wasn't following.

"See, I was wrong," Seth said. Amon widened his eyes, never having heard Seth admit an error before, and leaned in close. "I thought our loss in Triban meant it was over, but it had to happen to bring us to this ... this critical mass. This upswell." Seth grinned. "This one is ours, Amon."

"Glad you think so." Amon was still stuck on Seth's apology. "We should get going," he added.

Seth did not move. Something had just dawned on him. "Correction," he said and grinned again, turning his smile to Amon. "This one is *yours*, Amon."

"Mine?"

"We have enough fighters to split up. Look at them all! I can make my way to the Northwestern Key with half of them, and you can keep going to the Western Key with the rest."

"On my own?"

"But you wouldn't be." Seth swept his arm, taking in the entire sea of people. "You'll have your own army."

"I don't know if I'm ready."

"You *are*!" Seth clapped Amon's shoulder. "Come *on*. You lead this one and you'll come out a hero. You want that as much as I do, I know you do."

"A hero ..."

"A *hero*."

Not to mention the time it would save Seth. The time he needed in order to join up with Sabine at the Eastern Key, which is where he truly wanted to be. To have it out with Edmund, in private, once and for all.

"A hero." Amon grinned. "You and me both."

"So can I leave you to it?" Seth grinned back. Sure, he had his own motives, but it felt genuinely good to give Amon the chance to prove himself on such a large scale.

"Yes I can, Commander Seth. Won't be any more difficult than what we got up to in the city, eh?"

Seth wasn't sure about that, but he agreed anyway. It was one thing to defend your own city, and quite another to attack someone else's.

"You're heading to the Eastern Key, afterward. Aren't you? To find your father."

"Not right away, but yes." Seth nodded. "When we're finished with the rest of them."

"Then, unless we meet up again before then, I'll look forward to laying sore eyes on you at the Eastern Key."

"Until then." Seth saluted. "All the best, Commander Amon."

"Commander ..." Amon shook his head, beaming. "That sounds just about right."

Seth halted the march—no easy task, given their momentum—and informed the gathered troops of their new Commander. Then he sent the forward half onward to the Key, and diverted the rear half toward the northwest. All he had to do now was talk to Rosa. And so he would wait.

GUNFIRE CRACKED into the sky as the Guard took aim at the first fighters to reach the Key's walls. A flock of crows scattered from a dead horse not far from where Seth waited. Seth's horse didn't even flinch, so accustomed had it become to the volley of warfare. Seth squinted toward the Key. He could just make out its walls, yet he could hear the screams as the fighters fell to the better weapons of the Key. Pawns, just as in chess. Lose the pawns, deplete the enemy's cache of bullets and bows, then send in the rest to take the king.

The ground trembled with cannon fire. Soon, the din of battle was as ignorable as the buzz of the cicadas, which grew louder as the day set into dusk and the gunfire grew sparser. They'd be down to the hand to hand,

Seth imagined. That was where his soldiers and the Droughtlanders would win. When it came to scrapping it out, his people had everything to gain and nothing to lose.

ROSA'S FIELD HOSPITAL CARTS and wagon trains of wounded crested the hill behind him, kicking the horizon with dust. He rode to meet her.

She gave Seth a puzzled look as he neared. "Why aren't you fighting?"

"Oh, so you'll talk to me when you have a question, eh?" Seth replied with a smile. He told her his plan. Firmly. She would have to agree. She'd have to.

"And who will look after the wounded here?"

"I'm sure there are healers among them."

"But they have no supplies."

"They can raid the Key."

"If they get that far."

"If they get that far, yes."

Rosa slowed to a stop.

"You're coming with me," Seth said again. She didn't need to know he was quaking in his boots. To steady himself he turned to nod at his soldiers marching neatly in a great, straight line now, at least twenty abreast.

He turned back to Rosa. "At the rear." There. He'd managed another statement.

She stared at him, eyebrows raised.

Seth wouldn't—couldn't—force her to do anything. And yet, finally, there it was: the slightest nod of her head.

Silently exulting, he turned and galloped along the outside edges of the march until he came up at the front. The road stretched ahead with no end in sight.

THEY CAMPED THAT NIGHT on the edges of the village nearest the Northwestern Key. Seth had Ori and Finn set up his tent while he strode among the rows and rows of people who'd chosen to fight for him, who announced their solidarity with red bands tied around their sleeves. He liked to meet them, see their faces. Many of them would die, but he would at least know a few of them by name.

Frederick. Danny. Seamus. Lloyd, Adok, Alejo.

There were girls and women too. Elise. Nadine. He stopped at a Seduce game being played around a candle for light. There he met Goose and Preet, and a girl called Felicity. She blinked at him under long lashes shadowed by the light. Her red band was a dainty ribbon, tied in a bow around her slender arm.

"A name like that," Seth said. "Far too pretty to be fighting."

"Then maybe you should get me to do something else." She winked. "Hmm, Commander Seth?"

Seth clasped his hands behind his back. He'd walked right into that one. "Good luck with your hand."

"You have no idea what I can do with my hand," she purred.

"Your hand of cards, hon." Seth laughed. "Your hand of *cards.*"

He returned to his tent. One of the boys had lit a lantern; the canvas was glowing now with a soft orange light. Inside, a meal waited for him on an overturned crate, and his bed had been set up on two pallets. Seth had to smile. It wasn't much, but it made him think of Commander Regis, holding court in his tent on the outskirts of Triban, wanting for nothing.

Seth sat down to eat the chicken and potatoes. They had a cart full of chickens, each in their little cubby of straw, donated by a village along with all its able-bodied men.

Halfway through his meal, Rosa appeared at the flap. "Can I come in?"

"Of course." Seth stood, wiping his mouth with his handkerchief. "Come in! Come in."

She took a few steps and stopped. She eyed the chicken. "That's not for supper at my end of the camp."

"Have some, please." He gestured to the plate. "I would've invited you, but I just assumed you'd turn me down. Help yourself."

She just stood there, though, her hands clasped together at her chest, kind of hugging herself.

"Are you cold?" Seth pulled the blanket off his cot.

"No."

He draped it over her shoulders anyway, bending closer than he should, breathing in the smell of her. She turned, and he didn't step away. They stood so close.

"I said I wasn't cold." Rosa shrugged the blanket off and let it fall to the floor.

"I'm sorry."

She shook her head with a little laugh. "So you say."

"What did you come here for?"

"Shut up, Seth."

"What?"

She laid a finger over his lips. "Just shut up."

"But—"

She silenced him with a swift kiss, locking her hands behind his neck and pulling his head down so she could kiss him deep and long. When they came apart for air, and he parted his lips to speak, she shook her head.

"Not a word." Her voice was thick. "Don't speak. Promise?"

Seth nodded, stunned.

Rosa pulled him down onto the abandoned blanket, working his pants down to his knees as he kicked off his boots. He held himself above her with his hands, and dared not tell her everything he wanted to. He beamed at her and laughed warmly, but that was all. She shut him up with another kiss as she pulled him down to her and spread his legs with her own.

SETH WOKE with a start. Someone was calling his name. He sat up, rubbing the sleep from his face. He was alone. Rosa was gone. His limbs ached from the hard ground.

"What is it?" He covered himself with the blanket.

Ori stepped in, Finn at his side. "They sent a runner from the Western Key. The battle's winding down ... but they've taken Amon prisoner."

"*Commander* Amon." Fear stabbed at his heart. Seth pulled on his clothes. "Get my horse, and rouse the Fourth. I'll take them with me."

"You're going back?"

He was. Seth had sent Amon in with the confidence that he could take care of himself. And now, all the while riding back the way they'd come, Seth held to that confidence. He would arrive to find it not nearly as bad as had been reported. He would make sure that Amon was freed, if he wasn't already, and then he and the Fourth would return to the others and carry on.

They rode right into the Key and didn't see a single Guardy until they neared the centre of town. The bunting was still up from the legislature. This made Seth smile. It hadn't been business as usual for a while then, else they would've taken it down right after the annual session. The Keyland Guard must have been scurrying around, preparing to be stormed.

The battle at this end of the Key must have turned in their favour during the night, because as far as Seth could see, this area was theirs. Who knew how many Guard had fled before the fighting had really begun? Keylanders, too. Seth had to smile to think of them, trying to survive outside these walls.

He was led to the prison yard where captive Keylanders were packed in shoulder to shoulder, protesting and screaming and carrying on like so many angry pigs in a field of muck.

"Where's Amon?" he asked the BAT boys who'd led him there.

"Dead, Commander Seth."

"No." Seth shook his head impatiently. "No. Take me to him."

"But he's dead, Commander."

No.

Seth felt his eyes welling up. He would not cry. He never cried. He gritted his teeth and turned away from the boys. "Where is he?"

"With the rest," the first boy said. "We've been stacking them in the field behind. Is that okay? We figured you'd want 'em burned soon enough."

"Bring him to me."

The boys scurried off. Seth turned, and then turned again, stunned. A blast shook the ground, but it was on the other side of the Key. The front was advancing on it, and making good progress, or so he'd been told.

Seth turned again, not sure what to do. The pressure bore in behind his eyes, but he'd be damned if he'd cry. He backed into a doorway and bent his forehead to the wall. He lifted it up, and knocked it against the wall. Another time, harder. He growled. He made fists and pummelled his forehead until the pain distracted the tears.

Amon. Seth had screwed up. He should never have divided the troops. They'd needed all of them here. *If they had been here Amon would not have died.*

But Seth knew that wasn't true. They'd virtually won. He'd seen that immediately by the portion of the Key they already held, and by how few Guard were left.

Amon. Seth pressed his face against the wall, squinted his eyes tight against the tears. *Amon was dead.* His first real comrade in arms. His one true companion. The man whose loyalty, once proven, had never faltered.

"We've got him here, Commander Seth." The boys led him to a cart.

Amon stared up at Seth, eyes wide, mouth fixed in a grimace. His throat had been cut straight across. His BAT vest was soaked with a bib of blood. His hands rested at his sides, relaxed. Seth tried to reassure himself that it had been swift at least, but his guts rebelled, churning with regret. He fought to remain tall and upright when all he wanted to do was crouch and clutch his knees to his chest. "How did they manage to get so close to him?"

The boys shrugged. "We didn't see it."

"Find me someone who did."

He waited with Amon's body until the boys were back, with a Droughtlander man who'd joined them somewhere along the way.

"He got shot in the back of the leg and fell off his horse." The man heaved Amon gracelessly onto his side and pointed out the bullet hole. He stuck a finger in the ripped material of Amon's trousers. "See?"

"Don't touch him."

The man let go and Amon thumped back, supine again. "And when he fell they got his gun." The man twisted, pointing. "Back there on the first street they came in on."

"And they cut his neck," Seth finished with the obvious. The man nodded. "Thank you. You may go."

Now the boys stood at attention, waiting for orders.

"Give Commander Amon his own grave." Seth felt the threat of tears again. No, he would not cry. He thrust his hands behind his back and pinched the tender skin at his wrists hard, and then harder, until the pain surpassed the urge to cry.

"Go." The boys hesitated, uncertain. "Go! *Go now!*"

With his wrists still smarting and his heart hurting more than he'd ever admit, Seth rode out of the Key and galloped into the sunrise, heading back to his camp.

20

⚜

Eli thought the trip overland to the iodide depot should have been faster. Their horses should have gone farther before needing to rest. Their food should have kept. The sun should have eased its heat. Was this not a sacred mission? Shouldn't the highers bless it accordingly?

Instead, the horses had lagged after only a few hours, and couldn't travel in the daylight at all once they hit the plains on the eastern side of the mountains. And the saddlebags full of food went into a shallow stream when Mireille's horse rolled in the water, eager to cool himself. The horse would have rolled her right over too if she hadn't jumped off. Almost a week out, and they weren't even halfway there. And they were out of food. Not that any of them blamed the horse. He'd sniffed out the water and galloped for it, Bullet bounding after him, tail wagging. They would never have found water among the hoodoos; would never have even thought to look for it in the desert.

Travellers they'd passed, when they were back on the road, had told them there was a market ahead.

"We should see it on the horizon soon," Nappo said.

"Let's hope so." Mireille squinted in the dark. "Some lights, something."

Eli hadn't said much since losing the food. Mireille had told him he should go ahead and thank the highers for leading them to a much needed water supply at least. But losing the food? Eli didn't get it. What kind of lesson was that? He knew you could survive longer without food than water. Maybe that was it?

The market came into view over a small dip. Shaped like a wagon wheel, its covered lanes stretched out from the centre into the dusty plain. As they neared, the stallminders eyed them warily. Women and girls, old men and babies—everyone tracked the trio as they made their way to the market's centre.

"Where are the men?" Mireille made a point of looking for a boy their age, or a man who wasn't old. They hitched the horses and got down. "Half the stalls are shut up."

"They're off fighting." The man who spoke wasn't old, but he had no legs. He scooted toward them on a low cart he pushed with two sticks.

Eli perked up. "Have they been this way?"

"They?" The man arched an eyebrow. "Who do you mean?"

"The Triskelians," Nappo interrupted. "Or the Guard." There was no need for secrets now. "Have either come this way?"

"Well, the Guard skirted around." The man laughed. "Still worried about catching sicks, even now. The Triskelians came through over a week ago. Maybe ten days."

"Who was with them?" Eli asked. "A girl? Called Sabine."

"A girl?" The man smiled. "'Called Sabine,' he says, as if we've never heard of her!" When Eli didn't return the smile, the man continued. "We know who Sabine is here. We know who Seth is, too. And so we know who you are."

The friends shared a nervous look.

"Come, come." The man waved his hand at them and then scooted toward the plaza at the very centre. "Follow me. We'll be the best hosts you've had in the Droughtland. You must spend the day here with us. Tell us tales of Triban. And you ..." He waited for Eli to catch up, then tapped him with one of his sticks. "You can tell us stories of the Keyland, because soon stories will be all that's left."

"The Keys have fallen?" Eli had to jog to keep up. "Tell us everything."

"We've taken the Western, Northwestern, Southern, and Southeastern Keys."

"Yes!" Nappo punched his fist in the air.

"Wow." Eli tried to picture it: Droughtlanders storming the gates, scaling the walls, gunfire and bombs. Keylanders fighting, cowering, fleeing.

"That's amazing!" Mireille hugged Nappo.

All those people—people just like the ones he'd known growing up in the Eastern Key. People who didn't know better, who knew no other way of life. Innocent people. Nappo and Mireille and the man kept talking, but all Eli heard was a flat drone.

"Eli!" Nappo gave him a playful punch. "Are you even listening?"

"What?"

"Your sister is headed to the Eastern Key now." The crippled man grinned up at him. "Gathering people along the way, people hungry for Keyland blood."

"And Seth?"

"Conquered the Southeastern Key, last we heard."

Eli thought of Chancellor Southeast. The old woman had always been kind to him. He could imagine her standing at her window, watching it unfold below. What would become of her now, he had no idea. He would say a prayer for her, and hope that her tenacity would see her through.

"Good news, Eli, eh?" Nappo startled him out of his thoughts with a friendly slap on the back.

"So far, so good." The man reached up a hand toward Eli. "I'm Gogo." Eli stared at the man's dirty hand, its nails ground down to the beds. "Ah, no mind." Gogo dropped his hand. "Just showing off. I know a thing or two about how you do things in the Keyland. Pokin' fun."

"Let's get something straight, pal." Nappo grabbed the man's sticks from him and squatted. "He's no Keylander."

"Just having a little fun. Gimme."

"Show some respect." Nappo gave the sticks back. "This is Reverend Eli, brother to Sabine and Seth. Leader in his own right."

"Sure. Sure he is." Gogo nodded. "Only, we're not exactly a community of higher worshippers here."

"Eli, let's just get some provisions and keep going." Nappo gestured east. "We've got another two hours before the sun comes up."

"No, no." Gogo grabbed Eli's pants. "I meant no offence. Come on, let me be a good host. I'll take you to my brother's ale house. We'll drink, we'll eat. Maybe we'll play some cards. Okay?"

Eli lifted his eyes to Nappo, who was shaking his head. Mireille shrugged.

"It would be stupid to pass up a free meal," Eli said finally.

"Right!" Gogo clapped his hands. "Exactly. Okay then, let's go! You can even say grace over your mutton."

Nappo pulled Eli aside, out of Gogo's earshot. "We leave as soon as the sun goes down."

Mireille leaned in. "Earlier if we can."

"I don't like him any better than you do," Eli said. "But food is food, and I for one am not going to look a gift horse in the mouth."

Up from the centre of the plaza rose a thick pole that anchored a wooden pinwheel, from which stretched swaths of heavy fabric in a multicoloured canopy. The plaza floor was itself a patchwork of carpets, laid to keep the dust down. All around the open tent were hawkers' stalls boasting the sizzle of frying meat, the woody smell of roasting nuts. Eli's mouth was positively watering.

Gogo introduced his brother at the door to his ale house. "Come in, come in!" The man ushered them inside. "Everything is on the house."

Clearly, someone had spread the news about the Triskelians' arrival. Everyone in the place rose and started clapping and cheering.

"Long live Triskelia," the bartender boomed as he handed the trio their drinks. Then everyone joined in, glasses raised. "Long live Triskelia!"

They all wanted to know everything.... Where would Triskelia rebuild? Here, perhaps? Farther east? What was happening with the Keyland prisoners? When would their people return home? How could they get word to them? Was it true the Group of Keys had gone into hiding? Had Eli's father contacted any of his siblings to arrange a deal?

Eli had no answers, although he tried his best. How different it was now to travel openly as a Triskelian, with everyone knowing his family's story. The last time he'd been in a market out here he'd very nearly been killed. This time, he felt important. He felt like royalty.

WHEN THE SUN had set again and it was safe to set out, Eli roused Nappo from his stupor and helped him to his horse. Mireille laughed as Nappo tried once, twice, and then gave up swinging his foot up into the stirrup. He gave Eli a bleary-eyed smile.

"Gimme a hand, will ya?" His breath reeked of ale.

Eli locked his fingers together and gave Nappo a boost.

Their saddlebags were packed from supplies from the market people. They'd insisted on giving them as gifts, and refused payment whenever Eli pulled out the little pouch with the money Louis had sent them off with. They'd be good for the rest of the trip to the depot. After that, who knew?

WHEN ELI, Nappo, and Mireille finally reached the ridge above the depot they'd been travelling for almost two weeks. They'd passed only one other settlement on the way but had veered way south of it, not wanting to stop again.

They left the horses at the base. And now, side by side with Bullet trotting ahead, the three of them stinking to high heaven with more than a dozen days of sweat and grime, they crawled up toward the top of the ridge to await the dawn.

As the sun rose, a pillar of red rock sheltered them and served double duty as a hideout. The depot comprised a series of squat, drab bunkers behind an imposing fence patrolled by large black dogs with big blocky heads and barks to match. Eli had to keep ordering Bullet to lie down. Every time one of the dogs barked Bullet leapt to his feet, the fur along his back on end and his head lowered, ready to fight.

"I can't believe I'm doing this," Nappo said under his breath. He handed the spyglass to Mireille. "I must be crazy."

Eli let the comment slide. They were here. They'd carry out his ordained task. If he was right, they would free the weather, and if he was wrong, they'd be dead. He tried to feel sorry for himself—his life could end tragically here, on a doomed mission out in a sunbaked plain of dust, mercilessly torn apart by ravenous hounds—but he just couldn't see it. He trusted his vision. He trusted his highers.

"How did you know there'd be dogs?" Mireille rolled onto her back and handed the spyglass to Eli. He hadn't had a close look yet.

Eli had described the depot to Nappo and Mireille several times en route. He knew it inside and out, and he'd known about the dogs. "There are four of them, and one has a limp."

Mireille grabbed the spyglass back and had a look. "He's right."

"And from here you can see one of the doors. It's red, but the paint is peeling. There's a danger sign on it. And the numbers 387 below it."

Mireille gasped. "You're right, Eli!"

"Do you believe me now?"

Mireille lowered the spyglass. "I do." She offered him the spyglass, but he shook his head. "I don't need it."

"Maybe you're psychic," Mireille said.

"And that's easier to believe than the highers giving me a vision?"

"Yes. It is, actually."

Nappo was squinting at the depot now, the spyglass to his eyes. "The layout is exactly as you described it, too. There's even the pile of old fence sections like you said." Nappo nodded in amazement. "You were right about everything, Eli. Incredible."

"We wait until it's dark." Eli said it with renewed conviction. He felt puffed up and important now that his friends finally believed him. "Then we do as we'd planned. We should all try to get some sleep." He pushed himself up onto his knees and backed away from the ridge. You two coming?"

Mireille was gazing at him with equal parts confusion and admiration. "I'll stay up here for a little while longer."

"Me too." Nappo turned back to the depot with the spyglass.

Eli scuttled down the slope. He gave Bullet and himself some treated water, and then rolled out his sleeping bag right against the wall of the hoodoo, where it was cooler and would be in the shade for a few hours.

He thought he'd just lie there, anxiously going over and over the plan in his mind. Instead he fell fast asleep, and slept so hard that he woke up only when the sun was full on him. He glanced up the slope. No sign of Nappo or Mireille. With a yawn, Eli gathered up his bedroll and trudged around to the other side to follow the shade. As he turned away from the heat, he caught a glimpse of Nappo arranging his bag. Or so he thought. Another couple steps and he could see that Nappo was rolling away from Mireille, who was lying on her back, her hand at her throat, grinning at him. Eli pressed himself to the wall of the rock. His heart raced.

Nappo came around the corner just moments later. "Eli! I was just coming to wake you up and tell you to get out of the sun."

Eli gave himself a stern, silent lecture. Do not freak out. Do not say a word about it. Maybe it wasn't what you think. Maybe you've got it all wrong. You need these two and you need them to be alert. No distractions. No hard feelings. Do not mess this up. Trust that everything happens for a reason. A reason you might not be aware of.

Trust.

Trust.

"You okay?" Nappo took his bedroll from him.

"A little heatstroke. I'll be fine."

"I was asleep, or I would've come and woken you sooner."

"You were asleep." Eli followed him into the shade. Mireille was sitting up, hugging her knees.

"Eli! We were just coming to make sure you were up."

"Here I am."

"I'm famished." Mireille gathered her hair into a loose knot at the nape of her neck and rummaged in her pack. "I've got some halva left, and figs." She looked up, cheeks flushed. "You've got the jerky in your pack, Eli."

"I'll dig it out."

They sat together in the narrow wedge of shade, and then as it grew and there was room, Eli rolled out his bag and laid himself down away from the other two, his hands behind his head, working to keep his mind off what he'd seen. It shouldn't bother him so much. He'd already given up the idea of him and Mireille. But that didn't make the idea of Nappo and Mireille any easier.

HOURS PASSED, the shade stretched long, and when night finally fell Eli was still wrestling with his thoughts. Mireille and Nappo were sound asleep, Mireille curled onto her side, facing Eli, her hands under her cheeks, head resting on a sweater. Nappo lay on the far side of her, out of Eli's sight but certainly not out of mind.

As the stars shimmered above, winking awake, Eli sat up. They would do this together, and then they'd part ways.

Unity. It came as both a caution and command. *Unity.*

It would matter tonight, Eli reasoned. But not after that.

UP ON THE KNOLL AGAIN, everything at the depot was unchanged.

"Not a single person so far," Nappo said. "You don't think someone's been here before us?"

"Maybe they're busy inside," Mireille suggested. "Working."

Eli went over the details of the vision with them one more time. Bullet charges the front, causing the guard dogs to kick up a fuss, while Nappo and Eli scale the fence at the back and gain entry. Horrified by Nappo's skineater scars, the Guardies panic. After they surrender and the dogs are called off, Mireille is let in to deactivate the depot.

"I still say they won't surrender," Mireille said. And off she went down her list of concerns, as if repeating them for the umpteenth time would somehow change things. "Why would they? Why won't they just shoot us dead? They've got so much at stake: there's only that one other good source of iodide and it's already secondary to this one. And it's so far south it takes three times as long to ship it once it's extracted. Sure, we pay that transporter to have him skim off those shipments, but he says the supply is dwindling. And either he's lying or he's right, because we've been getting less and less over the last two years." Mireille paused for breath, and Eli waited for the final volley. "This is the *weather* we're talking about, Eli. This is about who owns the skies! There could be five hundred Guardies inside that building."

Eli, now as ever, had no logical response to her concerns, and he knew she wouldn't want to hear any more about his highers.

"I'm still willing," Nappo said with a shrug. "Get out the beet cream, let's make the scars look nice and fresh." Eli rummaged in his pack for the jar and handed it to Mireille.

"And what about Emma, Nappo?" Mireille dabbed Nappo's scars with the red paste, working it in gently along his old scars. "What about Teal?" Eli could see that now, at the final moment, Mireille was really getting scared and pulling out all the stops. "What *good* are you to them if you're *dead?*"

"I won't be dead." Nappo pulled away, his scars damp now, sticky with red. He dug in his pack and retrieved his gun. "And neither will you."

"Two against who *knows* how many?" She already had her rifle slung across her back.

"We fire first," Nappo said.

"You won't need to," Eli insisted. "Honestly."

"You take comfort in your vision, Reverend." Nappo checked the chambers, tucked his spare ammunition into the pouch on his belt. "And we'll take comfort in shooting first and asking the highers what went wrong later."

"Just promise me you won't fire if you don't have to."

"Self-defence only. We've talked about this. Okay?" Nappo pulled out a third gun and held it out to him. "Now, do me a favour and don't be a completely idiotic martyr."

"No violence." Eli shook his head. "I don't want it."

"Eli, come on, you can use the *threat* of violence. Intimidation, that's all." Nappo cracked open the chamber and tipped the bullets into his palm. "Not even loaded now. Happy?"

"Is the threat any better than the reality?"

"Eli!" Mireille raised her voice. "Now is not the time for philosophizing!"

"Listen to me, friend." Nappo gave him a dark look. "You got us out here, now let's just get on with it." He slung his own rifle across his back and started down the far side of the knoll. "Three lights, just like you said. Come on."

Just as in the vision, only three of the dozen torch lights were lit.

Eli and Mireille followed. The boys left Mireille some distance away while they carried on, half-crouching, toward the compound. Eli kept Bullet at a silent heel beside him until they were within fifteen metres of the fence, even though Bullet was trembling with excitement just at the scent of the depot dogs.

"Highers be with us now," Eli murmured. "See us through this safe and sound." He glanced up, half expecting to see the stars shift in acknowledgment, but the sky was calm, the stars twinkling in place, the moon hanging plump over the buildings.

Eli took a deep breath and braced himself.

"*Sic 'em!*" he ordered and released the dog. Bullet exploded from Eli's hold and tore off along the length of the fence, barking and snapping and leaping. The guard dogs, skinny and mangy as they were, slavered at the mouth and answered Bullet with their own menacing snarls, shoving their muzzles against the rusting chain link and pawing at it furiously.

Two more lights flared. Just as in the vision. Eli and Nappo raced for the rear of the compound. Eli tossed their rope up, missing the post he was aiming for. This was not in the vision. He yanked the rope back and tried again and missed.

"Highers, *please*," he pleaded. A door slammed, a man ran toward them with a holler, and just as Eli tossed the rope a third time, Nappo cocked his gun and pulled the trigger. The man reeled back and fell.

"No! What are you doing?" Eli tugged at the rope. It was secure. "I said no violence!"

"I'm doing the part that you can't do." Nappo handed Eli a length of cloth and the two wrapped their hands in anticipation of the barbed wire atop the fence. "Maybe that's why it was so important that I came."

The boys clambered up and dropped to the ground on the other side. Nappo cried out and clutched his ankle.

"Broken?" Eli asked, breathless. He was confused. So much of it was exactly what he'd been expecting, but so much else was coming as a surprise.

"Don't think so." Nappo straightened, not putting weight on the one side as two more men ran from around the side of the building. Nappo lifted his gun. Eli stepped in front of it.

"Don't."

With a fierce shove, Nappo pushed him aside. "I will, and you won't stop me, or I'll shoot you too."

"You wouldn't."

Raising the gun to his sights, Nappo took aim. "Now's not the time to test me, friend. I've got a daughter and a little brother to go home to." He limped forward, yelling, "Stay right there!"

"Wait!" The men stopped, waving their hands over their heads. "Don't shoot!"

"On the ground!" Nappo hobbled a few more steps.

Without argument, the men dropped and splayed themselves on the dirt. Eli and Nappo approached cautiously, until they were close enough to see the Guardy uniforms. They had no guns. Knives still in their sheaths and a club hanging from each of their belts, but no guns.

"Toss the knives and clubs," Eli said over the continuing din of the dogs. Glancing up, he spotted the guard dogs charging around the side of the far building and galloping through the dirt, headed straight for them. Bullet ran frantically along the fence on the outside, throwing himself at the chain link, trying desperately to put himself between Eli and danger. "Call them off!" Eli bellowed.

The men said nothing. With a wince, Nappo put his bad foot on the first man's back and the tip of his gun to the man's head. "Call them off!"

"He's got the skineater sick!"

"Call the dogs off or I blow your fucking brains out!"

"Dogs stand down!" the man shouted. "Dogs stand down!"

The dogs, all four of them, shut their barks into whines and lay down side by side, taut, waiting.

"Get up." Nappo jabbed the gun at the Guardy's neck. "You're going to secure the dogs." Nappo glared at Eli. Eli got the message. He fumbled for his empty gun and levelled it at the man still splayed on the ground.

As the first man ushered the dogs into a kennel at the side of the building, Eli questioned the second man.

"How many are there inside?"

"Get him away from us."

Nappo lunged forward. "Afraid you'll catch it?"

"Tell us!" Eli cocked the gun.

"Okay, okay. Four."

"That's all?"

"Yes!" The man lifted his head. "They're probably watching at the window."

All the lights had been extinguished, so Eli couldn't tell.

"Come out now, or we'll kill both of them!" he hollered as the first man came back. Nappo fired his gun into the air for effect, but still no movement came from inside. He cocked it again and aimed it right at the second man's gut.

"You've got until the count of ten!" Eli bellowed. "And if you don't come out by then, we shoot these two and bring in the rest of our soldiers to finish you off. And we'll make sure every one of you gets a hug from our friend with the skineater sick. This is your one chance to save yourselves!"

Mireille had climbed the fence and was coming up behind them. "If you don't come out now," she yelled, "we'll set the buildings on fire and the iodide will explode and there won't even be *bone shards* left to send back to your families!"

Eli waited a moment, and then started counting. "Ten, nine, eight ..." He was down to three when the door opened and the four men appeared.

"Throw down your weapons!" Nappo yelled. Guns and knives and clubs clattered onto the dirt. Mireille collected them, her own gun drawn.

"Why didn't you shoot?" she asked, incredulous, as she backed away.

"We ran out of bullets three weeks ago. People from the village got a little ahead of themselves," a man with hollow cheeks said. "Got a nice pile of corpses, if you want to see."

"And no one went for more supplies?" Mireille ushered the men into the clearing. "No one sent for help? I find that hard to believe."

The men said nothing.

"There are more of you in there, aren't there?" Mireille fired a shot between the legs of their spokesman. "You're lying to us, aren't you?"

"Stop!" The man shook his head. "We're telling the truth."

"Look at them," Eli said. "Closely."

The men's gaunt faces caught the shadows of the moonlight. Their uniforms hung off them as if they were two sizes two big. "Did the food run out then, too? Did your Guard forget you? Leave you here with nothing?"

"They're coming."

"So you *did* send for help."

"They could be here any minute."

"And so could your imaginary friends," Mireille said. "The truth is you've been abandoned, right? All the other Guardies are far, far away defending the Keys, right?"

The men stood in silence, chins up, eyes forward, trying to hold onto their dignity, if nothing else.

"You're probably hungry," Eli said. "Tell us the truth and we'll feed you."

"You won't."

Nappo strode up to him. "Funny thing is ..." The man stumbled back with a grimace. He fell. Nappo stood over him. "That he probably will. He's that kind of leader. Kind. A lot more forgiving than say, someone like ... Oh, I don't know." He squatted and cupped the man's face with his scarred hands. The man cried out, tried to wrestle away from him, but didn't have the energy to spare. "Me, for example."

Nappo jumped up then like a prize fighter in the ring. He bounced around, fists up. "Who else, huh? This is kinda fun."

"I'll talk!" The man at the end, cheeks hollow, eyes drooping, stuck up his hand. "You spare me the sick and I'll talk."

Mireille was mostly right. The last supply delivery never arrived. Whether it had been hijacked or rerouted to the Keys, the man didn't know. He was only two years out of the academy, so he wasn't in on all the details.

"It just didn't show," he said with a shrug.

"Show me to your kitchen," Eli said. The man limped ahead of him, led him to a huge room with three wood stoves and an empty walk-in cooler. "Is there water?"

The man shook his head.

Eli pulled out his own canteen and offered it to him along with the last of his hardtack. The man chewed slowly, wise to his stomach after who knows how long without food.

"Tell me the rest, and I'll feed the rest of your men." Eli glanced around. "A kitchen this size, there must've been hundreds of you at some point."

The man nodded. "When word came that they stormed the first Key, most of them took off to fight. Then others left when the food ran out. Then the water. We're the idiots who felt we should stay and protect the depot. We're the fools who thought they'd send for us. Keep us fed. Rotate us out with fresh troops." The man started to cry. "But they didn't! They left us here to die. Another couple of days and we were going to eat the rest of the dogs. We would've already, but they're our last real weapon. And now the depot is lost anyway."

"So the skies are free."

"Free? For you people to screw it all up? Waste good rain on the desert that won't grow anything anyway? We've got *two hundred years* invested in our projects."

"The heavens will decide where the rain will fall from now on," Eli said.

"No, *you* will."

Eli shook his head. "We're not staying here to extract the iodide. We don't want the iodide. We don't want *anyone* to have the resources to cloudseed. We're going to blow it up. Set the rain free once and for all."

21

❧

Sabine's plan to switch their horses at the transport-train stables had worked well—her troops had been able to advance almost constantly across the plain. Soon they'd be joining fighters amassed outside the market nearest the Eastern Key.

They had switched teams again that afternoon and kept going. Sabine had fallen asleep, her head bouncing against the wall of the caravan as it rumbled along. But now she awoke to an insistent tattooing on the wooden roof. Rain? Impossible out here. She unlatched the window and looked out. It *was* rain!

"Stop the coaches!" she cried out, waking up Jack and Trace as she did.

"What is it?" Trace instinctively reached for his gun.

"It's raining!" Sabine leapt out and spun, delighting in the cool drops hitting her dusty skin.

The convoy creaked to a stop, and soon everyone was out, marvelling at the shower.

"Rain or not, we need to keep going."

"Do you think someone sent it for us?" Sabine stuck out her tongue, tasting the plump drops. "Or is it some freak occurrence?

Up and down the line of carts and caravans her troops stared skyward, some stripping off their shirts, others dancing, arms out, cheering. And then it was a downpour, with whoops of delight as grown men stomped in the mud, tossing handfuls of it at each other like little boys.

Sabine was soaked to the skin now, her hair stuck to her head in long wet sections—for one who hadn't bathed in almost a month, it was the very definition of bliss. She stripped down to her underlinens and ran into the wide open plain. The wet earth was still hot underfoot, but the rain was gloriously cool. She turned her head up and let it fall on her face. A miracle. Maybe there *were* highers after all.

TWO NIGHTS LATER it rained again. And then it kept raining. Then it stopped. And then it rained again. Sabine and the others were awestruck—and thoroughly confused. Not in over a century had it rained like this in the Droughtland. Clouds filled the wide-open sky; entire fronts passed on random routes.

Then a messenger rode into the camp and told Sabine the wildest tale she'd ever heard. Eli, along with only Nappo and Mireille, had captured the main iodide depot and blown it up.

"*Our* Eli?"

The young boy standing tall inside her tent was covered in the filth of the road. He clutched his hat in his hands, thrilled to be the one to have brought the news.

"Yes. Your brother, right?"

"Yes ..."

"No way." Trace guffawed behind her. "*Reverend* Eli?"

"So they say." The boy's eyes darted with doubt. "I'm saying it just like they told me to."

"And who's *they*?" If the story had leapt from messenger to messenger, growing and mutating, it could surely have become this far-fetched bit of make-believe.

"Reverend Eli himself. Said it was a mission from his highers, which is how he knew they could do it, just the three of them. That's why it's been raining so much. It's true they blew it up, too. The mushroom cloud from the explosion was so big they could see it in the nearest village and that's over a day's ride away, Auntie."

"What did Reverend Eli look like?" She cocked her head at the boy. "Describe him, and maybe I'll believe you."

"Looks just like you, Auntie. And his friend has the scars, and the girl has long dark hair. And they have a dog called Bullet." The boy's eyes widened as Sabine's supper was brought in on a tray. With his gaze locked on the food, he continued. "And he had a medallion 'round his neck, with the symbol of Triskelia and all your names on it. Like yours."

"All right. Thank you." Sabine touched her own medallion. "Go ahead and eat."

The boy ripped into the chicken with his hands, scooped the stew up with a tear of bun, and chugged back the cider in one go.

"Our little pacifist." Jack started clapping. "Blowing up buildings. Well done."

"Hard to believe," Trace muttered, grinning nonetheless.

"Incredible!" Sabine laughed in sheer delight. Gentle Eli—freeing the continent's weather in one big bang! "But why didn't I think of it first?" She laughed again.

"Because it was sacred, Auntie. That's why." The boy looked up earnestly from his meal. "A sacred mission. He was called by his highers— like Joan of Arc." Now the boy smiled, pleased with his analogy.

"Hmm," Sabine said, amused. "Well, let's just hope he doesn't end up sharing her fate."

When the boy left, Sabine and the others didn't say anything for a long, stunned moment.

"It's for real." Sabine shook her head in renewed disbelief. "We have the weather back."

"It would appear that we do," Jack said, equally flabbergasted.

"And even more amazing," Trace chimed in, "is that it was Eli's doing."

"Wonders will never cease," Sabine said. "Wonder will *never* cease."

AS SABINE'S ARMY drew closer to the Eastern Key, more and more people joined. Makeshift camps, set up to wait for them, were dismantled as the convoy passed through, the Droughtlanders falling in behind. By the time they reached the market closest to the Key the forces they'd gathered stretched out in all directions, as far as the eye could see.

Along the way Sabine had organized the unruly masses into legions. Forty men and ten women were named captains, all having proved their strength and loyalty many times over. The captains in turn chose their own officers and corralled their assigned legion. Only then did the army seem manageable—Sabine would communicate with her chosen fifty, who would disseminate orders to their troops.

"What must they be thinking," Sabine grinned as the little market community came into sight, "to see a sea of people marching over this ridge like a storm rolling in?"

"Let's hope it has the same impact on the Key," Jack said.

Trumpets sounded, heralding their arrival. Sabine felt like a royal princess out of a fairy tale, so grand was their reception. The market people had set up a long silk canopy garlanded with crocheted flowers. Platters of food had been laid on long tables set on wooden planks over the mud. The market too had been blessed with rain.

"For you, Auntie!" The leader of the market was a tall woman, much older than Sabine, and so the term of affection sounded quite strange coming from her. With Zenith it had always sounded right—to most of her admirers, she'd been ancient. "We had no idea there would be so many," the woman said by way of an apology. "I am only sorry we cannot provide for them all."

Sabine gave her a warm smile. "I wouldn't have asked it of you, Rhyssa."

"Anything you need, Auntie." Rhyssa beamed. "Make yourself at home here."

"Thank you." Sabine took a seat halfway down one side of the table. Rhyssa looked at her funny. Jack cocked his chin toward the chair at the head of the table: the one draped with satin, with the Triskelian symbol embroidered on its cushion. "Oh. Of course." Sabine perched on the edge of it and ran her fingers over the symbol. *Sabine, Seth, Eli*—the names had been stitched atop the branches of the triangle, just as they'd been engraved on the medallions their grandfather had made.

Sabine felt a sudden constriction in her throat. "How did you know?"

"They say you each have one like this, right?" Rhyssa looked so pleased. "When we heard, I had my husband refinish this chair for you. And I did the embroidery myself."

"It's beautiful." Now Sabine felt a little uneasy. Was it right that everyone knew about the medallions? Were they courting danger by lifting up Sabine and her brothers like this, placing them on pedestals?

"And of course it's yours to have in your home when you set up New Triskelia."

"Thank you." Sabine tried to imagine this "New Triskelia" the people had started talking about. She summoned an image of a table, a hall, a fire ablaze in the hearth, but she could only imagine the ruins they'd left behind. "I'll send for it," she said softly. "Wherever we end up."

LATER, AFTER THE FEAST, Rhyssa took them on a tour of the little market. Jack and Trace walked on either side of Sabine, eyes ever watchful. The crowds that followed filled the narrow lanes, conducting a busy, boisterous commerce in the stalls.

They spoke, of course, of the weather, and the war.

From all directions people kept coming at Sabine, wishing her well, offering her teacakes, mugs of ale, and in one case an entire lamb with a bow around its neck and a bell that rang as it butted up against her.

"Back off!" Trace bellowed.

"It's all right," Sabine said. She took the lamb into her arms, not quite sure what to do with it. It was a generous gift, though, and she didn't want to offend. They carried on for another short distance, but she really was attracting too much attention. Her heart pounded hard every time the crowd surged toward her, and she clutched the lamb, who bawled in protest.

"I've had enough, I think." She apologized to Rhyssa. "Thank you for your hospitality, but this is a bit overwhelming."

"Ah, they're only thrilled to see you, Auntie." Rhyssa hustled her through a cobbler's berth and into a slender alley separating the back ends of two rows of stalls. "Only the stallminders back here. Much quieter." Rhyssa escorted them back to their camp this way, and then left them.

Now with only her dearest friends to see, Sabine fell gratefully onto her cot and exhaled noisily. "I'm exhausted." She draped her forearm across her brow. "There must be ten thousand people here! All milling around, waiting."

"That means twenty thousand hands to fight," Trace said. "Or less, if some of them only have one."

Jack laughed.

Sabine sat up. "Trace, did you just make a *joke?*"

Trace shrugged, but he was smiling. He pulled a stool up to the flap and parked himself there on self-appointed watch.

Tomorrow they would begin the last leg of their journey: a two-day ride to the Eastern Key. They would advance under cover—through the very tunnels Eli had taken when he fled.

They'd received word that another camp of Droughtlanders was already waiting for them outside the Key walls, on its south side. Meanwhile, the Guard—now tripled in number—had set up on its north side, regiments arriving piecemeal from the other fallen capitals: Western. Northwestern. Southern. Southeastern. All had fallen.

The Eastern Key was the last one standing. The Guard, Sabine had no doubt, would fight to the death for it.

She leaned back in her cot, listening to the revellers outside, hooting and whooping in their frenzied excitement. The throngs were straining for battle: a great multitude of Droughtlanders who had nothing to lose.

"We should just storm it," she said suddenly.

"What?" Jack frowned. "But we agreed: the tunnel will give us cover. The Guard won't be warned of our approach. Surprise attack: it's the only sensible way."

Sabine shook her head. "The people want to storm it, so why not let them?"

"They'll fall like so many matchsticks," Trace said from the door flap.

"They likely will anyway." Sabine didn't like to think of it, but it was true. "And at least they'd be going into battle in a way that's true to themselves." She paused, staring resolutely at the swaying canvas above her. "It's their revolution, not ours."

Now she stood and went to the door. Their tent was set well back, but still had a view of the west side of the market. A row of hawkers formed the outside edge of its official boundaries, although it was much more swollen now. The aromas from their enormous kettles and clay ovens lifted over the sea of people. Across from Sabine's tent a launderer was hanging a basket of clothes. A little girl stood at his side, handing him pegs from the bulging pockets of her apron. The wind was stiff, and he wrestled to secure the pins. The clothes snapped and danced toward the east.

Jack stroked his biceps reflectively. "It *would* be quicker overland," he said. "Half a day."

"Can't travel during the day," Trace said. "Too hot, genius."

"We can if it's raining." Sabine stepped out and looked west. A bank of dark clouds was pushing their way. "And it looks like it will be. Thanks to Eli."

Trace stood. "I'll send word for the legion captains to gather."

BY THE TIME all fifty captains had assembled the sun had set. It was cooler now; clouds had settled overhead, bringing a swift breeze with them.

Sabine laid out the new battle plan and told the captains to be ready to set off at sunrise.

"With all due respect, Auntie?" A man with a long beard stood, his hand up. "During the day?"

"If this front stays overhead, we'll be fine."

"Catch them by surprise," the bearded man said, grinning.

"They won't be expecting us to attack in broad daylight." Sabine looked calmly out at the group of captains.

The men and women looked at one another, nodding their assent. Some raised their eyebrows in mild surprise. This slip of a girl *did* have a mind made for revolution.

Now the captains fanned out to inform their legions. They would leave first thing in the morning. "I'd advise you all to get a good night's sleep!" Sabine called after them. "It will be your last for a while."

Trace tapped her on the shoulder. "A good night's sleep? What are you, their mommy?"

"Sounded just like Zenith there, *Auntie*." Jack took her hand to lead her back to the tent. "You can pretty much bet that they'll be up all night, wired and ready, playing Seduce to wile away the hours."

"Well, I for one," Sabine said, putting on airs, "will sleep like a lamb. Or, um, with the lamb."

BUT SHE COULDN'T SLEEP, and neither could Trace or Jack. And, having checked that Stephane had his lifeminder cart in order and his helpers ready to leave, they did end up playing a short hand of Seduce in the tent, by lantern light.

They didn't say much. Sabine's thoughts were careening every which way, eventually bumping head first into the inevitable.

"Where do you think we go when we die?"

"Heaven," Trace said firmly. "To your highers. Where else?"

She picked up a card. "But where is that exactly?"

"You're not going to die," Jack said. "The rest of us, maybe. But not you."

"She might," Trace said.

She might. Die. Sabine rubbed her arms against a sudden chill. "Do you wonder about heaven, Trace?"

"It's a good place," he said with a catch in his throat, Charis ever in his thoughts. "A holy place. Peaceful. Plentiful."

"You are not going to die." Jack lifted her hand and gave it a quick kiss. "I promise."

But she didn't want to be placated. Sabine pulled her hand away. "Do you think we end up somewhere where we can look down on all this? Like flipping the pages in a picture book, or watching a play?"

"Yes," Trace said.

Jack shook his head. "I don't know."

"I'm sure of it." Trace nodded, his face set with determination. "Charis is up there being looked after by Zenith herself, ever busy quilting her baby blankets." Trace touched the small painting of his daughter he wore on a leather cord around his neck. "And Quinn and Gavin teaching her the circus arts. Only cloud to cloud, and they don't need any trapeze because they can fly."

Jack and Sabine shared a glance. It was odd hearing something so sentimental from Trace, even about Charis.

"You have to believe it, or else it doesn't exist." Trace laid down his hand with a slap, the Queen of Hearts lying atop a spread of aces. "I win."

While Jack shuffled the cards and dealt again, Sabine tried to imagine a place where Jack's two lovers were swinging a giggling Charis between them while Zenith sat in her rocker working on a quilt and Papa grumbled about the state of things as he packed his pipe with tobacco. It was so preposterous that she almost laughed. Still, she hoped she was wrong. Because then Quinn and the others would have a family up there. They wouldn't be alone. And maybe, if she did die, she'd join them. Would that be so bad?

Suddenly a gust of wind cut into the tent, scattering the cards from the overturned crate they were using as a table. The patter of rain sounded on the roof, the canvas darkening in splotches as it dampened.

"How can you *not* believe in the highers?" Trace said with a grin. A sheet of lightning brightened the sky. Thunder followed shortly, rumbling the ground under their feet.

"Hello?" A woman's voice came from outside the flap. Trace leapt up, hand hovering above his gun, and went out to speak to her. Moments later he led her in. She had a long brown braid and skin the colour of wet Droughtland earth.

"She says she knows Eli," Trace said by way of introduction.

"I'm Gidah." The girl curtsied.

"No need for that," Sabine said with a smile. "You're among friends."

"If I could just be forward and say, Wow, do you two ever look alike."

"Come, sit."

Gidah settled herself nervously on a stool. "I helped Eli when he first got out here."

"Oh! He told me about you. Our mother is buried in your village. You're a herbminder, right?"

"Only an apprentice, really."

Sabine offered her the bowl of nuts.

"No thank you." Gidah blushed. "I couldn't eat a thing, my stomach's all in a flap meeting you."

"The curtsy ... Eli told me you have a bit of a crush on the Keyland—"

"No, no." Gidah's blush deepened. "When I was a little girl, because of the dresses and parasols and fancy talk, but I'm over it now."

"And you have a cousin in the Key?"

"Yes, that's why I'm here: my cousin Gulzar. He works for your father."

Sabine bristled at the word. He wasn't her father. Not really.

"Gulzar and one of the maids—her name's Francie—they're both rebels and they're both still there. They're to be married—when all this is over."

"We'll see they're kept safe," Sabine said.

"That's not what I came about, but thank you. I know they can take care of themselves. I came about the baby."

"Your cousin's baby?"

"Your father's baby."

"What?" Sabine's gut twisted into a knot. She stared at Gidah, speechless. "What baby?"

"I brought someone else, who can tell you more." Gidah waved for a man standing by the flap to come in. "He worked in the laundry at the estate, took off through the tunnel two weeks ago."

"Auntie," the man mumbled, his chin ducked respectfully. "It's an honour."

"Tell her," Gidah urged, seeing Sabine's eyes darting in confusion.

"It's a boy, about ... maybe five months old? Something like that?"

"The mother is ... ," Sabine rummaged through all that Eli had told her so long ago. "Allegra. Right?"

Another nod.

"What's the baby's name?"

"Charles, after the ex-Chancellor."

"This is news. Thank you for telling me," Sabine whispered. She thought quickly, her mind whirling. With fifty legions of a thousand fighters each and countless hangers-on, there was no way to get word to them all to keep an eye out for one lone baby. She could alert the captains, but beyond that there was no hope of saving this little boy, her very own half-brother. She could only hope to get to him first. Sabine took a deep breath to steady herself. "He lives at the Maddox estate, of course?"

"Yes. Under the care of a nanny mostly. Sleeps in the nursery. Second floor, west corner."

"Thank you again ..."

"Miles," Gidah supplied.

"Thank you. Miles." Sabine smiled, not wanting to let on how upset she was. "You're coming with us in the morning?"

"Yes. Up at the front, if I can."

"Best of luck."

"You too, Auntie. May the highers keep an eye on you."

"We'll leave you now." Gidah could tell that the revelation had hit hard.

"Gidah ..." Sabine called after her. "Our lifeminder carts will be bringing up the rear. We'd be honoured if you'd join them. Contribute your herbminder skills."

"I will," she said, her face suddenly beaming with pride. "We'll see you after."

"Yes. Take care."

"And you also." With a little wave, Gidah and the man left the trio alone once more.

AS THE RAIN pounded down harder, Jack silently fiddled with the deck of cards. Trace drummed his fingers on the crate. Sabine's brow furrowed as she thought hard.

"We have to find him," she said finally.

"They won't be at the house. That's too easy."

"We'll gather the captains again," Jack suggested.

"Sure," Trace said with a laugh. "*You* try rounding up fifty people partying like it's their last day alive."

"I want that baby kept safe."

"And so do I," Trace said. "But you have to realize that we might not get to him in time. We can only hope he's taken prisoner. Our people wouldn't kill a baby, Sabine. You know that."

"I don't," Jack said. "Actually, I don't think we're really holding the reins any more." He shuffled out another hand of Seduce, but none of them wanted to play.

Eli dug his heels into his horse's flank, urging him to go faster. Mireille and Nappo rode on either side, the three horses kicking up the mud as the rain fell. When a crack of thunder boomed ahead Nappo's horse reared up with a terrified whinny, his nostrils flaring.

"We should camp!" Nappo shouted. "The horses are terrified of the storm!"

"You can camp if you want." Eli snapped his reins. "Hee-*yah!*" With his other hand he held tight to Bullet draped over his lap.

"Stop!" Mireille cried.

Eli didn't want to stop. He was as compelled to go east now as he'd been to destroy the depot. The relentless drive that drew him forward wasn't coming from his highers this time, though: it came from his sister. It was ... a pulling. As if he were at one end of a thick, taut, insistent rope and had no other choice.

After they'd set off the explosion he'd told Nappo and Mireille that he would continue on to meet Sabine at the Eastern Key. They'd tried to convince him to return to Cascadia, but Eli would not waver. And then Nappo and Mireille had chosen to ride with him. Nappo out of a sense of obligation, no doubt. And Mireille? Eli wasn't sure. To be with Nappo? For the adventure? To avoid looking after Rainy?

"Stop!" Mireille screamed again.

Eli eased up until his horse stood still, panting hard, coat slick with lather. Steam from sweat and rain lifted off him as if he were a ghost.

"Look, we have to camp sooner or later," Nappo called out as they approached. "Even bullet is too tired to keep going."

"You two can do whatever you want—"

"How long are you going to pout?" Mireille said, bringing her horse up beside Eli's. "We've both said we're sorry. We didn't mean to hook up!

It just happened. I'm a horrible person, I get that, but even horrible people need to rest!"

"I'm not stopping."

"Just for a couple of hours," Nappo urged. "Come on, we'll have something to eat, catch a bit of shut-eye."

"I'll see you there." Eli pulled the reins taut. "May the highers be with you."

He rode off, half-expecting them to follow. He wasn't surprised, though, when an hour later he was still alone with his dog and horse.

Eli galloped on furiously through the night, for no reason he could ever have put into words.

THREE

THE EASTERN KEY

22

ance and his men veered as far north as they could without losing too much time. Now they joined the road again above the Eastern Key and thundered up between Guardy camps sure to rival the Droughtlanders' on the other side. The troops stretched out for the last ten kilometres at least. There had to be tens of thousands of them.

The canvas tents set up in proper rows, the men in their crisp Guard uniforms and ready to fight at any moment—the very sight steeled Vance's resolve. He would not let Chancellor East give this last Key to his children, if that's what he had in mind. Vance would personally see to it that Edmund's hands were tied. Literally, if it came to that.

Vance and his men were let into the Key just after nightfall, the rain still falling steadily. Vance broke away at once, cutting across the quiet streets and well-trimmed lawns and drawing up to the front of the Maddox estate within minutes. He burst through the front door without so much as a knock.

"Where are you?" he bellowed. "If your people haven't jailed you by now, I'll do it myself, you son of a bitch!"

"Sir!" Francie hurried down the hall. "Can I help you, sir?"

Vance grabbed her arm. "Where is your master?"

"I'm here," Edmund said from the top of the stairs. "No need to shout."

Vance cast Francie aside with a shove and took the stairs two at a time. He pinned Edmund against the wall, his hand at his throat.

"Tell me the truth," he growled. "Or I will snap your neck right now."

Edmund's face grew red then deepened to purple as Vance leaned on his windpipe.

A baby cried behind them. Vance turned his head. Allegra stood at the foot of the next set of stairs, the baby in her arms.

"Release him."

Vance dropped his hand. "We have business, your husband and I."

Edmund clutched at his throat and gulped for air.

"Not like that, you don't." Allegra's tone was as cool as each word was sharp. "Not in my house. Not in front of my child. Not at a time like this."

"My office," Edmund croaked.

Allegra followed the men downstairs and took a seat on the couch. "I'm staying," she said firmly when Edmund made to protest.

"She stays," Vance concurred.

Edmund turned to him haughtily. "You're wondering why I'm still Chancellor," he began.

"I know why you're still Chancellor." Vance leaned forward, practically spitting as he spoke. "Because you sabotaged the ceasefire, which set off a cata*strophic* series of events that has brought us here." He pounded a fist on the desk. "Right here, today. With two Chancellors prisoners of your son Seth. And the others dead. There is no Group of Keys left to force you to stand trial in a Chancellors' Court. Which had to have been your intention."

"And you propose what?" Edmund leaned back, his face pale. "To kill me now? Never mind a trial?"

"I want the *truth*."

"The truth," Allegra said from the couch, "is that his first wife was the traitor, not him. The truth is that he had no idea about the third child. The truth is that you are a fool if you think you can find a more loyal Keylander in all the world than Chancellor East. This mess was inevitable. My husband's only mistake is that he tried to manage it in isolation." Charlie started fussing. Without missing a beat, Allegra stood and swayed with the baby, soothing him. "He is guilty of ignorance, and arrogance. But I can tell you now, Commander Vance, that he would sooner be willing to kill Seth and Eli and that ... awful *Sabine* with his own bare hands than give over the Eastern Key to Triskelia."

Edmund watched Vance's face while Allegra lectured him. Not a single muscle twitched.

"As granddaughter of the ex-Chancellor, I give you my solemn and respected word that Edmund is—and has always been—a true, if not always honourable, Keyland patriot," Allegra went on. "It is not his fault that we have a legion of rebels trying to topple us on one side and a legion of Guard trying to hold it all up on the other. We are the last stand. And we all can admit, I think, in the privacy of this room, that this has been a long, *long* time coming."

Vance stood. He leaned over Edmund's desk until he was only inches away from his face. Beads of sweat rolled down Edmund's forehead. "And what do you have to say for yourself, or does your *wife* always speak for you?"

"Everything she says is true." Edmund pulled back. "I had no idea who Lisette was when we married. She was already pregnant. By me, yes. But I knew nothing of the third baby. She sent her away to be raised by the rebels."

"Ah ha!" Vance slammed his hand down on the desk. "So Sabine *is* your daughter. And still you take no blame? None at all?"

"I take responsibility for not having control over my household." Edmund rose up, met Vance face to face. "I take responsibility for my poor choice of a first wife. I regret having let her make such a fool of me. But I am no traitor."

Vance strode away from him. He yanked aside the drapes and looked out across the moonlit lawn to the Key centre, lights ablaze in windows, and then the wall beyond that. "And what do your people make of you?"

Allegra spoke first. "They're confused—"

"I want Edmund's answer." Vance unlatched the windows and pushed them open.

"They don't know what to think. The rumours are rampant."

"They think you are a traitor."

"Likely."

"And if you're not?"

"I can only hope they have the chance to live to realize it."

"When we come out of this triumphant, you will stand in front of the Chancellors' Court. As soon as they are freed."

"I will."

"I will see to it myself. Even if you flee, I will hunt you down and bring you in. You will let them decide your fate."

"So be it."

Vance gripped the window sash and leaned out. He took a deep breath. "I can smell them. The Droughtlanders. Carried on the wind and the rain. It's as if every drop of it slings in a drop of their disease, their desperation." Vance took a step back. "Con*found* this rain!"

EDMUND KNOCKED LIGHTLY on the bedroom door before opening it. Allegra sat at the window, looking out at the rain. He let a small smile shape his lips. He understood the lure of the wide, open sky, the possibilities it seemed to offer.

"We should flee." Allegra shook her head and pressed her hand against the window. "They're out there, I can hear them, howling like wolves."

He could hear them, too. Just barely, across the distance and despite the rain. It was a dull thrum, as though they were out there with drums, banging away like savages. He wouldn't be surprised if they were doing just that.

"It's just the rain." Edmund crossed to the bed where Charlie lay asleep, one fist curled under his chin, the other flung over his head. And yet there should be no rain. This week's schedule had been set ages ago. Everything was out of whack, and the weather worst of all.

"Don't lie to me!" Allegra practically shouted. The baby stirred and she brought her voice to a whisper. "Not now. Not after how I stood up to him for you."

"I'm *not* lying." Edmund joined Allegra by the window. "It *is* just the weather."

The sky, as if on cue, suddenly hurled the rain down with added vigour, slapping it against the window. The wind kicked up and throttled the trees at the edge of the estate.

"We should flee." She shook her head. "You're wrong about staying. I am not an idiot, Edmund." She stared at him, eyes bright with fear. "We must *go*."

"Like some of the others have? Straight into the clutches of the Droughtlanders? How do you think they've fared, Allegra? Imagine the punishment. Imagine the sicks, if nothing else."

She held her stare, harder at the edges. "We might have a chance out there. Try to blend in until it blows over. At least that way we'd be alive."

"We can't leave now," Edmund said flatly. "The time for that has passed."

"Anything ... *anything* is better than this waiting." She dropped her hands to her lap. "This is horrible." She shook her head. "You have failed us all, Edmund. You have failed."

Edmund looked at his hand on his wife's shoulder. He wanted to dig his fingers in until they left marks. He wanted to grip the other one too and shake her until she was silenced. Instead, he flexed his fingers one at a time and then let them rest again, still gently, on her shoulder.

"You should try to get some sleep." Jaw clenched, Edmund returned to the bed, lay down, and shut his eyes. Allegra's skirts rustled as she crossed the room to stand over him.

"I should have left with the Chenowyths when the first Key fell. They offered to take me with them, you know. What a fool I was to turn them down."

Edmund snapped his eyes open.

"Your friends the Chenowyths made it out." Edmund rolled toward Allegra and took hold of the baby's leg. "This is true."

"What do you know?" Allegra calculated Edmund's tone, his firm hold on the baby. "What aren't you telling me?"

"They were captured by the Droughtlanders, not a day's ride away."

"You're lying."

"I'm telling you the truth. Had you gone with them you would be dead. And my son, too."

Between them, the baby simpered. Another moment and his face crumpled into a grimace and he started to cry.

"Let go," Allegra growled. "You're hurting him."

"Allegra, listen to me." Edmund sat up. "There is simply nowhere to go. Do you want to risk the sicks? I've done all the thinking I can do on the subject and this is the best I have to offer."

Edmund laid out his plan: to hide, to ride out the worst of the battle, in the sewer.

"The *sewer?*" Allegra glowered at Edmund. Her voice rose despite herself. "To wallow in feces? What kind of plan is that?"

With a sigh, Edmund closed his eyes. "A singular plan, the benefits of which are clearly lost on you."

"You are right there." Allegra stomped out of the room. Francie had just passed and was on her way back down the stairs.

"Francie, wait!"

"Ma'am?" Francie turned back, her cheeks flushed. Heart beating. She'd overheard it all. She arranged herself in a deep curtsy, trying to calm herself. She'd only just lifted her ear away from the door when the handle turned and Allegra came out.

"You may rise," Allegra said now.

Francie straightened.

Allegra handed Charlie to her. He'd stopped crying and was happy to find himself in Francie's arms. He reached out, locked her collar in his fist, babbling happily.

"Find Nanny and have her bathe him. The highers know it may be his last. I'll be in the drawing room. Nanny can bring him to me there."

"Yes, ma'am," Francie said with a more modest curtsy.

"Turn the sheets down in the lavender suite." Allegra gave a distracted wave of her hand. "I shall sleep there tonight. Bring in his crib, too. I want him close to me."

"Yes, ma'am."

When Allegra had turned on the landing and was out of sight, Francie cooed at Charlie. "We'll keep you safe, little man. Don't you worry." She gave him a kiss on each cheek, settled him in her arms, and headed off to find Nanny, and then Gulzar.

It had rained all through the night. That was good news: it quelled the heat; and bad news: the ground was now a sea of mud. Sabine rose just before dawn and got dressed slowly. Fresh underlinen—Rhyssa had arranged for the laundering—leggings and tunic, socks, boots. Leather cuffs to protect her forearms. She had a helmet and a cumbersome leather vest, but she would wait to put those on.

"You decent?" Trace waited for her reply before he entered. "Brought you this." A coat hung over his arm, brown and waxy. A horseminder's coat from the other side of the mountains. Rain proof.

"Where'd you find that out here?"

"I didn't. Bloke chucked it at me. Said it was for you." He held it up and she slipped her arms in.

"Very generous." She had to roll up the sleeves three times to get the right length. The shoulders hung halfway down to her elbows, and it nearly dragged on the floor. "I feel like I'm a kid playing dress-up."

"Figured as much." Trace pulled his knife from his belt and sized off the extra material at the sleeves and hem.

"Hope he doesn't want it back."

"We could do your belt up on the outside," Trace said. "To cinch it in. Once you've got your vest on."

Sabine felt a sudden wash of sadness flood over her. She gripped Trace's hand and looked at him with wide, wet eyes.

He folded her to him in a tight hug. Sabine closed her eyes and breathed in the stink of him. She could hear his heart beat, feel the rise of his chest against her.

"Now then, Auntie." Trace kissed the top of her head. "It is time to go."

23

❧

In the far distance, the Eastern Key looked very much like Triskelia had from the ridge above the Colony of the Sicks. The mass of Droughtlanders spreading away from it stood in for the Colony's messy streets, while the Star Chamber jutting up in its centre resembled the rebels' former home. Seth ordered the driver to stop. He jumped out of the cart and gazed at the vista as the rain pounded down. Sabine had done it. All these people were gathered to fight for her.

He looked back and marvelled at his own troops, thousands strong, who had followed him across the plains after the Northwestern Key along with so many more who'd fallen in along the way. Still, it was nothing compared with the numbers Sabine had amassed to fight this final battle.

Like Eli, Seth had pushed hard to get here, propelled onward from deep within his gut as if it were a command.

And now he knew why. A black line appeared to the southeast. Other soldiers now gathered around him, watching as it progressed. Ori and Finn pushed through until they were at his side.

"What's going on, Commander Seth?"

"Sabine's army. They're advancing on the Key." He spun, determination steeling his gaze. "To battle, soldiers!"

A cheer rose up from the ranks, spreading back like a wave.

Seth traded the cart for the nearest, strongest horse. He settled himself in the saddle and then kicked his heels in. *"Charge!"*

A battle cry erupted up from his troops, fists and guns and machetes thrust in the air as they rushed to follow, the ones on horseback keeping up, the carts and caravans falling in behind, those on foot bringing up the rear. Just as Seth had calculated, he and his soldiers would arrive just in time to take over when Sabine's fighters were too fatigued to carry on. His troops would capture the Key. He would claim victory.

The walls of the Key had finally come into sight. Sabine drew up at the outskirts of the makeshift Droughtlander camp, the fifty legion captains gathering around her.

"Rouse them," she ordered.

The captains rode off to send their men into the camp. Despite the waterproof coat, despite the stifling hot humidity, Sabine felt a chill right down to her bones.

Jack and Trace both saw her shiver.

"We'll be right beside you," Jack said.

"I know." She stood up in her stirrups, scanning the crowd.

"You have thousands of people here, ready to fight for you."

"I'm looking for someone specific, actually." She squinted, but with the rain, and the steam rising off the mass of people like a fog, she couldn't see much. "I have a feeling that Eli and Seth are here."

Before she could explain, the Droughtlanders behind them came to life as one massive beast, roaring out a terrible, guttural cry—a dragon woken from slumber.

"Whether they are or not," Trace yelled above the din, "there's no time to start looking now!"

Jack pulled his horse up closer to hers and tapped his chest. "You've still got to put your vest on."

Around them, fighters pushed forward, angry and oblivious, until someone shouted her name.

"Sabine! Sabine!" they chanted as they passed her. Jabbing their weapons into the air. "Sabine! Sabine! Sabine!"

She shucked off the horseminder's coat and buckled up her vest. It was too hot, too humid, and she wanted to be able to move easily. A glance to the skies, willing the rain to stop. The supply carts had fallen way behind, getting mired in the mud. They would need the ammunition they carried. They would need the lifeminder's equipment, the food.

"I ordered the advance in one hour!" She turned to Trace in dismay as the fighters pushed past her.

The chanting changed. "Kill the Key! Kill the Key!"

"We need the carts to catch up!"

"There's no stopping it, Sabine." Trace shook his head. "Not now. Not even if you tried."

"This is bigger than you," Jack wiped a splash of mud off his face with the back of his hand. "Bigger than all of us. Bigger than Triskelia."

Sabine set her jaw. "And so it is. Let's go!" She kicked in her heels, driving her horse through the tight, furious crowd.

THE CAPTAINS had managed to hold their fighters in formation. Sabine could see the legions fan out as they neared the wall, ten flanking off to the west, another ten to the east, and the rest marching north, straight forward. But their progression halted, and within minutes, Sabine realized why. The Guard was pushing from the northeast side of the Key, driving them back.

Suddenly everything felt suspended, as if the highers had levitated them all just inches above the ground for a long, collective moment of graceful weightlessness. Then, with a wrenching blast of cannon fire, they were slammed back down into the mud.

Sabine was momentarily transfixed by the sight of bodies flying through the air. They were like Night Circus acrobats—but aloft in a grim purpose not their own. The cannon had exploded its charge from the top of the Key's wall right into the troops at the front. She gritted her teeth and drove forward.

The battle had begun.

The rain was like bullets ricocheting off her helmet. A sheet of lightning cracked to the south, followed by a boom of thunder that rolled over the battlefield like a curse. Mud sprayed where bullets landed. Sabine's horse reared up as the one in front of her fell to the ground, taking the rider with it. Sabine stopped short as the man writhed in the mud, clutching at his chest. Trace grabbed her reins and yanked her away as another volley of gunfire arced overhead.

"Jack!" she called behind her. When she looked back again he was nearing her side.

Sabine clutched the reins with one gloved hand and her gun in the other. Not twenty metres ahead Guards and Droughtlanders were locked like elk, their antlers tangled. Gunfire was as steady as the pounding rain, cannon blasts as frequent as the thunder.

"Duck!" Jack yelled as a cannonball whistled overhead, shot from behind. It exploded just into the Guard side, scattering the men like sticks of kindling.

"Your carts have arrived," Trace hollered as another cannon cracked above.

Now a volley of cannons blasted the Guardy hold at the gate. And with a sudden, frantic surge forward, the Droughtlanders at the front stormed into the Key, sucking in those behind them as if a dam had broken and there was nowhere else to go.

"Trace!" Sabine screamed over the stampede. "Go left! *Left!*" She kicked her horse and bent forward, urging him to follow Trace, who'd managed to cut away. Sabine kept an eye on the glint of his helmet and could only hope that Jack was doing the same. She fought her way against the push of fighters, and only slowed when the crowd thinned enough to let her.

"The legions on this side have gotten farther than the others," she panted out. "We'll go through the service gate."

Sabine could just make out the cut in the wall that marked the service entrance. She pushed forward alongside the legion fighters, forming an enormous scrum.

The front line was well beyond the main gate now, forcing the Guard back as they advanced.

Now a cart bearing a cannon rolled through the throngs nearing the service gate, stopping only a metre away. A legion captain bent over its fuse.

He straightened, waving two red flags furiously over his head. "Cover!"

Sabine fell back and crouched down along with the others as the fuse was lit. The blast blew a great hole into the wall, sending a rain of stone over them. The worst had blown through into the Key side, killing the dozen Guardies who'd been firing from atop that section of wall. Like a flood forcing a new course, Droughtlanders poured through the jagged gap.

"Stay close," Trace instructed Sabine and Jack at the mouth of the hole.

They urged their horses past the Guardies killed in the blast. Blood mixed with mud, creating a gruesome soup. The horses' hooves sank in it but they scrambled for purchase, kicked up the muck, and galloped on.

A bullet whizzed past Sabine's ear, so close she could feel its heat. She raised her gun and cried out. A Guardy was running toward her. Sabine took aim, fired, and he fell forward into the mud. Now three more, and then still more, stumbled into view behind him. Sabine fired off furious rounds, panicky now, spraying gunshots into the Guard's advance. Jack and Trace let loose their own fire, and one by one, even as the bullets zinged in her direction, she watched the Guardies fall.

When it was briefly safe again, she twisted in her saddle to see Jack bent over, clutching his side. Blood oozed between his fingers.

Sabine leapt off her horse and ran to him as he eased himself to the ground. She loosened his buckles, but he pushed her away with his other hand. "I'll be fine," he said through gritted teeth.

Trace dropped to his knees in the mud and started searching for the wound in Jack's side. "You're not fine."

Sabine looked around, frantic for somewhere to take cover. Suddenly she heard a voice behind her. "I saw what happened, Auntie." The Droughtlander spoke urgently. "Follow me. Our safehouse is close. Our battle headquarters. Come quickly!"

The Droughtlander led them into a nearby estate, its windows blown out and its front half collapsing onto the absurdly manicured lawn. Another Droughtlander led them down a luxurious corridor at the rear.

"The battle's moved into the Key centre," he said as they followed him into a spacious kitchen. A knot of rebels turned to the newcomers, gaping at Sabine. "You're safe here for the moment," the Droughtlander continued, "until the Guard give up outside the walls and move in."

Now Jack sagged his shoulders and crumpled against a filigreed tea wagon that stood near the doorway. While Trace steadied him, Sabine unfastened his vest and tugged it off.

Jack shook his head, keeping his hand tight over the wound. "It'll stop bleeding soon." His breath caught in his throat. "Just leave it."

Trace yanked Jack's hand away. Sabine pulled his shirt up and gasped. Blood pumped from a hole at his side.

"Get me a towel!"

The Droughtlander rushed for a clean dishcloth and she pressed it to the wound, feeling the crunch of broken ribs as she did.

"I'll stay with you." Tears coursed down Sabine's cheeks.

Jack laughed, his face pale. "You can't run a war from in here. You—" Jack coughed wetly. "You have to go." He coughed again, and then spat onto the floor. Blood. He was bleeding badly inside.

"Jack!" Sabine stared in horror at the red stain. "We have to get you help!"

A commotion sounded at the door, and now another Droughtlander burst into the room.

"He's here! Commander Seth and his army!"

"What?" Sabine turned.

"Advancing on the Key as we speak!" The messenger was breathless. "Thousands of soldiers! And the Guard—they've seen the advance—they're heading out to stop them!"

Sabine's mind whirled. Seth and his army. It would mean everything. Together, their forces joined, they would have a chance. "Bring him to me. And his lifeminder. At once!"

Trace sprang toward the Droughtlander. "I'll go with you," he barked, hustling the man out into the hall.

Sabine's heart pounded as she sat on the floor with Jack curled up beside her, his head on her lap. She kept a hand on the cloth over his wound and watched his chest rise and fall unsteadily.

A girl squatted beside her. "Let me clean it," she said. She glanced over her shoulder at the man standing behind her. "We need a bowl of water and a new towel."

As he hurried off, the girl turned a fierce gaze to Sabine. "I'm Francie," she said simply.

Sabine's eyes widened. "From ... from the Maddox house."

The girl smiled and turned her eyes up to her companion as he returned with the water and fresh towels. "And this is Gulzar."

"Auntie," Gulzar said with a nod.

Gidah's cousin. The very man who'd taken Eli to the tunnels. He and Francie—rebels in Edmund's unwitting employ. At another time, Sabine might have laughed in delight. Now, as she waited desperately for Seth, she could only stare as Francie deftly cleaned the wound while Gulzar reported what they knew: Edmund ... in hiding ... in the sewer.

The *sewer.*

HEAVY BOOTSTEPS hurried toward them from the hall, and suddenly there was Seth, wild-eyed and out of breath, his face flushed and filthy. His eyes found Gulzar first. "You!" He moved on to Francie, who fixed him with a proud glare. "His—" He pointed to Gulzar, then Francie. "You two—" He broke off in confusion.

"Seth!" Sabine eased Jack's head onto a rolled-up blanket and rose up to greet her brother with a hug. "Where's Rosa? I need her here."

"As do the thousands she's helping as we speak. She can't come, not yet."

"But what about Jack?"

"For the moment, he's in good hands here," Gulzar assured her.

"But Rosa—"

"Listen to yourself, Sabine." Seth gripped her shoulders. "We're in the middle of a *war.*"

"Auntie," Gulzar pressed. "We must act."

Seth glared at him. "What the hell are you talking about ... *we?*"

Francie appraised Seth with a critical sweep. "How many soldiers did you bring?"

"None of your business," Seth barked. "I don't really get what's going on here, but Sabine, we—"

"Everyone here is a rebel. Francie and I are rebels," Gulzar said, lifting his chin. "Always were."

Sabine turned to Seth, the words tumbling out. "He led Eli out. Through the tunnel."

"Tunnel? There is no tunnel out of here. I would know. He could be lying, Sabine. He and Francie are Edmund's *servants*. We don't know he's really a rebel—"

"More rebel than you'll ever be," Gulzar growled.

Seth clenched his jaw. "There are no tunnels out of here," he repeated.

Sabine ignored him. "Where does it come out?"

"Two places," Gulzar told her quickly. "I led Eli out the access near the wall. There's another access by the gardens, near the centre of the Key."

"We'll bring Seth's troops in that way." Sabine's mind spun ahead of her. She could see it clearly, as if it had already happened and she was remembering it. "Right under their noses. The same as they did to us."

"You'll have to blast a way in on the other side of the gate!" Gulzar burst out. "There's no way in on that side for a long distance. A day's ride at least!"

"Seth?" Sabine looked at her brother.

"We'll do it." Seth's words came fast and even. "The Guard's coming at my troops from the northeast. We'll cut around them, southwest, in arc formation."

A crack of thunder boomed overhead, followed from a blast nearer than the last two. Glass shattered in the next room. Everyone ducked. "We go now."

24

⚜

Eli had no idea how far Mireille and Nappo were behind him. He rode ever eastward through the night, Bullet across his lap like an exhausted sheep, stopping only to beg a fresh horse from a woman fleeing in the other direction.

He did not stop when he reached the southern plains outlying the Key he no longer recognized. The once-mighty wall had fallen in several places. The mud underfoot was strewn with bodies like the pictures in history books about war. Eli kept his head up, hands gripping the reins, and did not stop until he came upon the bodies of two boys, folded across each other in death. Their clothes were saturated with blood, but Eli recognized the BAT vests. Red, from Seth's main regiment. And if his boys were here, Seth was here too.

Eli glanced all around. The eastern side of the Key had fallen; he could make out that much. Small groups of Droughtlanders moved slowly among the soldiers sprawled out on the muddy ground, collecting the bodies onto carts, lifting the wounded onto other carts. He should stop. He should help. He should pray.

Keep going. This is not what you came for.

It wasn't. He knew that. He fixed his sights on the crumbling wall. Gunfire sounded from a distance. Inside the Key? He wasn't sure. In the farther distance—the west side, outside the wall—more gunfire, and larger explosions. Now Eli rode straight for it, veering along the outskirts of the Key, rounding the corner until the western plain came into view before him. A crowd of people—and masses more gathered farther out on the plains. Suddenly the ground between the crowd and the wall exploded in a blast of mud. Eli's horse reared up, Bullet's paws scrambling as he dropped to the ground. Eli's ears rang. He called for Bullet but couldn't even hear his own voice. As the mud rained down Eli calmed the trembling horse and coaxed him forward, Bullet sticking close at heel.

Then he spotted the BAT vests again. Seth's boys—making their way at a run toward the blast site. Eli kicked in his heels and urged his horse into a gallop.

This is the way. You are close.

The BAT boys were armed with shovels and picks, and as they came upon the pit carved out of the mud, they set in, digging furiously. Right above the tunnel that Eli had used to escape the Key.

And now someone was running toward him. Sabine!

"Eli!" Sabine waved furiously.

Almost.

And then Seth was striding toward him too.

"Eli."

At last.

Despite the rain and the rattle of gunfire, Eli felt an enormous sense of contentment wash over him. His highers had led him here, back to his brother and sister, for *this* moment. This reunion, right here outside the Key, the three of them covered in mud and rain as the sky slid back toward night. Eli jumped down from his horse in time for Sabine to fling herself at him in a fierce hug. Seth stood off to the side.

"Seth!" Sabine broke away from Eli. She grabbed Seth by the hand and dragged him over. She put an arm around each brother's waist and pulled them closer.

Eli glanced at Seth. This was not the brother he'd grown up with. This boy—nearly a man, really—had sloppily shorn hair now and was covered from boot to brow in mud and filth and his old sick scars. This was not the Seth whom Eli had long since learned to hate and fear. This was a new person.

And you will embrace him as such.

So he did. He gripped his brother's shoulders and pulled him into the hug. He could feel Seth tensing up, resisting, but he didn't care. Seth was the one to pull away first.

"You know this tunnel."

"I do."

Seth gestured behind them at the soldiers digging into the wrecked earth. "Then you can lead the way." With that, Seth went back to his boys, picked up a shovel, and began lifting away great clumps of mud and clay.

Eli marvelled at this stranger. His brother. At how all three siblings had come together here, outside the walls of the Eastern Key, in the midst of a storm, at the edge of a battle. Sabine was talking to him in a rush of words. He forced himself to listen carefully as she told him what had happened so far, and what their plan was now.

"Jack is hurt badly." Sabine gripped Eli's wrist. "Pray for him. Please?"

Commander Vance heard the blast but could not place its location. Nor could he afford to send any of his men in that direction to investigate. He couldn't spare a single soul.

This battle had been going on all day, and now, as night approached, he had lost his grip on it. The day light rebel attack had taken them by surprise, no matter how prepared they'd thought they were. Still, he and the other Commanders had launched into battle, confident of its outcome.

Now Vance had no idea how many men he had left, how many had fallen, or how many had simply fled for their lives. Word had come that Seth and his army were approaching from the west. This was the worst news. And with so many Guard siphoned off to repel them, he would focus his forces on holding the centre of the Key.

The night was going to be long and bloody, he could be sure of that. At least Seth's troops wouldn't have anything near the firepower the Guard had. For now, he'd hole up in this storefront at the edge of the fighting. He didn't dare light a candle or lamp while he took some time to organize his thoughts.

It grew dark outside. Vance slumped in a chair, muscles aching as the gunfire carried on. The street out front was clear. The fighting had moved to the end of the block. But why? That was a narrow street, hedged by buildings on both sides. Not a smart move.

Vance snugged his helmet onto his head, checked his gun, and slid out the door, keeping his back in the shadow of the building. There wasn't much moonlight, what with the cloud cover, the incessant rain. He made his way down to the end of the street, gun at the ready, visor flipped up, eyes searching for likely places where rebel snipers might be hiding.

25

❧

The blast had knocked the tunnel from a solid, well-built route into a creaking, muddy mess in danger of collapsing entirely. Eli led Seth's troops through the winding passageways, reversing the route he'd taken from the Key so long ago. He prayed all the while that the tunnel ceiling wouldn't fall in on them now, suffocating them in a soup of mud and wood.

Now Eli pressed himself against the wall as the silent soldiers crowded in on him, the thick, humid air making it hard to breathe.

The highers will it so.

This is exactly where he was meant to be, at this very moment. In the company of these people, these boys and men, women and girls, about to enter battle.

And you are here as witness.

Seth shoved his way up to Eli. "You're staying down here." Not a question, not an order, just a fact.

Eli nodded. And then Sabine too was by his side. "Gulzar will open it from above if the lever down here was damaged in the explosion."

The three of them, talking easily, as if it were an ordinary day.

"I'll see you later," Seth said, making off toward the great wooden door that now loomed before them at the end of the tunnel.

"I'm coming with you." Sabine gave Eli a quick hug and ran after Seth. As if they were going for a walk, or about to play a game of dominoes. Have a cup of tea.

Eli stood still, breathing in the smell of sweat and fear as Bullet whined by his side. The soldiers filed past him quickly now, an endless river of fighters. Then a creak as the ramp was lowered to the floor of the tunnel. Eli closed his eyes, leaned his head against the damp wall, and prayed some more.

The moonlight was shy behind low cloud cover, hiding behind the steady, shimmering veil of rain. The battle raged on in the centre of the Key, intensifying now as Guard and Droughtlander forces alike converged upon it.

Seth fell in behind the first wave of troops to emerge from the tunnel. They did as they'd been told, keeping silent, moving stealthily as they turned the corner from the gardens into the street. On and on they came, the tunnel mouth a flaming dragon, its fire the troops that rose ceaselessly from below.

It took a moment for it to sink in. The Guardies looked up, perplexed. Where had these rebels come from? And in such numbers!

The surprise was all it took. The boys at the front erupted in primal yells and battle cries as they raised their weapons and leapt into the thick of it. Behind the boys came even more rebels, Droughtlanders who'd followed Seth across the plains and were now on BAT's heels, pouring out from the tunnel, running and screaming headlong down the short lane that opened onto the street. They wielded machetes, clubs, guns with or without ammunition, it didn't matter. This was the final claw at revenge, and each wanted to tear it out in whatever way possible. By fist, by foot, by teeth.

"Stay here." Seth left Sabine in a doorway and vanished into the angry mass.

Sabine clutched her gun at her side. Eyes wide and heart pounding, she felt overwhelmed, paralyzed by the primal display of rage all around her.

But then something inside her shifted. Suddenly she felt loose, as limber as if she were about to reach for the trapeze. She stepped into the street and lifted her gun. Letting herself be ushered forward in the mass, she turned her head this way and that until she caught a flash of Guard-issue blue. A Guardy, bent over, pummelling a BAT boy with the butt of his gun. She set her sights on him, and in one fluid motion twisted in his direction and pulled the trigger when she was close enough to watch the bullet blast into the back of his head.

It felt as graceful as if she were moving in time to the earthy sound-track of the circus. She closed her eyes for the briefest of moments, the staccato of gunfire melting into the steady heartbeat of the drums. A crack of thunder. The shudder of rain a crescendo on the cobblestones.

"Sabine!"

She opened her eyes to a curtain of rain and a blur of motion beyond.

Seth shouted her name again. "Sabine! Watch out!"

She spun. Vance towered over her. He was so close that the whites of his eyes stood out in the shadows of his helmet, his visor raised. Rain streaked over his shoulders and trickled down his armour.

"Auntie. That's what they call you."

Where was she? Barely moving, she looked left. Right. The dead Guardy. The cowering boy soldier, hand to his head, standing beside Seth. An alley, narrow. Buildings tall on either side. The dissonance of thousands of fighters clashing in the street beyond. The smell of blood mixing with the loamy stench of mud and wet stone.

"Isn't it!" Vance raised his gun. "That's what they call you!"

"If you harm her," Seth shouted, "I will kill you with my bare hands, I swear!"

Vance laughed. "Is that so?" Then, lowering his voice, he addressed Sabine. "Edmund's daughter. In the flesh. Not for long, though." He put the gun to her temple.

A crack cut the tension. Vance reeled back and cried out, clutching at his thigh. Everyone turned. Eli stood at the mouth of the alley, gun raised.

"Eli!" Sabine ran toward him. She took the gun from his shaking hands and then pulled him away as a group of Guardies, eyes ablaze with panic, rushed into the alley.

"Commander Vance!" One of them caught Vance as he stumbled. Sabine spun. Where was Seth? And the boy? Only the Guardies and Vance remained in the alley.

"Come on!" She grabbed Eli's hand and pulled him into the street.

THE MOON, fat and sluggish behind the storm clouds, cast a dull pallor over the Key. From up that high, the warring armies below resembled opposing tides, each pulling with it an entire ocean as it surged forward and fell back, volleying for dominance. Each sea was thousands strong and swelled with its own momentum: from the north, the blue uniforms of the Guard, practised and afraid; from the south, the pell-mell of the rebellion, disorganized and furious. And on both sides, adrenalin tainted the waters, whipping every fighter into a mad frenzy.

The rain beat down hard on Guardies and rebels alike. Thick mud sucked at boots, tripped BAT boys as they wrestled Guardies to the ground, splattered down with every blast of cannon. The storm washed over bewildered Guardies as they spun, guns raised, out of bullets, looking for backup, allies, help of any kind. Thunder drowned out the last words of BAT boys as they begged for mercy, looking down the barrel of a Guardy gun. And always the staccato of lashing rain competed with the tattoo of gunfire.

If the highers were to search for Seth, they would find him reaching for his last clip of ammunition, yelling behind him at Ori and Finn to get more. And then two Guardies grabbing for him, throwing him to the ground. The one gripping his ears and bashing his head against the cobblestones, the other throwing punches at Ori and Finn, cracking them both squarely across the jaw. With his head ringing and his face ablaze with pain, Seth would find his determination and use it to haul the man off, to turn and fight back, the rain and mud flying off him from the force. Thunder booming overhead, the flash of lightning: Seth would fight on.

And if the highers looked for Eli and Sabine, they would find them together, at the front of an enraged mob, pursuing throngs of mud-soaked, uniformed men toward the west gate as the Guard ran for their lives.

Sabine would pull Eli out of the unstoppable flow just before they spilled out into the Droughtland. She wouldn't want to be there when the rebels caught the Guards, when they exacted their bloody revenge for all their years of misery—not when the Guard were already running away.

THE MOON arced down in the sky and the night gave way to the coolest glimpse of dawn.

Everywhere Sabine looked, the people were rejoicing. "Eli!" She gripped his arm. "It's over!"

"Thank the highers," Eli said. "At last."

NOW THE CROWDS multiplied, thronging toward the centre of the Key, filling its ravaged streets.

"Auntie!" One of the revellers had spotted Sabine. Suddenly she was aloft, held up by a mass of merry fighters.

"Hip hip, hurray! Hip hip, hurray!"

She bounced along, down the street. They were heading for the Key square. Sabine twisted, tried to sit up. She teetered awkwardly, but never once worried about being dropped. Higher now, she could get a better look. Everyone who had been outside the walls was inside now, all pushing into the small square.

"Sabine!" Eli shouted.

"I'm all right!" she yelled, trying to turn.

And then she gave up and let herself be carried. She threw back her head and let the rain pound down on her face. She took the deepest breath she could summon and let loose the most glorious scream.

"AHHHHHHhhhhhhhh!" Her bearers joined in, bellowing triumphantly at the top of their lungs.

And then she was being tugged down. "Let her go," a deep voice instructed. "For now."

Trace! She threw herself into his arms.

The two clung to each other for a long, suspended moment.

"Gulzar sent word," Trace said at last, in answer to her unspoken question. "Jack will pull through. Rosa's with him now."

"That's wonderful!. We'll go to him...." But the crowd would not let Sabine go just yet. More hands, reaching to touch her, kiss her. Sabine let herself be pulled into the euphoric throng once more, Trace close behind now. A shower of candies fell upon her. Candies! A sweet shop on the corner was filled with people looting the colourful displays; someone pressed more candy into her hand as she passed.

The parade pushed on toward the square as more and more revellers joined them from beyond the walls. And now, everywhere Sabine looked, were Droughtlanders: their smiles as wide as rivers, their eyes shining with victory. Running, walking, arm in arm, singing. Everyone, it seemed, was singing. It was the sound of a nation rejoicing.

26

꙳

S abine recognized the two boys. The pair were standing guard in the early afternoon light outside the sewage treatment plant, where Eli had led her and Trace. Ori and Finn. Seth's pets. The boys held themselves at attention, guns drawn.

"Boys," Sabine said. "Where's Seth?"

"Inside," Ori said.

"And we ain't supposed to let anyone else in," Finn added. "Not even you."

Trace took a menacing step toward the boys, but Sabine reached out, holding him back. "No need, Trace."

The boys were shaking their heads. "Can't let anyone in. Commander Seth's orders. Sorry, Auntie."

"Step aside," Sabine said with a smile. "Now."

Ori and Finn shared a look.

"She said now!" Trace bellowed.

Sabine dug out the candies in her pocket and offered them to the boys. They hesitated, whispered something to each other, and then accepted them, ripping off the wrappers and stuffing them all into their mouths at once.

"Let us pass."

More whispers, then the two boys stepped aside, eyes cast down, ashamed.

"No one will blame you," Eli assured them as Trace swung open the heavy door. "You were only obeying the leader of Triskelia."

Still, the boys' shoulders slumped, disappointed in themselves.

Sabine touched them as she passed. "I'll tell him we forced you aside."

"No!" Ori blurted. "We stand by our decision. Commander Seth would expect no less." His words rolled into a swooning slur as he sucked on the candy.

INSIDE THE FIRST DOOR was a small anteroom. Beyond that, a heavier door. When Trace pulled that one open the smell of shit smacked them all in the face. He slammed it shut and let them all recover before slowly opening it again.

Sabine stifled a gag, took a few practice breaths through her mouth, and pushed past Trace, who was pinching his own nose.

There was a shallow shelf just inside the door, lined with lanterns, a box of matches at one end. Eli lit one and led the way down a dark corridor.

He'd been here twice in his life. Once with Seth when they were ten, for the new system's ribbon-cutting ceremony, and then again, just a couple years ago. A field trip cooked up by their tutor at the time. The rush of water in the distance echoed against the walls. There was no need to whisper; they could have shouted if they'd wanted and not been heard over the roar.

"Do you see anything?" Sabine asked, squinting into the dark. A platform reached out below them and across the water.

"No."

Another corridor, another ladder, and they were on a landing overlooking the holding pond. On the catwalk below them, lit by a lantern each, stood Seth and her father.

"Seth!"

Sabine leapt onto the catwalk, then froze. Eli took her hand and they walked together. The space between seemed to stretch on forever, and for this, Sabine was glad.

Eli stopped now. Seth and Edmund were still just shadow masses in the dark.

"You go ahead."

"Come with me."

"No."

"I need you." Sabine fingered her medallion. "Please, Eli."

"So you're the girl!" Edmund called into the dark. "Well, come on! Let me have a look at you! The prodigal daughter returns at last."

Sabine swallowed back a bilious swell at the back of her throat. She squeezed Eli's hand. "I *need* you, Reverend."

Go.

But Eli didn't want to go. He didn't want to ever set eyes on his father again. He didn't want a confrontation; he wanted to be left alone. He didn't want to know what he had or didn't have to say to the father he'd last seen so long ago.

For your sister.

Eli squeezed her hand back and took the first step forward. He kept walking, Sabine at his side, until they were both looking at Edmund. The lantern played shadows across his pale face. His eyes betrayed nothing.

"Father." Eli felt like there was an electric field between them, and that if he dared reach across it, he would perish. Edmund didn't even turn his head in Eli's direction. His eyes were locked on Sabine.

And her eyes were locked on his.

"At last we meet," Edmund finally said.

She stared at him, trying to glean, by sight alone, who he was to her.

"The almighty girl leader has nothing to say?"

Sabine still stared. She wanted to know everything about this man, and at the same time nothing. She was full of rage and she was full of sadness. She missed her mother. She wanted her here while she met her father for the first time. How was it for Lisette to have been with him? How could she not have slashed his throat and ended the long life of lies and loss?

"Say something!" Edmund leaned toward Sabine but now Trace cut between them, holding him back with a strong hand against his chest.

Sabine shook her head. The realization had hit her: she didn't want to speak to him. She had nothing to say. This was all she'd needed: to show him that he held no power over her. That she didn't need him for anything. Not for an explanation, not for an acknowledgment, not for any admission. He was nothing to her.

She moved away, her hand at her medallion.

"Sabine?" Seth lifted his lantern. "Don't you want to talk to him? Tell him what you think of him? Ask him about our mother? What he did?"

"No." Sabine shook her head, damning the tears that rolled lazily down her cheeks, blessing the dark for hiding them from Edmund. "No, I don't."

"What about Seth?" Another chuckle from Edmund. "Ask me about him. Don't you want to know about our little arrangement?"

Eli backed away with her. "She doesn't want to talk to you, and neither do I!"

"You will when I tell you what Seth had cooked up."

"We don't care!" Eli shouted back. "He's proven himself as a fierce and loyal rebel, and there's nothing you can say to change that."

"It's true." Trace leaned into Edmund's face. "He might have been on your side once. I'd be the first to say so. And I have. Many times. But not now. And nothing you can say will change that."

Seth's heart pounded. He *had* been a traitor. He'd wanted to reconcile with Edmund, combine their skills and savvy and rule the people with Maddox flair. When had that changed? Could he even pinpoint the shift? No matter, he was a true Triskelian now. He'd fought a war against his father. And he'd won.

Sabine lifted her lantern now, looked inquiringly at Seth.

"I'll take care of him," he said simply.

Sabine nodded. Her throat swelled with emotions of all sorts, glomming together in a big ball. She could hardly swallow. Hate and sadness, pride and fear, all pushing, pushing. Her limbs felt heavy. She let the lantern down and willed herself to walk away.

But now, with a sudden wash of clarity, rage took over.

"Take this." She thrust the lantern at Eli and stalked over to Edmund. "Where's the baby?"

Edmund said nothing.

"Tell me!"

"Make me."

It was such a childish response from a grown man, Sabine had to laugh. "*Make* you?"

Seth gripped Edmund's collar and shook him. "Where are Allegra and the baby?"

"Gone. Fled. I don't know where."

"You're lying!" Sabine jabbed Edmund's chest. "They're here somewhere, aren't they?"

Silence.

"If they are, we'll find them!"

"I'll scour the place, Sabine. You go." Seth gestured to the ladder. "They'll be looking for you. Go up and celebrate your victory."

"*Our* victory."

"Yes." Seth grinned.

"Come." Eli took Sabine's hand. "We're done here."

Sabine took what she hoped would be one last look at the man who had caused so much pain and misery. Then she leaned in, and trembling with fury, spat in his face.

Then she turned on her heel and left him there.

Vance and his rescuers had shed their uniforms and pulled on the drab, filthy clothing of fallen Droughtlanders. They'd fled out the east gate and thundered away from the Key as fast as their horses could go. Eli's bullet had only grazed him, leaving a jagged tear on his thigh.

They had lost. But just as the Triskelians had resurrected themselves from the ruins, so would he. He would find allies, gather fellow Guard who had fled for their lives. Rebuild a new, fierce battalion. He would not give up. He would not live in a Droughtland world. If the sicks didn't take him first, he would do his best to overthrow that wretched Sabine and her vile brothers. Or he would die trying.

Allegra woke when the rain stopped. Someone was jostling the carriage. Charlie was still sleeping soundly but she picked him up anyway, clutching him to her as she pulled aside the curtain and peeked out.

It was only her driver. She sighed with relief and pushed open the door. He helped her down. He had come to the Maddox house when she did, and had been her grandfather's driver until he died. His name was Alonso, and while he too was dressed in Droughtlander rags, he still treated her properly.

"It's stopped raining," Allegra remarked.

"Yes, ma'am." Alonso's sleeves were pushed up, his arms covered in mud up to his elbows.

He'd been smearing mud onto the carriage walls. They'd been stopped several times the day before and had convinced people the carriage was stolen. Last night Alonso had found a rock to scrape away the fine paint job. Now he was dirtying the outside, making it less recognizable as a Keyland carriage.

"Shall I help?"

Alonso blushed. "No, ma'am. I wouldn't think of it!"

Allegra smiled at him. "We will have to make adjustments, Alonso."

"Ma'am?"

"First off, no more *ma'am* or anything like it." Allegra gestured at the barren wasteland around them, a veritable sea of mud. "We may not have company now, but we are likely to at some point. And so we must practise blending in."

"What am I to call you, then?"

"Allegra. That will have to do." Charlie stirred in her arms. "Now, how about I put together some tea?"

Alonso stared at her.

Allegra smiled weakly at his obvious doubt in her domestic abilities. "All right, then. You do it."

He wiped his muddy hands and set about heating up some water while Allegra climbed back into the carriage to nurse the baby. Outside her window, Alonso set up the little cooking stove. She watched, intent on learning. He fit together the pieces and put—what was that? a piece of coal?—in the bottom, and water in the pot, and lit it with a match. She'd seen staff do the same at picnics. She was certain she could have figured it out. Maybe. Charlie fussed, tugging at her and arching his back. Allegra sat back and tried to relax. "There, there, pet. Mummy's here. We'll be all right."

She hummed his favourite lullaby, and he calmed. Allegra did not, though. She had left behind everything she'd ever known. Secretly, not telling a soul, and especially not Edmund, she had asked Alonso to prepare for their flight. That was almost a week ago, and thank the highers that she had!

And now here she was, in the Droughtland. Alone. Or, almost alone. With a helpless baby to care for and one lone servant. She had nowhere to go.

And yet. She was free. She would make her own way now, no matter what.

Allegra began to feel something ... unfamiliar. A pleasing sense of contentment. Was this ... happiness? Or beautiful denial? Only time would tell.

27

꙳

Rosa brought Sabine to the tent where Jack was sleeping.
"Can I wake him?"

Rosa shook her head. "He needs to rest. I've given him a sleeping powder."

Sabine took Jack's hand in hers. "Can he hear me?"

"I think so."

Sabine leaned over his pale face. "I love you." She kissed his cheek.

Jack stirred, his brow creasing.

"We should really let him rest...."

"I'll be back in a few hours," Sabine whispered in his ear. "You better be healed by then, or there will be hell to pay." She winked, and then added, "I just winked. But you couldn't see that."

"Sabine—"

"I know. I'm going." She leaned in one more time and whispered, "We won, Jack! We did it! We toppled the Keys!"

Again, Jack stirred, this time squeezing his eyelids, as if straining to wake.

"I must insist," Rosa said softly.

Sabine kissed him one more time and then pushed away. She lifted the rough wool blanket to see the wound. It was bandaged neatly, but was seeped through with blood. "He'll be okay?"

Rosa grinned as she backed out of the tent to join Eli and Trace. "If you leave him be."

Sabine tucked the blanket back over Jack's shoulders. "We won!" she whispered again as she followed Rosa. She wanted Jack to wake up and go with her to the festivities. In good time. She was just thankful that he'd made it this far.

"You can't put it off any longer," Trace said, turning to Sabine. "Your people want to see you, Auntie. Can you hear that?"

Sabine strained. She could hear a dull roar coming from where the revellers were partying in the square. *Auntie, Auntie!*

"What about Seth?"

Eli grinned. "They want you."

"Then they shall have me!" She hooked arms with Trace and Eli and practically skipped toward the horses that stood waiting. "We won! We won! We won!"

THE CELEBRATIONS carried on for hours. A bellowing oompah band had set up in the square, where joyous dancers spun and reeled to its merry rhythms. A giant bonfire crackled in the middle of a side street as people hurled ornate Keyland furniture atop it and dried their sodden selves with its warmth. Every ounce of Keyland liquor had been liberated, from estates and shops alike, and was being passed around with a rare disregard for catching sicks. Now wasn't the time for worry. It was time to celebrate!

MUCH LATER, when the rejoicing had quieted down a notch and Sabine could feel exhaustion finally creeping into her bones, she asked Eli to take her to the Maddox estate. She wanted to see it. She wanted to know where her mother had lived. Where her brothers had grown up.

"We could stay there," she blurted out. Suddenly, she felt a little shy. "Um ... if that would be all right with you?"

Eli agreed, but wasn't sure he'd even go inside. Once at the gate, though, he knew he would. He climbed the front steps ahead of his sister, awed that he felt nothing. Not yet anyway. The door swung open before they reached it.

Francie grasped Eli and hugged him. Gulzar have him a hearty slap on the back.

"You look a little worse for wear," he said, grinning.

"As do you," Eli grinned back.

Francie led them to the elegant parlour, where Eli and Sabine sunk down gratefully on the deep, richly woven couches. Eli smiled to think of how often his mother had encouraged them to use this room, how warm and welcoming she had made it, not all stuffy and austere as in other Keyland homes. There was her piano, still taking up one whole corner.

And then, for a fleeting moment, he saw her: Lisette, sitting on the piano bench, studying the music sheets before her. She looked up, gazed into his eyes, and then, smiling, she winked at him. Then she was gone.

"Eli?" Sabine laid a hand on his arm. "Are you okay?"

"... Everything is under control here," Gulzar was saying. "The house staff that refused to acknowledge you have fled."

"The rest are happy to stay and work for you," Francie added. "So long as you'll have them."

"No one has to 'work' for us," Sabine protested. "We are all free people now."

A plump woman in an apron appeared at the doorway, a tray in her hands, a pot of tea in the middle, the steam curling away from the spout. "However," Sabine smiled generously at the woman, "if that is a pot of tea, I would accept it with much gratitude."

Cook stepped into the room, eyes agog, the tray shaking in her grip.

"Dear Cook!" Eli jumped up and took the tray from her, setting it down just in time for her to tackle him with one of her big-hearted hugs.

"Eli!" Cook gripped his shoulders now. "You're safe! And they'd said you were dead!"

"Here I am, Cook. Alive and well."

"And you're so tall!" On tiptoe she kissed one cheek and then the other. "Oh my grace! Oh my highers! My boy!"

Then she turned to Sabine. "My eyes are lying!" Cook leaned over and grabbed her, squeezing her tight as if she were checking that she was real.

"Cook, this is Sabine." Eli stammered out an explanation; for Cook, Sabine must have seemed an eerie apparition. "We were triplets. Not twins." He clarified the story as succinctly as he could. The colour slowly returned to Cook's cheeks, her confusion transforming into delight.

"I always wondered," Cook said when Eli's words had finally trailed off. "Your mother was so big when she was pregnant, and then you boys were so small!" Cook sighed. "And later, she'd been so sad."

Now she stood back and shook her head. "Your mother, bless her soul, would be so happy to see you."

Eli took Cook's hand in his and led her to the sofa, urging her to sit.

As she plumped down awkwardly on the ample cushions beside Sabine, Cook went on marvelling. "I can't believe ... all this time ..." She folded Sabine's hand into hers. "A daughter. Your mother kept such a big secret. All this time. And now here you are." Her cheeks were flushed, her eyes damp with tears. "And your father! He never knew."

Now Cook pulled a handkerchief from her apron pocket and dabbed her eyes before blowing her nose with it. She stood.

"Won't you sit with us?" Sabine asked. "You can now. Everything is different."

Fresh tears coursed down Cook's cheeks. "Oh dearie no, but thank you." She made her way to the door, then turned back. "You know, I'll miss the way things were." And with a warm smile for Eli, she trundled off down the hall.

EARLY EVENING and the streets were filled with people celebrating. Eli leaned against the window, Bullet at his side, watching the merrymakers as they made their way to and from the central square. Then he spotted Nappo and Mireille, on horseback, near the front gate.

He stood rooted to the spot, his heart pounding. "How can I still care that he won her over?" he asked his highers with a whisper. "How can I still care about such things when the world has taken on a new shape?"

Then Eli paused in wonderment. Hadn't he taken on a new shape, too? He could feel it now: he loved his friends. All the jealousy, the resentment he'd felt, had left him. They were alive, and they were right outside the window! He rushed to the door and flung it open, his heart as wide as the skies.

"Nappo! Mireille!"

SABINE SAT ON THE COUCH in the front parlour, the house quiet now. Everyone else had long since gone to bed. She didn't know how long she'd sat there by herself, unable to sleep, reliving the fear, the panic, and finally the exhilaration of all that had happened. She'd kept shaking her head, marvelling at it all. They had won. Triskelia would live again. They were free.

She went to the window. A glow rose from the square. A bonfire? The noise had died down somewhat, but she could still hear a steady undercurrent, like the crowd in the stands before a circus performance was about to begin.

Fumbling in the dark, she found a robe in the closet and slipped into it, hugging the heavy fabric around her as she stepped out into the hall. She turned around, not sure where to start, before deciding to head down the hall in the opposite direction.

Sabine opened every door, casting a glance into darkened rooms, trying to make out the shadows within. A harpsichord in one room. A wall of books in another. A loom. A statue of a maiden reaching up. She climbed the stairs and tried the first door. The nursery. She stepped in and pulled the door shut behind her. She would have spent a great deal of time here, had she not been secreted away as a newborn. She crossed the room and leaned over the empty crib. She brought a little blue blanket to her face and breathed in the smell of talc. Holding on to the blanket, she toured the room. A rocking horse. An overstuffed chair with a soft throw draped over one arm. An elaborate playhouse whose kitchen contained miniature pots and pans, a pantry of pretend food. A basket of stuffed animals. A dresser full of carefully folded tiny clothes in an array of blues. Charlie's clothes. He should be asleep in this room. Not out there somewhere.

Still clutching the blanket, Sabine turned the knob on a door in the middle of the back wall. It opened into a bedroom. The master bedroom?

It seemed manly, with dark wood and boldly striped wallpaper. Nothing frilly about it. She closed the door and tried the one on the other side of the room.

She knew right away. She could smell her mother in the air, the rosy scent of her perfume lingering still. This had been her mother's room. Was this Allegra's room now? She trailed her finger along the dresser top, marking a slithery trail through a thick coat of dust. She didn't think so, even though the dresser was still full of clothes. Her mother's clothes. Sabine leaned in and gathered an armful of dresses. She took a deep breath. With tears in her eyes, she let go of the rich fabrics and turned away. A four-poster bed cast a daunting shadow on the far wall, like an angry skeleton. But it was exactly what Sabine was looking for. She slipped under the heavy quilt, curled up, and promptly fell asleep.

28

S eth straddled a wooden chair and stared at his father. He'd brought Edmund straight from the sewer to the Justice Hall's prison, slipping through buildings and along back lanes to avoid the revellers. Seth wasn't ready to celebrate. Not just yet.

"How does this cell compare to the one you kept Pierre Fabienne in?"

Edmund sat on the edge of a hard bench, his head in his hands, stinking of the sewer. He didn't look up.

"When you cut off his fingers, did you use a hatchet? Or more of a clipper, like secateurs?"

"I want a basin of water, and a bar of soap."

"I'm guessing you cut them off when he was still alive, right?" Seth rested his chin on the back of the chair. "So that he'd tell you where Triskelia was. Am I right? Do I know you, or what? Or maybe it wasn't you. Maybe you just stood there, looking all smug, *supervising.*"

Now Edmund looked up with a glare. "Bring me soap and water."

Seth got up and walked out without a word, clanging the barred door shut behind him. Edmund half-stood, craning his neck to see where Seth had gone. The two soldiers assigned to keep watch glared at Edmund from behind the desk and their hands of cards.

"What're you looking at?" the first one said.

Ten minutes later and Seth was back, clutching the arm of a filthy old man covered in the oozing wounds of the skineater sick. Edmund jumped up and pressed himself against the wall, his face pickled with horror. The soldiers too leapt from their seats, letting their cards fall to the desk.

"Commander Seth?" one of the jailers inquired, controlled panic in his voice.

"You may leave." As the jailers rushed away Seth pushed the old man into the room, clanging the door shut after him.

The Droughtlander was barefoot and bow-legged, dressed in tatters, his eyes cloudy with fever, grey hair damp with sweat, plastered to his flushed brow.

"What is the meaning of this?" Edmund demanded.

"I thought you'd like some company."

Edmund paled. "Just what do you mean by that?"

Seth pulled a chair up and took a seat outside the bars. He crossed his legs and bent forward, chin on his fist, elbow on his knee.

"We had a deal, you and I." Edmund enunciated his words sharply, carving each one out of the tension. He did not move away from the wall, though. He would not step one inch closer to the sickly man. "You portray yourself to be an honourable leader. A noble soldier. Yet you reneged on your word. And here you are now, toying with a helpless man." Edmund paused. "You have all the power now. So there's no need to threaten me with the likes of him." He nodded in the old man's direction.

"You know nothing about me, Father." Seth gripped the bars now, his knuckles white. "I've changed. Which is more than I can say for you."

"If I held the balance of power now, I would be gentleman enough to honour our arrangement."

Seth threw his head back and laughed. "That's right: Edmund Maddox, pillar of the community." Now Seth spun to face the Droughtlander. "Get up!"

The old man lifted his head slowly and blinked at Seth with red-rimmed eyes. He pushed himself up, bracing himself against the wall with a hand covered in weeping wounds.

Edmund drew his legs up onto the bed now, anything to put more distance between him and the skineater sick. "Put me on trial, then. Keep me locked up forever. Banish me to my own devices in the Droughtland!

But not this. I know what you're going to do. It is not humane. It is not fair. It does not befit a gentleman of war."

"You talk to me of *fairness*?" Seth shook his head in disbelief. He put his face to the bars and pointed at his own scars. "Did you put him up to it?"

"What are you talking about?"

"Commander Regis!" Seth gritted his teeth. "Did you order him to make me sick?"

Edmund shook his head. "No! No, I had no idea."

"Just as you had no idea Maman was at the gardens that day."

"Exactly like that!"

Seth sighed. "If you survive this, I'll set you free in the Droughtland. That, Father, is sufficiently fair."

"Please, Seth!" Giving the sick man as wide a berth as he could, Edmund scooted down the bed and clung to the bars. "You are not this person!"

"Oh yes I am. All thanks to you."

The Droughtlander looked at Seth, a question in his eyes. The old man had not done well under Rosa's care. He would die anyway. Seth had assured him that what he was being asked to do was for the good of Triskelia. His death would not be in vain.

Seth nodded, giving him the signal.

Now the old man summoned his last ounce of his strength and launched at Edmund, fists raised.

"Get him off!" Edmund cried out in horror, covering his face with his hands.

The Droughtlander bit down on Edmund's bare arm. Edmund balled a fist and punched him hard in the face. There was a crack and then the old man crumpled, his nose bleeding profusely.

Now the old man flexed his jaw, fixed Edmund with a glare, and launched at him like a wild cat, the blood spraying everywhere. He pinned Edmund to the floor and let the blood rain down as Edmund struggled beneath him.

"First the fever will come." Seth cocked his head. "Along with hallucinations. You'll shit yourself and puke like mad. You'll want to tear off your skin with your bare hands, but you'll be too weak."

With one great heave Edmund finally pushed himself away from the man. "You're insane!"

"That very well may be," Seth said with a grin. "Who knows?" He got up and turned to walk away.

"Come back here!" Edmund grabbed the bars. "Take him away!"

"I will," Seth said. "Eventually."

Droughtlanders were everywhere, camped on the estate lawns, spilling out from the majestic houses, tottering down the street, drunk from partying all night. Traders had already set up stalls along the main street. It was as if the highers had lifted up a Droughtland market in one almighty hand and a Key in the other, jumbled them together, and tossed it all down.

"Even with the smoke still settling," Eli marvelled as he and Nappo strolled down what had once been a tidy row of fancy shops. Bullet trotted between them, tail wagging.

Nappo shrugged. "Can't blame them."

The yellow and blue Keyland banners that had flown from streetlamps now lay strewn about, trampled with mud. Everywhere Eli looked it was the same as he remembered it, yet entirely different. The gardens, for example, where his mother had died. They were now a campground of sorts, dotted with canvas tents and low tarps and people everywhere, trampling the grass and lounging among the topiaries shaped like elephants and giraffes. Eli's mother had been on the committee to decide how to shape the trees. They'd chosen exotic animals so that the children of the Key would have something strange and wonderful to visit, even if they were only trees.

The children of the Key. Where were they now?

"How does it feel to be back?" Nappo interrupted his thoughts.

"Like I'm not back at all." Eli shook his head. "Not back to anywhere I belong, anyway. Or anywhere I recognize. It just feels strange."

"Tell me about this place," Nappo said. "What it was like to grow up here?"

Eli shook his head. "It doesn't matter."

"It's where you're from."

Eli stopped at the gate in front of the rebuilt solarium. To look at it, you'd never know it had been a bomb site just over a year ago. "Not really," he said quietly. "It's not the same any more."

"It *is* where you're from," Nappo insisted. "You can't change that."

"And why does that matter?" Eli gripped the cool metal of the fence. "You never talk about where you're from."

"I'm not a Keylander."

"Neither am I!"

"But you *were*, is all I'm saying." Nappo shook his head. "You can't erase it just because you wish it were different."

"I'm not a Keylander."

"I get it, Eli."

"I don't think you do." The gate swung open easily. "This is where my mother died."

Nappo followed Eli up the path. Bullet sniffed the air and then took off at a run into the bushes. Eli stopped at the door to the solarium. It was wide open, and he could hear children playing. He went around to the side and put his face to the steamy window. He could see Droughtland children running around inside, laughing, chasing each other through the jungle of fragrant green, marvelling at the butterflies and songbirds flitting overhead. He didn't want to go in. There would be no secret underground room this time.

Someone called for Eli. He turned to see Gulzar, on horseback, dressed in Key finery: high socks and cropped riding pants, a vest made out of rich, heavy fabric. Edmund's, most likely. It looked funny on the stable-minder. Eli smiled.

"Your brother and sister are looking for you Eli." Gulzar didn't notice Eli looking at him strangely. "They're at the house."

ELI FOUND Sabine and Seth in Edmund's office. Seth had taken their father's chair for himself and leaned back in it now, feet on the desk.

"So you lived to tell the tale, Reverend." Seth rested his head against the chair and crossed his arms. "Congratulations on the depot siege. Or should I congratulate your highers? I hear it was a—" Seth made quotes with his fingers, "*sacred mission.*"

"It was."

Seth smirked. And yet, he was proud of Eli. He would never have thought him capable of such a daring feat. Still, here he was, mocking him. It was all he knew how to do. Seth shifted uncomfortably in his seat.

Now Sabine leaned forward, brow furrowed in thought. "We need to talk about where to go from here."

Eli couldn't help but notice how much she looked like their mother. These long months had changed her, carved edges where she'd been soft before. Lisette, his beautiful mother, had always harboured a darkness about her, and now Eli could see the same haunted quality in Sabine.

"I want to keep going east," she said now.

"What for?" Seth asked. "We could stay right here."

"I don't want to stay here."

"Why not?"

Sabine rose and crossed the room to the window. She put a hand to the glass and looked out. "This will never be home for me."

"It can be. Now," Seth said.

Sabine shook her head. "It can't. To me it will always be Maman's prison."

"She could've left." Seth's voice hardened. "There was no one forcing her to stay against her will."

Sabine turned away from the window, her eyes dark. "She stayed for the two of you."

Eli looked from Sabine to Seth and back again. *Forgive.*

"We could go back west," Eli blurted out, trying to shift them away from the shadowy place they were headed for.

"Where exactly? There's nothing left at Triban." Sabine shook her head. "And as for Cascadia, we can't rebuild Triskelia on the top of a mountain. I want the people to be able to come to us. Like before. And I want to build a permanent home for the circus. I want to go farther east."

"The arms traders might still hold the coast," Seth cautioned.

Sabine smiled at him. "You can deal with that, can't you?"

"I could." Seth frowned. "If they're still there. You want them dismantled?"

"Yes," Sabine said. "I don't want any Guardy survivors to have any access to weapons. If we settle the seaboard, we'll have the entire continent. Cascadia will govern the west, and we'll set up Triskelia in the east."

"I'm going west," Eli said, more emphatically this time.

Sabine looked at him thoughtfully, eyebrows raised. "Well then. You could be the leader at Cascadia."

"No. I'm going back to Triban."

"Triban?" Sabine gave Eli another quizzical look.

"To offer salvation to the proletarians?" Seth smiled.

Eli looked at him. It was Seth's customary sarcasm, but there was something else in his eyes, in his tone of voice. A new regard. And the funny thing was, Seth was right. The highers were calling him back to that broken city.

"Well. Of course you're free to go where you please," Sabine said. "But not until I don't need you any longer."

"You don't *need* me at all."

"I do."

Eli crossed his arms. "There's nothing here for me."

"*We're* here," Sabine said. "And I want you to bless New Triskelia before you leave." She paused. "I need you because we are a trinity. Like Zenith said." Sabine gripped her medallion. "And while I can't make the three of us stay together forever, I am asking that you two agree to do this with me."

Seth dragged his feet off the desk, letting them thunk onto the floor. Eli kept his arms crossed.

"Agreed?" Sabine glanced first at Seth, then Eli. "We'll do this together, then we can go our separate ways. If that's what you want."

Now Seth and Eli shared a long look. "Agreed," said the brothers in unison.

29

Two days later Seth was back in Edmund's study, concentrating on a map that laid out the route from the Key to the seaboard. He would take Ori and Finn, of course. And as many more as would volunteer. They would leave within the week. Rosa wanted to go with him, and would not take no for an answer.

"They don't need me here any more!" Rosa was perched beside him on the desk. "I can be of more use to you."

"You want to know the truth?"

"Of course."

"The truth," Seth pulled her onto his lap, "is that I love you, and I want you to be safe."

Rosa, who'd been prepared to argue, leaned back and stared at him. After a long silence she finally spoke. "And I love you."

"So you see?" Seth kissed her temple. "I want to keep you safe."

"And don't you see?" She pulled away. "I want to be *with* you. And you need a proper lifeminder."

He squeezed her tight. "I still have time to convince you to stay. For now though ..." Seth kissed her wrist, and then again, trailing kisses up to the crease of her elbow. "For now, let's not try to convince each other of anything. Okay?"

Rosa's breath caught in her throat. She shivered under his kisses, her arm long with goose bumps. "Okay." She lowered her lips to his, and kissed him hard.

Suddenly a loud knock sounded at the office door. "Commander Seth?" The voice in the hallway was urgent.

Rosa scrambled up from Seth's lap as he straightened his shirt. "Come in, Ori."

Ori flung open the door. He looked wide-eyed at Rosa, but faltered only a moment before turning to Seth.

"It's your father, sir. He's sick."

ROSA HURRIED TO THE JAIL with her bag of supplies, Seth at her side. Ori had told them that Edmund was in the clutches of a horrible fever, his skin already reddening in welts that would soon begin oozing. It was the first Rosa had heard that he was even sick. Still, it was early days. He might be saved yet.

As they rushed down the corridor they heard shouting, and then the clatter of the cell door being opened and more shouting. Onward they went down the hall and around the corner directly to Edmund's cell.

The door was locked, and so they could only watch through the bars as Seth's boys cut the man down from where he'd hanged himself with his clothes, ripped into strips and tied together to form a noose. Edmund's body fell to the floor with a thud.

"Open the door!" Rosa rattled the bars. "There's still time!"

One of the BAT boys stared at her, dumbfounded, while the other fumbled with the lock. When the door opened, Rosa rushed into the cell and fell to her knees beside Edmund. She took a second to pull on long, leather gloves, and then dug her fingers into his neck, searching for a pulse.

Seth had not planned on this. "Why weren't you watching him?"

The boy blanched. "I only stepped out to fetch some food, Commander Seth. They didn't bring us none at supper."

The shorter one's cheeks reddened with shame. "I fell asleep, Commander Seth."

"You had one prisoner to watch. One! And you couldn't even—"

"Seth!" Inside the cell, Rosa sat back on her haunches. "His neck is broken. There's no use."

Seth came into the cell and offered her a hand up. They stood side by side and looked down at him. Edmund's face was grey, his lips colourless, the welts already drained and pale.

"I'm sorry, Seth."

He shrugged.

"No matter what, he was still your father." Rosa stripped off her gloves and leaned into him.

Seth embraced her but could not take his eyes off the man lying before him. Edmund was dead. Yet Seth found himself waiting ... for what? The realization stunned him. After everything that had happened, everything Edmund had done, he still ... he still wanted his father to say something to him.

There would be no service for Edmund, all three siblings agreed on that. Sabine and Eli sat together in the study, still shocked by the news.

Eli's highers had been silent. He had expected something, some appeal to compassion at least. A call to pray for Edmund's soul. But his highers were mute. Did that mean he was excused from praying for his father? Or that Edmund wasn't worthy of it? That didn't make sense. Eli prayed for everyone, regardless of their affiliations, regardless of their sins. Shouldn't he pray for Edmund too?

"Do you hate him?" Sabine asked after a long silence.

Eli shook his head, perplexed. He didn't hate him, so why not pray for him? He turned the question over in his mind, examining its rough edges. "No."

"I do. I'm glad he's dead." Sabine nodded curtly. "Does that upset you?"

"No. You can't make yourself feel something that you just don't." Thinking of Mireille, he added, "And I can't make anyone else feel something I think they should."

Sabine understood what Eli was thinking. "Back at Cascadia ..." she began with gentle caution, "you and Mireille seemed like a sure thing. I'm sorry it didn't work out, Eli."

Eli smiled sadly. "Thank you. But it's okay, really. Nappo's my best friend. I love them both." And with that he got up slowly and left the room.

Sabine shook her head. She didn't think she'd ever truly understand Eli. Her whole life she'd thought she was the outsider. And then, when she finally met her brothers, she decided that it was Seth who took that role. But really, all this time, it was Eli. She couldn't help but worry about him. Sensitive, spiritual Eli. Always on a quest for something just out of his reach.

Sabine sat in the calm quiet of Edmund's office until the day faded into evening and another storm cracked open overhead, assaulting the Key with a sudden barrage of rain. She hurried to close the window, the floor already damp. She could see Seth's army gathered in the distance, scurrying for cover from the rain. They looked like toy soldiers from this far away. Seth and his soldiers would leave in two days, and she and the others would follow a day later. She wished she could leave this house of ghosts and go now.

30

They rode out of the Key as the rain pounded down, the horses straining to pull caravans and carts through the soupy mud. "Are you going to miss it?" Sabine asked Eli as the Key receded behind them.

"No."

Sabine settled back, drawing a blanket over her lap. It was warm, humid, but the damp chilled her, and the thin walls of the caravan didn't keep out the wind, which sliced low across the Droughtland like a machete. "Gulzar and Francie will take good care of it, should you ever want to go back."

"I won't."

Sabine resolved to leave Eli with his thoughts. She wished she'd ridden with Jack instead. He and Trace were bringing up the rear, behind Rosa and her cart of supplies. In front of her spread out more carts and horses and wagons, full of Triskelians and Droughtlanders who would join them in rebuilding Triskelia. Or building it anew. New Triskelia.

Sabine frowned at Eli as he gazed behind them. Perhaps it would be better to distract him. Bring him back to the present, in this caravan, the two of them together. "Did you see the lines at the polling stations?"

Eli nodded, but didn't look away from the window.

"What do you think the new name of the Key will be?"

Eli shrugged.

"Do you want to know what I voted for?"

"What?" Eli sat back with a slump.

"Lisetteville."

That got a smile out of him. "Me too."

Then his smile faded, and his face screwed up as if he were in pain. His fingers leapt to his medallion as a wash of déjà vu chilled him from the inside out. Just as Sabine was about to ask him what was wrong, she felt it too. She clutched at her medallion and gasped as a blast of pain exploded in her leg.

"Seth!"

Eli's heart pounded. *A bomb, mud raining down, boys in the air, screaming. His leg! His leg!*

"Make it stop!" Sabine cried out, her heart thudding so hard she thought she'd pass out. The driver heard her cries and slowed the horses. He flung open the door to find brother and sister slumped together on the floor of the caravan, pale and frightened, both of them clutching their left leg.

"Are you all right?"

"No," Sabine cried. "His leg! His leg!"

"I'll go get Rosa!" The driver took off, splashing through the mud, waving his arms for the others to stop.

Vance and his men had spent two days and two nights in the coulee, hunkered under tarps, hiding out both from the rain and the world at large. They were nearly out of food, and the only water they had was what they could collect off the tarp by directing the runoff into their canteens. Yet still they waited.

He might have lost to the Triskelians, but he would claim their leader as his own. Sabine or Seth: it didn't much matter to him now. He'd blow that leader to bloody smithereens. And then he could accept whatever fate brought him.

Most of the surviving Guardies had long since fled, and Vance couldn't blame them. As a group, they garnered suspicion. They way they talked, the dark shadows of suspicion and fear under their eyes, their difference standing out like a bad smell.

Now, as the rain slapped them hard, Vance and his six men shared the last square of Guardy-issue emergency hardtack.

"Vance!" One of the two lookouts shimmied down from the ditch by the road. "I think it's Seth!"

Vance leapt to his feet. The others did too, grabbing their gear. Between them they had thirty-two bullets to share between four guns, a grenade each, and an assortment of tripwire, knives, and clubs of varying quality.

Vance shimmied on his elbows beside the others as they made their way up the embankment and peered over.

The BAT boys were in high spirits as they rode atop the handsome horses they'd been issued before leaving the Key. They chatted about the battle, boasting of their kills and one-upping each other's already tall tales. Vance crouched out of sight, breath held, eye on the road, looking for Seth.

And there he was. Three-quarters of the way to the rear, riding the biggest horse, gun slung across his back, a hat keeping the rain off his scarred face.

"It's him," one of the men said. "It's really him."

With a silent hand signal, Vance ordered his men into place.

"Word gets back to your families that you died taking down *the* Seth Maddox, Triskelian traitor ... destroyer of the Keyland ..." Vance checked his gun. "You will be heralded."

"What families?" the Guardy beside him grumbled. "They're probably all dead."

"Valour outlives us all," Vance said quietly.

He waited for his moment. Then he lifted his arm high, and with one practised movement lobbed a grenade overhead and into the road before him.

THE BLAST THREW Seth high into the air and down, down into the muck of the road. Now he tried to stand. What had happened? Landmine? He couldn't get up. Mud exploded around him as another blast cut into the road. He glanced up at a shape arcing overhead. A boy. Finn, flying as if he'd been launched from a cannon. Screaming. And hot, angry pain. He glanced down at his left leg. It wasn't there.

A bullet zinged past him. Seth flattened himself into the mud. More screaming. More gunfire. And then Vance standing over him, glaring down with eyes full of hate, mouth twisted, yelling at him, but Seth couldn't hear a thing. The pain was too loud. It pounded through him like ceaseless thunder.

Suddenly Vance arched his back, flung his arms out, and fell back. Seth twisted, searching for the shooter.

Ori. The boy lowered his gun, his arms trembling.

"It's over, Commander Seth."

The boy's words were just echoes. "We killed them. It's over."

Seth tried to sit up, but he couldn't. He wanted to stand, but his leg was out of reach. It lay back by the dead horse, his boot still in the stirrup. It made no sense. None of it made sense. He gave up and fell back once more. Mud and rain and sky and blood. And Rosa. Always Rosa. Forever Rosa.

When they pulled into the village Rosa leapt down with her bag before the caravan came to a stop.

"Where is he?" she cried. *"Seth!"* She was led to a shack of tin and scrap wood. Sabine and Eli ran after her into the dim hovel where they found Seth writhing on the ground, an old woman dabbing the stub of his leg with a dirty rag.

"Get away from him!" Rosa shoved her aside and fell to her knees. "Oh, Seth." She untied the tourniquet above the wound. He mumbled gibberish, not recognizing her at all. He swatted at her with hands dark with dried blood. "Hold his arms," Rosa ordered Eli and Sabine.

Neither sibling could watch as Rosa inspected what was left of Seth's leg, a skirt of ripped flesh around it. Sabine clenched her teeth and stared at the wall. Eli squeezed his eyes shut and prayed.

Let him live. Let him live. Let him live. Let him live.

He remembered the dream he'd had. Of this. Of Seth with one leg. It hadn't been a dream. It had been another vision.

"It has to come off at the knee," Rosa said as she gulped back a sob.

"What do you need?" Sabine let go of Seth's arm and gripped Rosa's chin in her hand. "Look at me. You can do this. Tell me what you need."

"A-a-a table. And boiling wa-wa water. More light."

Jack lit the fire while Trace sent for more water and a table. When it came, the villager with him mumbled that they had no firewood.

"The caravan," Sabine said. "Take it apart for the wood."

When the water was boiled, Rosa took a deep breath and asked them all to stay and help. They lifted Seth onto the table. He murmured a delirious protest, but was limp.

Trace replaced Eli and Sabine at the head of the table, the better to hold Seth's arms during the surgery. Sabine held his one good leg. Jack manned the fire. Pouring a noxious liquid onto a bit of cloth, Rosa handed it to Eli and told him to hold it over Seth's mouth. After a few moments Seth's head lolled to one side, his eyes closed. Rosa cut into him gingerly, and when he didn't rouse, she let go a captive breath.

She cut again, this time deeper. "Boil the saw blade," she said as blood oozed along the scalpel edge and ran down Seth's mangled leg. Eli swooned a little and the walls warped. With one hand he steadied himself against the table, and with the other he picked up the crude-looking tool and dropped it in the roiling pot hung over the fire. *Let him live. Let him live. Let him live.*

SABINE HAD NO IDEA how much time had passed before Rosa was suturing around Seth's raw stump. She gathered the soiled towels in a heap and took them outside.

The remains of the caravan looked like a skeleton scattered by scavengers. Someone had even detached the canvas cover and propped it up outside the little hut as shelter from the rain. Sabine sat beside Eli on a stool set to one side and hung her bloodied hands off her knees.

"I had a vision of this," Eli said, staring ahead.

"Of what?"

"It was more like a dream. Seth had lost his leg and was carrying it around, slung over his shoulder. And there was a hole in his head, and when I looked in there was an army of boy soldiers marching along." Eli hung his head when the tears finally came.

After a long pause, Sabine asked quietly, "Did he live?"

"Yes." Eli nodded. "He did."

"Well, thank the highers for that." And now it was Sabine's turn to cry.

EPILOGUE

New Triskelia looked freshly polished under the glint of the midday sun. The carnival buildings had been washed, and the worst freshly painted. The boardwalk had been swept, and colourful sashes had been strung between the lampposts and were flapping in the ocean breeze. People strolled along, looking in the shops, eating warm pretzels with mustard, some stopping to watch the bustle inside the gates of the carnival yard as last-minute touches were added to the booths and the carnies set up their stacks of balls and meagre prizes of candy sticks and ribbons. The sound of hammering and shouting from the theatre competed with the gleeful cries of the children playing in the surf.

Anya was in charge of the children, although she was too pregnant to run after a single one. Effie and Althea collected the wanderers. Anya looked up now as a shadow cut into her sunshine.

"Sabine!" Anya shielded her eyes. "*Quelle surprise.* I would have thought you were too busy to take a walk on the beach."

"I am, really." She sat beside Anya on the sunbleached quilt, folding her knees under her. "Nana is ready for the little ones."

Celeste was organizing the costumes, and had wisely left the children's until last. The grand reopening of the Night Circus was only a few hours away. New Triskelia was abuzz, with visitors from far and wide here for the special occasion.

It had taken much longer than Sabine had hoped for the circus to be ready. She couldn't have anticipated the sluggishness that would plague them all as they dragged themselves up from the horrors of war and toward a new life. She herself had found her limbs heavy when she climbed the trapeze again for the first time, her balance skewed, her confidence frayed. Thank the highers it had all come back, with time and effort.

"Where's Emma?" Almost a year old, she clung to Anya when not in Nappo and Mireille's care.

"There." Anya pointed to where Teal and Toby held her hands as she tottered unsteadily at the edge of the surf. She was new at walking, or falling mostly. Her hair had lightened with so much sun, and Sabine could easily see Tasha in her now.

"I should get back." Sabine stood, brushing the sand off her long, flowing dress. She called for the children who were performing that night, leaving the rest to build their castles and dig for clams.

Now she let the children tug her along, past the theatre entrance with its glossy red door and ornate trim. It had been built in the time of vaudeville, so long ago that Sabine had never heard the word before. They'd restored the old wooden stage and now it gleamed, richly stained and freshly polished.

Tonight's gala would begin on the beach, when the tide was lowest. A lantern procession would start off the proceedings, and then Seth would do his part. Sabine knew that Seth was planning something big, but he was keeping it a mystery, his boys sworn to secrecy, even as they trooped every day from their barracks to the old casino on the far side of the carnival yard.

ELI OPENED THE DOOR to his room to change for the circus. His blessing was rehearsed, his costume was laid out, and his bag was packed. He would be leaving in the morning.

He would miss this place. He would miss his people. New Triskelia had been a healing waystation along a much larger journey. And it would be here for him to return to, should he ever be drawn this way again.

THE CROWDS BEGAN TO GATHER on the beach. Word had spread through New Triskelia that Seth was planning a surprise, and now everyone pushed forward, trying to catch a glimpse of the carts laden with strange wooden structures as they were wheeled out through the wide doors at the back of the old casino.

"Commander Seth!" The crowd caught sight of his uneven gait as he emerged from the building on his crutches. Seth stopped, and lifted a hand to wave. Ori escorted him, scanning the crowd. One never knew what loony might show up at a time like this.

And there was Rosa at the end of the boardwalk, waiting for him. She hadn't been sure she could get there early, what with all the patients to see in her clinic at the other end of town. She ran to him now, hooking her arm in his. She knew what he'd been constructing all this time. She had helped.

The sun was setting as the carts made slow work of rolling through the sand. Seth had arranged for one end of the beach to be cordoned off, his boys keeping watch to make sure everyone stayed behind the ropes. The carts convened there now, and the boys went to work unloading the parts and laying them out.

"We haven't got much time," Seth said as the crowd drifted onto the beach, all eyes on his boys as they wrestled the wooden pieces into place. From afar, the rickety-looking structure they were building looked like a tower of matchsticks.

THE INDIGO of early night pressed in from the ocean. And now the lantern carriers began to parade out of the warehouse, accompanied by the melancholic whine of accordions. The lanterns were lit in quick succession, the fire swinging between them like a winged animal. The crowd drew in a deep, collective breath.

The fire spinners—local girls—followed the lantern bearers onto the sand, gathering in a wide half circle near the surf. One by one their poi were lit. They swung and twirled the balls of fire at the ends of their lengths of chain, their movements graceful and timed perfectly with the band of drummers that emerged now from the boardwalk, splitting the crowd in two. A burly, bald sailor was at the lead, whacking on a marching drum, followed by a motley crew of men, tattoos of stars at their temples, armed with a mishmash of instruments. A tuba, a trombone, more accordions, a row of didgeridoos, and then bringing up the rear, more drums. As higgledy-piggledy as the marching band looked, the sound they created was haunting and provocative, the drums a rushing heartbeat, the melody hot blood coursing through veins.

In the deepening dark the girls looped fire and trails of hot orange as fleeting as shooting stars, as stirring as a flurry of kisses from a lover. The air filled with tendrils of acrid smoke as the lanterns burned out and were lit again in sudden, artful bursts. Two of the younger girls wove easily between the others, their fire cast lower, drawing the eye down at the same time as it was lured up, up to watch the languid arcs overhead. The music meshed symbiotically with the pulses and twirls of light and flame, as seamlessly as passion realized. These girls were sorceresses, casting a spell over the crowd with their wands aflame, in a sultry nonchalance.

When the last poi was allowed to burn out on the last note from the band, the surge of silence spilled into a chaos of joyous praise. The clapping and cheers left a wake like a bell.

Then came a *whoosh* from Seth's side of the beach and everyone turned to see a cascade of red light raining down in a staccato of cracks and pops.

"Fireworks!" Jack marvelled beside Sabine. "Did you know about this?"

Sabine shook her head in wonder. The crowd was moving now, this time toward Seth, where a fence of boys held them back. Then, when the fireworks faded and the sky grew dark again, the gigantic wooden structure suddenly came into view. Those orderly but anonymous pieces had been assembled to take the shape of a man. Boxy and austere, towering twenty metres high with bully fists at his hips, his chin turned arrogantly to one side—there was no doubt what this effigy represented.

"I give you ..." Seth stood on one of the flatbed carts, a bullhorn to his lips. "The Group of Keys!"

The crowd hesitated, unsure how to react, curious murmurs rustling the quiet. Then Ori, high up and suspended by a harness of canvas and rope, set fire to one arm. The flames gnawed hungrily at the wood as he scaled to the ground and ran for the cart. He leapt on, and as the cart pulled Seth and Ori to safety, the effigy crawled with fire.

The people understood now. This was Seth's offering to them. Everyone knew of his Guardy past, and of all he had accomplished since. This was a way to reconcile the two: a proper and spectacular death of his life as a Keylander.

"It's brilliant," Sabine yelled over the crowd's bellows. She pulled Eli to her. "Look!"

Eli couldn't help but look as the first arm fell. As it toppled to the sand the crowd roared with delight. It landed with a *thwack* in a crash of ash and sparks. Then the other arm fell, and the fire reached its hot tendrils into the crude ribcage and clutched at a black box there.

It caught, and in a pulse of white heat, an explosion blew off the head and shoulders with a tower of fire that reached up to the sky. The blast sent the waves back out to sea and rolled out an awesome mushroom cloud overhead. At first the crowd cowered, but then the thrill of it hit home and they rose up, fists pumping the air, their voices one collective, triumphant holler.

The marching band started up again, giving them all a memory of song for this moment. The rest of the effigy fell in fits and starts until it was a pile of rubble, a bonfire that hypnotized the crowd as it drew nearer. Seth's boys broke their human fence and let them through. People ran across the sand, desperate to feel the heat on their hands and faces.

SETH HAD JOINED his siblings now, although neither Sabine nor Eli could have said when, exactly. He was just suddenly there. With Rosa, who grinned at the three of them and pointed.

"You're all doing that thing again," she said.

"What?" Sabine cast a glance at her brothers before noticing herself. All three were grasping their matching medallions.

Seth let go of his at once and draped his arm across Rosa's shoulders, pulling her to him for a kiss.

Sabine closed hers in her fist. "That was spectacular, Seth." Stunning and cathartic, the explosion had moved her more than she could say.

"Thank you." He made a little bow, teetering a little on his one leg, even with his crutches. "When it dies down the boys will direct everyone into the theatre."

Sabine nodded. "Yes. In good time."

Eli stood slightly apart, his medallion clasped lightly in his hand. The metal was warm, the carved surface comforting in his palm. He closed his eyes, but he wasn't praying. He pictured the small room that had been his since they had arrived. He'd left his bed neatly made, his bulging rucksack at its foot. Bullet would be on the bed, his head on the pillow, waiting. He would have woken for the explosion, but such noises didn't bother him now, not after all that dog had been through.

Eli wouldn't make a production of goodbyes. His time on stage would be his farewell. He turned his mind's eye to the theatre, pictured where he would stand on the stage to deliver his formal blessing for New Triskelia. He could hear the rehearsed words spill out, envisioned them rolling into the crowd. And then the curtain would rise with a flourish, and the orchestra pit would swell with music, and the Night Circus would begin. When it was his turn, he would climb the rope ladder and launch into the air, fists closed on the bar, swinging back and forth, gathering momentum. And then he would let go and fly.

Acknowledgments

I am ever so thankful for Penguin, of course, and everyone there who has used their brains and savvy to make the Triskelia books shine. The most hyperbolic appreciation goes to Barbara Berson, who had the bright idea to bring me under Penguin's wing in the first place. She makes a darn fine cheerleader.

Neatly printed Thank You notes also go to Tracy Bordian for such masterful coordination and skilled tweaking, and to Shima Aoki for her careful attention, and to Tina Sequeira for her masterful interpretation of my imaginary world.

Jennifer Notman and Nicole Winstanley ... thank you, and might I say that your new hats look very good on you, ladies.

Now that I have your attention, I must profusely thank the goddess called Karen Alliston. She is the master manuscript mechanic. Someone give her a gold-plated red pen and a raise, please. Karen, you are my detail-oriented hero.

I am most thankful for my personal chef and gin rummy partner, Jack Demers. She's been nothing but patient and supportive, and always knows when to whisk me away from it all just when I'm about to set fire to everything I've ever written. Viva Las Vegas!